THE ROAD UNSALTED

Other books by Sonja Hakala

Your Book, Your Way: How to Choose the Best Publishing Option for Your Book, Your Wallet and Yourself (Full Circle Press LLC)

Teach Yourself Visually (Wiley Publishing)

Visual Quick Tips Quilting (Wiley Publishing)

American Patchwork: True Stories from Quilters, editor (St. Martin's Press)

Forthcoming:

Thieves of Fire: A Novel of Carding, Vermont

A Queen Without a King: A Novel of Carding, Vermont

Damienne Hawke and the Dragon's Embrace

The Independent Publisher's Handbook: A Fingers-on-the-Keyboard, Step-by-Step Guide to Independent Publishing

You can join the adventures in Carding, Vermont any time
by visiting www.CardingVermont.com.

THE ROAD UNSALTED

A Novel of Carding, Vermont

SONJA HAKALA

Cover image © 2013 by Nancy Graham

Cover and interior design by Full Circle Press LLC

Editing by Ruth Sylvester

Proofreading by Kris Lewis

Full Circle Press LLC
441 Pomfret Road
West Hartford, Vermont 05084

Library of Congress Cataloging-in-Publication Data
Hakala, Sonja.
  The Road Unsalted : a Novel of Carding, Vermont / Sonja Hakala.
     pages cm
  ISBN 978-0-9790046-8-1
  1. Quilting--Fiction. 2. Vermont--Fiction. I. Title.
  PS3608.A54538R63 2013
  813'.6--dc23
                              2013029406

    Like all works of fiction, the characters and events in *The Road Unsalted* have been inspired by real life. While some of the locations noted in this book do exist, Carding, Vermont, its denizens, and what happens in this extraordinary town are purely works of the author's imagination.
    Or are they?

DEDICATION

In loving memory of my mother, Marcia Luey Hakala, who would have enjoyed shopping in Carding, Vermont, and for my aunt, Edith Ballard Stoddard, to whom Edie Wolfe owes so much.

THE AUTHOR WOULD LIKE TO THANK...

In my non-Carding life, I help other writers independently publish their books, and it's almost inevitable that they are taken aback by the immensity of their projects. For those who have never published a book, it may seem as though this should be a quick and easy task in the digital age, something you can get done over a couple of free weekends.

But books take time, and they don't happen without a lot of help. These are the people who helped me with *The Road Unsalted*.

My husband, Jay Davis, who always asks good questions, makes me laugh when it's important, and never gives up on me.

Editor Ruth Sylvester, who always makes me look better on the page, and who enjoys talking about good writing.

My proofreader, Kris Lewis, who has a very sharp eye. Any typos still on these pages are my responsibility alone because I changed something after he applied his red pencil.

My cover designer, Nancy Graham, the creative person extraordinaire who made the quilt that appears on the front of this book.

Carrie Fradkin whose proficiency with Photoshop amazes me, and whose chat over coffee keeps me moving.

My friends and fellow quilters in the Upper Valley whose interest in this book and "attagirls" mean so much.

My son Jesse, his fiancée Jessica, my siblings, in-laws, nieces, nephews, aunts and cousins who add such richness to the definition of family.

I am so grateful that all of you are in my life, sharing this journey.

Sonja Hakala
on a river in Vermont, August 2013

Contents

PROLOGUE

"So why do you want to blog about Carding?" Faye Bennett asked her brother. "It's not like anything ever happens around here."

Wil sighed the sigh of the artistically misunderstood. "Because I'm gonna be a writer," he said. "This'll be good practice."

"I thought you wanted to be an archaeologist," Faye said.

"Hmph."

"Well, that's what you said last week."

"So maybe I changed my mind," Wil said, leaning closer to his laptop's screen.

"What are you going to write about?" Faye asked, picking burrs off her socks.

"Hey, don't drop those things on my rug."

"Hmph, since when do you care what your room looks like?"

"I said…" Wil's voice took on a warning tone.

"OK, OK." Faye sprinkled the burrs into her brother's waste basket, making sure at least one of them hit the floor. "So what stuff are you going to write about?"

"Whatever I want," Wil said.

"But what if someone doesn't want you to be interested in their business?" Faye peered over her brother's shoulder. "You could get yourself into a lot of trouble with this blog thing, you know."

Wil sighed again. "Faye, you are always scared of getting into trouble." He placed his fingers on his keyboard and began to type—New post on *Carding Chronicle* blog: September 1.

"*Carding Chronicle*?" Faye said. "Why are you calling it that? Why not just the Carding bloggy thing?"

"Don't you pay any attention to Grandma Edie when she talks?" Wil asked.

"I pay lots of attention to Grandma Edie. I visit her a lot more than you do," Faye said.

"I'm not talking about hanging around her house eating cookies," Wil said. "I'm talking about when she tells stories about the way Carding used to be. Her grandparents ran the first newspaper in town, you know, and it was called the *Carding Chronicle* so that's what I'm calling my blog. It's in our family, don't you see?"

Faye flopped back on her brother's bed, and flicked up the end of one of her braids to extract a bit of tree bark. "Well, I think you're wasting your time. No one's ever going to read the thing."

Wil laughed, a bit uncertainly because he hadn't thought about how to get people to read his blog. But there was no way he would admit it to his little sister. "You wait," he said. "People will find it, and they'll read it."

"Are you gonna put your real name on it?" Faye asked.

"I don't think so because if I do, people might hide when they see me coming," Wil said.

"Ha, some people already hide when they see you coming," Faye said.

"Yeah, like who?"

Content to have gotten the rise she wanted, Faye turned back to the subject at hand. "So what are you going to call yourself if it's not Wilson Bennett?"

"What do you think about Little Crow? You know, because this is..."

"...the Corvus Valley, and we own the Crow Town Bakery," Faye said. "Yeah, I get it. I live here too, you know."

Suddenly another voice barged into their conversation. "Faye! Wil! Supper," their father called.

"Coming!" they chorused.

"So, what do you think about Little Crow for a name?" Wil asked as they headed downstairs to the family kitchen.

Faye shrugged. "As good as any, I guess."

ONE

THE BEDSIDE CLOCK

New post on Carding Chronicle blog: September 14

Carding Fair Best Ever

by Little Crow

Good morning Carding:

Carding Academy's executive director, Edie Wolfe, says this year's Carding Fair was "the best ever."

Since the parking lots in town were full all weekend, including the spots up at Harry Brown's garage that he charged people $20 for, it's easy to believe.

"The weather was perfect," Wolfe said. "That little crispness in the air made people think about autumn and the coming winter so getting outdoors was on everyone's mind."

Vendors at the fair reported record sales, and Ruth Goodwin, who was in charge of the Green Apple Crafts shop at the academy, said their stuff was nearly wiped out by Sunday morning.

"We want to thank absolutely everyone who helped out," Wolfe said, "from the folks who worked at the satellite parking lots down by the lake and in the Campgrounds and the shuttle bus drivers who got people back and forth and the performers who juggled and walked on stilts, the members of the Carding Quilt Guild who decorated the whole green, the artists who did demonstrations, the setup team, just everyone who pitched in to make it all work."

Is it too early to say: "See you next year?"

Little Crow | September 14 | Categories: Local News

Well, I guess marriage hasn't dulled my edge when it comes to the ladies, Gideon Brown told himself as he stretched his arms overhead. I still have it when and where it counts.

He turned his head to the side in order to admire the curvy structure lying under the sheets next to him, backlit by his bedside clock. What was her name? Nicky? Vicky? Awwww, it didn't matter.

Now wide awake, he stretched again, wondering if he should rouse his play date for another round before hustling her out of the house while it was still dark. He raised his head to see the clock's face. There was still time.

He laid a hand on the woman's shoulder, maneuvering himself closer. Ricky, that's her name, like the singer Ricky Lee Jones, the one who sang "Chuck E's in Love." Haven't heard that one for a while.

"Hmm, what time is it?" the curvy woman asked.

"About 4:30, give or take a few minutes," Gideon said, sliding his hand down to caress her backside, always one of his favorite female parts. He squeezed. "What do you think?"

"Hmm, whatcha have in mind?"

Gideon never had the chance to answer Ricky's question because at that very moment, he heard his wife turn the key in the lock of their back door.

New post on Carding Chronicle blog: December 1

Winter Driving Reminder from Carding Police Chief
by Little Crow

Good morning Carding:

Just passing on a friendly reminder from our chief of police:

"We hope everyone has their winter driving groove back, and their snow tires on," she said. "We'd also like to remind everyone that the speed limit on Academy Road is 25 mph, and when Carding Academy is in session, foot traffic is heavy so extra caution should be taken."

Here's an update on the traffic accident where a woman got hit on that same Academy Road. Last reports are that the victim, Peggy Martin, age 53 from Philadelphia, was treated for a bruise on her knee at the Dartmouth-Hitchcock Medical Center and released.

The driver of the pickup truck that hit her, Gideon Brown, age 32, was cited for speeding and failure to yield to a pedestrian. Brown claims that fresh snow on the steep twist in Academy Road made it impossible for him to stop. He also claims he was distracted by a tour group on the sidewalk in front of the Carding Academy for Traditional Arts.

The academy has arranged for Mrs. Martin to take her art quilting class at a later date.

Little Crow | December 1 | Categories: Local News

New post on Carding Chronicle blog: December 3

Academy Road Closed to Traffic When Academy in Session
by Little Crow

Good morning, Carding:

All five members of the selectboard voted last night to grant the request of Carding Academy's executive director, Edie Wolfe, to close the section of Academy Road in front of the school to traffic when there's a lot of students. The selectboard granted the request for 90 days, and said they'll look at the situation again at that time to decide whether to make the closing permanent.

Harry Brown, owner of Brown & Sons, Inc., whose trucks use Academy Road all the time, was at the meeting to talk against the closing. He claimed it would have a negative impact on his business. One of the selectmen pointed out that closing Academy Road when there's a lot of students does not mean that Brown's trucks are blocked from getting where they need to go.

"They just have to make a small detour," the selectman said. "The trucks can turn right and go around the town green instead of turning left. The safety of academy students has to be protected. These are people who travel from all over the country to Carding just to take classes at the academy. We can't go knocking them down with pickup trucks. What kind of a reputation will that give us?"

Mr. Brown promised to sue the town for what he called "restraint of trade." He owns 89 acres of land behind the academy's main building but the only way in or out is by Academy Road because every other way out is blocked by the school or the big wetlands that's up there around Watson Creek.

Mr. Brown has sued the town of Carding two other times, once when the conservation commission said that the area around Watson Creek, which is on Mr. Brown's land, is a wetlands. The second time he sued the zoning board because it ruled that Brown & Sons can't build a road through the wetlands. Brown lost both of those suits.

The selectboard gave Edie Wolfe the authority to decide the hours of closure for that section of Academy Road because she knows when the student traffic is going to be heavy.

Little Crow | December 3 | Categories: Local News

"You did that just to spite me," Harry Brown roared as he followed Edie Wolfe out of the selectboard meeting.

"Spite you? Your son can't stop his pickup truck from hitting a woman who's nearly six feet tall and wearing a red coat because he's too busy ogling the backside of a twenty-something on the sidewalk, and you think I asked for this road closing just to spite you?" Edie picked up her pace in an effort to get away from Harry but he stuck like a burr. "It's been decades since I cared even a little about your feelings, Harry Brown, good or bad. There are only two things I ever get out of knowing you—heartburn, and a pain in the area of my body that touches a chair when I sit down."

He crowded in to her shoulder, and Edie whirled on him. "That is too close," she hissed. "You always get too close."

Harry backed away, his face red enough to pass for a tomato. "I won't forget this, you know. I never forget."

Edie stopped for a moment, struggling to control her fury. Don't get so upset, she told herself. He's not worth it. You divorced him more than forty years ago, and he's nothing to you. Her lungs pulled in about a gallon of air, and it helped. A little.

"What does it matter if I close that part of Academy Road in front of the school for a couple of hours now and again?" she asked. "Your trucks can still get in and out of your garage easily enough. Why does it matter to you?"

Harry took a step forward but stopped when he remembered that the selectboard had given Edie Wolfe—this woman who used to be his wife—the right to close Academy Road any time the desire hit her. And you never knew what she'd do when she got angry. "Now Edie," he began. But he was too late. She had already slammed the door to the town hall behind her.

New post on Carding Chronicle blog: December 21

Solstice Dance Tonight at Carding Academy
by Little Crow

Good morning, Carding:

The decorating crew showed up early this morning at Carding Academy to deck the halls for tonight's annual Solstice Dance and fundraiser. Music from Thieves of Fire is sure to set people's feet tapping, and Peter Foster—the leader of the Thieves—asked me to remind everyone to bring a pair of clean, soft-soled shoes if you're planning to get out on the dance floor.

Admission to the Solstice Dance is $10 per person, $25 for a family. The fun begins at 6:00 with a supper put on by Cate Elliot and her cooking crew. Dancing starts at 7:00 with a family dance, and then the grownups take the floor at 8:00.

I'll be looking for you.
Little Crow | December 21 | Categories: Local Fun

When Chloe Brown unlocked the door to her studio on the second floor of the academy, the sun still had hours to go before sharing its weak light with Vermont's hills. For the first time in her life, she hated the very idea of the annual Solstice Dance. Last year, she and her good-for-nothing husband Gideon had whirled about the floor, his brown eyes sparking each time he spun her around so that her dark green dress swirled about her legs. This year...well this year there would be no pretty dress, no dancing, and no husband who pretended to love her above all others.

Chloe winced as she remembered the shock of seeing that woman's backside disappear into her bathroom as her husband struggled to pull on a pair of pajama bottoms to hide...what exactly? His nakedness from his wife?

She closed her studio door but didn't bother to turn on the overhead lights. Maybe I'll just hide in my stash closet all day so no one will ask me if I'm going to the dance. As one self-pitying thought chased another, Chloe stood staring out her floor-to-ceiling windows at a clear, starry sky. Orion and his famous belt had nearly disappeared over the horizon trailing the ovoid shape of the waxing moon behind him. Across the lake, snow guns sent up plumes of crystallized water to coat the trails on Mount Merino. With a jolt, Chloe suddenly realized she hadn't skied since she met Gideon because he didn't—and didn't want to learn. "There's no way I'm going to fall on my face in front of the whole town on Merino's bunny slope," he'd said. "But you go ahead. I know you love it."

Chloe squirmed as a new thought insinuated itself into her mind. She had stopped skiing—something she'd enjoyed since she was a little girl—because of Gideon. He hadn't demanded she stop but as she thumbed through the years of her marriage, she remembered how much he fussed whenever she talked about taking an afternoon off to schuss down Wooly Mountain, as the locals called Merino, without him.

What else, she asked herself, what else have I stopped doing since I married Gideon?

With her eyes adjusted to the dim light, Chloe found her way to the tea kettle, the sink, and the hot plate. As she waited for her water to boil, she fished a block of cheese out of the tiny refrigerator under her cutting table, and retrieved a box of crackers she'd opened the day before. Or was it the day before that? She sighed as she cut a slice of cheddar. Today I'm going to get myself a real breakfast at the Crow Town Bakery, she promised herself as she appeased her growling stomach.

I'm sick of cheese and crackers.

I'm sick of not skiing.

I'm sick of Gideon, and his horrid father, Creepy Harry, and his mother, Louisa the Fainthearted.

Thinking about Gideon's mother sent a chill across Chloe's shoulders. That could have been me, she thought. I could have become Louisa Brown, all Cadillacs, cheap jewelry, and no soul.

Chloe picked up the remains of her nibbly food and threw it into a wastebasket. Then she snapped on all her studio lights and stood close to her windows to welcome the late-rising sun. "I'm going to that dance tonight," she said out loud. "And I'm wearing my green dress, and I'm doing up my hair, and bringing my soft-soled shoes. Somebody will ask me to dance."

She turned up her jacket's collar, pushed her hands into its pockets, walked out of her studio, down the stairs, and across the green toward the beckoning smells of cinnamon and bacon.

New post on Carding Chronicle blog: December 21

Parking Advisory for Tonight's Solstice Dance
by Little Crow

Good afternoon, Carding:

There's no snow, rain or sleet in the forecast, and that probably means a big crowd for the Solstice Dance tonight. Chief-of-Police Carla Davenport reminds everyone that parking is prohibited on Academy Road due to pedestrian safety concerns. The academy's executive director, Edie Wolfe, emailed the *Chronicle* to say that volunteers will circle the parking areas around the green to give rides to people who need them.

And Cate Elliot says there's lots of lasagna and salad to go around plus Carding's pie ladies have been busy so there's plenty for everyone to eat.

I'll be looking for you.
Little Crow | December 21 | Categories: Local Fun

"But why should I go?" Lisa whined. "No one will ask me to dance, and I'll be bored. I might as well stay home and watch reruns of *Friends*." She let her lower lip hang. "It's no fun being the wife of a band member."

Peter tried not to let his irritation show. Until he married Lisa, he never knew women could pout so much. Really, Lisa's act had become tediously routine. "I understand," he said.

Lisa's eyelids snapped up, and Peter knew immediately that his comment was not well received. He barely suppressed his sigh, wondering whether she'd choose to complain he didn't love her any more or flounce off to the bathroom and lock the door behind her. He hoped it would be the bathroom. If she complained he didn't love her, he might tell her the truth, and he didn't want to deal with that just before the Solstice Dance. Then the telephone rang, and when Lisa dove across the bed to answer it, Peter escaped to the kitchen. With any luck, he'd be out the door before she finished talking. He grabbed the case with his bass guitar, the Thieves of Fire banner, and his jacket. But he wasn't quite fast enough.

"That was my sister," Lisa said as she sashayed into the room. "Chloe's going tonight, and she wants me to come with her. So I'm going, Petey. Isn't that wonderful? What do you think I should wear?"

He hesitated at the door, wracking his brain to remember any outfit of Lisa's that didn't make her look as though she'd rather be naked. "You know, I like that dark green dress, the one with the skirt that flares out a little," he said as he leaned over to give her a quick kiss. "I'm sorry, Lisa, but I've got a sound check to run. I'll see you there, OK? And I'm glad you're going with Chloe. She needs the moral support."

Lisa stared as her husband closed the door behind him. Then she stared some more as she watched him drive away. "I don't own a dark green dress," she said. "I look terrible in green. Everyone knows that."

"Oh, wouldn't Mom love to see us going to the Solstice Dance together?" Lisa asked as she clutched her sister's arm.

"Well, she could see us if she hadn't left Dad, and gone to live in California," Chloe said, sniffing.

Lisa laughed. "But she had to go, don't you see? It's where she belongs. But even when we were little, Mom wanted us to be close in spite of the difference in our ages."

"Difference in our ages? I'm only three years older than you, Lisa. That hardly makes me ancient," Chloe said.

"Well, I guess you're right. So catch me up on your Gideon situation," Lisa said as they turned the corner of Academy Road to see the brightly-lit school at the top of the hill. "Are you going to keep him in the basement until he gets moldy?"

"Not a bad idea," Chloe said.

"Mom says you should forgive him because Gideon is just like his father, and everyone knows it," Lisa said. "Besides, his daddy is rich which means Gideon will be some day."

Chloe fixed her eyes on the sidewalk. "Rich doesn't make up for what he did. Putting another woman in my bed was unforgivable. Do you know, he couldn't tell me her name. At least she had the decency to look ashamed, which was more than he did."

"Oh, I'm sure they introduced themselves to one another at some point," Lisa said as they ducked through the school's front door. "Those things always start, with an introduction. He just forgot, that's all. Oh look, there's that cute dark-haired guy, you know the one who's doing the oil deliveries in town now. I wonder if he'll dance with me."

As they turned into the cloak room, Chloe was amazed to see how readily the top buttons of her sister's coat opened to reveal what lay beyond. "I'm amazed you don't catch more colds," she said.

"What? Oh, I don't mind the cold if it's for a good cause." Lisa shed her coat and boots then slipped on her party shoes. "Well, come find me when you're ready to go home, OK Chloe?"

And with that, Lisa bounded across the floor in a trajectory sure to bring her within the orbit of Carding's new oil delivery man.

"I'm surprised you asked your sister to come with you. She's hardly what I would call a good companion," a voice said.

Chloe smiled. "Hi Dad. I know what you mean but I just couldn't make myself come alone so I figured if I asked Lisa, I'd at least get here. I'm tired of sitting home waiting for something to change."

Charlie Cooper leaned down to kiss his oldest daughter's cheek. "You know you can make a change any time you want."

"Spoken like a true lawyer," his partner, Agnes, said. She leaned over to give Chloe a hug, and the two women smiled at one another. Chloe admired the tall, graceful woman who made her father's eyes twinkle.

"Not just like a lawyer," Charlie protested. "Like a father, too. Seriously, Chloe, why are you staying in the same house with him? Do you want to stay married to Gideon Brown?"

"Charlie, not now." Agnes took his arm, and then grabbed Chloe's hand. "Come on, you need to find your two favorite women a glass of wine. And no more lawyer talk tonight. Save that for the daylight hours. Tonight, we're doing our best to make sure your daughter has a good time." Then she beamed at Chloe. "I'm so glad to see you wear that green dress. It looks so good on you."

Once his band started playing, Peter saw nothing beyond his own fingers on the strings of his bass. While he enjoyed many things in his life—good food, skiing, fishing for trout in Half Moon Lake, playing softball on the Fourth of July, running Carding's half marathon on Columbus Day weekend—he lived for his time with the Thieves of Fire. When they started, the Thieves played straight Celtic music on the contradance circuit but now their repertoire included African rhythms,

Latin instruments, and a mix of Cajun and Québecois songs. As their website proclaimed: When the Thieves play, nobody sits down.

Peter never saw his young wife arrive even though lots of other male eyes took notice. He never saw Lisa's flirty dance with the new oil delivery guy. Nor did he look up when she flounced to the opposite end of the room when that same young man didn't ask her for a second dance.

But Gideon Brown noticed everything his sister-in-law did. Why wouldn't he when she made it so easy?

"Kind of boring being a band wife, isn't it?" he asked as he handed her a glass of wine. "Do I remember right that you like chardonnay?"

"Yeah, I do, and yeah, it sure is boring," Lisa said as she accepted his gift. "I hate sitting on the sidelines." She let her lower lip droop when she spotted her sister laughing with their father while he swung her about in his arms. "I don't know why I came in the first place."

"Well, I'm glad you did," Gideon said. "I don't have much company lately. Your sister's opinion pulls a lot of weight in Carding."

Lisa turned her two most prominent assets in her brother-in-law's direction, and smiled. "I don't mind being seen with you, Giddy. Chloe has taken things a little too far, in my opinion."

Gideon smiled, and then let his eyes slowly trail down the curve of Lisa's cheek to her neck, and then to the generous arc of her breasts. "How far do you let things go?" he asked.

"Well, let's just say that I'm serious about my fun," Lisa said. Then she raised her wineglass to her mouth, and let her tongue trace its rim. Gideon's smile widened, and he raised his glass in a salute.

"To fun," he said.

"To fun," she replied. Then, just for emphasis, Lisa snuggled up close to her brother-in-law as they stood in the darkest corner of the room. And when he ran his hand casually down her back to rest where no one else could see it, Lisa smiled over the tingle it gave her.

I'd never cheat with my sister's husband, Lisa told herself. Besides, Giddy's over thirty. Too old. Still, this is the most fun I've had all night.

TWO

A FAMILY REUNION

New post on Carding Chronicle blog: January 20

Where Is She Now?
by Little Crow

Good afternoon, Carding:

Remember Allison Owens, the one-time Carding Regional High School cheerleader who moved to California? Alli-O, as she likes to be called now, became the star of the hit show, *Pretty as a Picture*, on the Mixed Media channel.

We haven't heard anything about Alli-O since her show was cancelled but today, Lisa Foster (who says she's a real fan) forwarded an announcement from Alli-O's website about the fact that the former star of *Pretty as a Picture* is headlining a show at Carmen's Casino in Las Vegas.

Good luck to her, I guess.

In news closer to home, there's another storm with our name on it rounding out of the Great Lakes region, scheduled to dump about a foot of snow in the driveway you just got cleaned up from last weekend's storm. As always, the road crews appreciate it if you wouldn't park your cars or trucks around Carding Green because it makes plowing a nightmare for everyone involved.

It looks like it's going to be another good night to hunker down to play cribbage by the woodstove if the power goes out. And that reminds me, Andy Cooper says the store has replenished its supply of flashlight batteries so we should be all set.

I'll look for you again when the roads are clear.
Little Crow | January 20 | Categories: Local Weather

"Excuse me?" Alli-O said. "You're doing what?"

"Firing you." The tall man pinched a piece of invisible lint off the sleeve of his jacket. He was glad he'd chosen the more subtle pinstripe for his newest suit. In a city that gloried in ostentation, subtlety got you noticed.

"You have twelve hours to get your stuff, yourself," he continued, "and that kid of yours out of my hotel." He pulled a piece of paper from the inside pocket of his jacket, glad to be rid of the slight bulge it made. "Here's a check for what I owe you through the end of next week. It should be enough to get you well away from here."

Alli-O stiffened into her affronted princess pose. "You can't treat me like a dead armadillo in the middle of the road," she said. "Everyone knows who I am."

The gentleman sighed. "Well, you see, that's the problem: nobody knows or cares who you are any more. You say the word 'Alli-O,' and people say 'who?' *Pretty as a Picture* went off the air ages ago, and you haven't done anything since. I need bodies in Carmen's, and I need entertainment that's going to draw bodies to it."

"But I've only been here for ten days. That's not enough time for word to get out that I'm here," Allison said. "Besides, I'm a celebrity."

He put the check on a nearby table. "Only to the totally clueless," he said as he strolled out the door. "And don't even think about leaving without paying for your room. I do have ways of finding you." He turned the corners of his mouth up. "I'm sure you understand."

Hidden deep in the walk-in closet in her mother's room, Suzanna Owens pressed her hands to her stomach, trying to will its pain away. Every time her mother got fired or had a fight with a club owner, Suzanna knew she'd be stuck in the back of some car driving who knows where to face who knows what. And that always made her stomach hurt.

Not that she would be sorry to leave Las Vegas. Of all the places her celebrity mother had worked, Suzanna considered this joyless desert city the worst. No friends. No place to hang out. And the adults acted like puppets.

Suzanna listened to her mother's high heels tap back and forth as she muttered to herself. Then the tapping stopped, and Suzanna heard the scrape of a match. Well, there goes the non-smoking status of this room, she thought. As her mother drew in a lungful of tar and nicotine, Suzanna detected the quiet beep of her cell phone.

"Ted?" Allison said. "No, please don't hang up. I need your help. It's

Suzanna. I need someone to take care of her for a while, and I thought… Well, I know I haven't been in touch for a long time. I have been working, you know. It's just that…well…things are a little tough right now, and I thought that with you being my brother and all…"

Suzanna listened in shock as her mother talked. In all her twelve years, she'd never heard her mother speak about a brother. Or any other family member, for that matter. She wondered where he lived, and hoped it was better than the yucky desert.

"Where are we going?" Suzanna whined when her mother woke her up in the middle of the night.

"Out of here," Allison said. Suzanna wrinkled her nose. She hated the smell of her mother's breath after she'd been in a bar.

"Can't we go in the morning? I'm hungry."

"No, we're going now, and we'll stop to get you something to eat on the way out of town," Allison said. "Now come on, get dressed while I pack your clothes. And don't cry about it. I don't have time for that."

Suzanna saw the shadow of a man moving back and forth in the other room of their suite. "Is that a new Bruno?" she asked. "What happened to the last one?"

"Don't call my boyfriends Bruno," Allison snapped. "His name is Haywood Collins, and he's very important. So you call him Haywood, hear? Now, go wash your face, and put your jacket on."

"Are we going down the back stairs like we always do?" Suzanna asked as she stumbled out of bed, shivering in the air conditioning that was always turned too high.

Allison gave the girl a small push toward the bathroom then turned to yank the blanket off the bed. "We're going to take the pillows, too," she said to the shadow. "That way, Suzanna can sleep in the back while we take turns driving, OK?"

"Yeah, but let's be quick about it," the man said. "I want to be in Vermont by Sunday, and then out. Why in the world would your brother live in that godforsaken place? It snows there, and it's cold."

In the bathroom, Suzanna turned on the hot water, soaked a facecloth, and then buried her tears in its folds. Where in the world was Vermont?

New post on Carding Chronicle blog: February 2

Groundhog Day Specials at Crow Town Bakery
by Little Crow

Good morning, Carding:

Thom Olson reports that the ice is over three feet thick on the south side of Belmont Island in Half Moon Lake. At last count, there's 47 bobhouses out there, and Thom says the perch were hitting pretty good yesterday.

He wants me to remind snowmobilers and cross-country skiers to stay on the same side of the island as the fisher folk. We all remember what happened to the Wheaton boys last winter when they decided to race their snowmobiles on the other side of the island. Dick Wheaton's snowmobile never recovered from its swim in the lake.

If you're off to fish or to church this morning, remember there's plenty of warm cider donuts at the Crow Town Bakery to go with your coffee. Owner Diana Bennett has a special on for today—buy an extra large coffee and get a donut for just another dime. What a deal!

I'll be looking for you.
Little Crow | February 2 | Categories: Local Food

"Your sister is coming here, to Carding?" Peter Foster looked over his coffee at his friend to make sure Ted wasn't kidding. "Last I knew, she said she'd rather be dead than in Vermont. So what gives?"

"Her daughter, apparently," Ted said. "I don't know what happened, and I don't really care. But Allison's in some sort of jam, and she wants me to take care of her kid."

"For how long?"

Ted shook his head. "Who knows? With Allison, time is relative as long as it doesn't inconvenience her."

"Have you even met her daughter? How old is she?" Peter asked.

"Nope, never met her. The only things I know about her are that she's twelve, and her name is Suzanna," Ted said. "I read in *People* magazine that she was born not too long after *Pretty as a Picture* started. Allison's never said who the father is." He shook his head. "Poor little kid."

"So when does your stint as Uncle Ted start?" Peter asked.

"Late this afternoon, I guess," Ted said. "At least that's what Allison said when she called this morning. They had just crossed the border from Ohio into western New York."

"They? Is she coming with an entourage of some sort?"

"Probably not an entourage because she's beyond getting that kind of attention. It'll be whatever guy she's picked up lately." He shook his head again. "Poor little kid."

"Where are you going?" Allison started out of her doze.

Haywood pointed to the dashboard. "Gas," he said. "Got any money?"

"Of course I have money," Allison said. "Who do you think I am?"

"Someone who just got fired from the lamest excuse for a casino in Las Vegas," Haywood said. He eased beside a pump, and turned the car off. In the back seat, buried under a pile of hotel blankets, Suzanna kept her eyes closed, her hands on her stomach. "I'll pump. You go in and pay," Haywood said as he opened his door.

Allison pushed her hair off her face, reached for the door handle but then stopped. "I can't," she said, pointing in front of the car. "Look."

Haywood obeyed. "I don't see anything."

"Those birds," Allison whispered. "Crows."

"Yeah? So?" He walked toward the three black birds, waving his arms in a shooing motion. The birds hopped out of range then strutted back toward the car. "Go on, shoo!"

Once again, the birds moved out of range then strutted back. Haywood looked at Allison cowering in the front seat. "Come on, it's just crows. Get out, and pay for the gas already."

Allison shook her head, rolled down her window, and held out a hand full of money. "You do it," she said. "Please."

Haywood was so surprised to hear that word come out of Allison's mouth, he did what she asked. Suzanna squeezed her eyes together tighter than before, praying her mother would think she was still asleep. Life was easier for Suzanna if she let her mother ignore her.

"So what was that all about?" Haywood asked when he slid back into the driver's seat. "Since when are you afraid of a couple of black birds?"

Allison looked over her shoulder. All she could see of Suzanna was the rise of a cheek and a tuft of curly hair sticking out from the pile of stolen blankets. "I hate crows. I think they're creepy," she said in a low voice. "When I was a kid, I knocked their nests out of trees whenever I could. I thought it was funny, you know? But then the crows started following me."

"Following you?" Suzanna heard the crackle of a candy wrapper, and knew she'd soon smell peanuts. Her mother's latest Bruno lived on Snickers and coffee. "You've been watching too many Alfred Hitchcock movies."

"No, not Hitchcock," Allison said. "I read an article about a scientist who studied crows, and he discovered that they remember the faces of people, especially people who do things they don't like. And somehow, they tell other crows about the people they hate. By the time I got into high school, crows showed up everywhere I went. People in Carding knew I was coming before I got there because the crows got there first. My brother thought it was hilarious." She shrank into her coat.

Haywood snorted. "Well, you have to admit it is a bit weird."

"What makes it even worse is that Carding is in the Corvus Valley," Allison continued. Suzanna heard the click of a seat belt, and the car started moving again.

"So? What's that got to do with crows?" Haywood said.

"Corvus is the genus name for crows and ravens," Allison said. "The first white guy who showed up in that part of Vermont, some mapmaker named Ovid Tilley, loved the damn things, and the story goes that he found hundreds of them nesting in the trees on top of this cliff. There's a river that falls from the cliff into a lake, and Tilley was interested in biology too so he named the river the Corvus River, and that's why the whole area became the Corvus Valley." Allison sighed. "I can't wait until this is all over. Do you think we'll get to Carding by dark?"

New post on Carding Chronicle blog: February 2

Strolling Heifers on Belmont Road
by Little Crow

Good afternoon, Carding:

This just in from the Carding police: Drivers are cautioned to be extra careful on Belmont Road, particularly near the Ledbetters' farm because three of their Holsteins decided to take a stroll just after milking. And yes, one of them is that pesky Gypsy who makes a habit of living up to her name. I think this is the third time she's gotten loose this week.

The Ledbetters say the Holsteins should be back in the barn soon but do be careful.

I'll be looking for you.
Little Crow | February 2 | Categories: Local Food

Try as he might, Ted could not sit down. He paced from window to door, door to window. Why was Allison doing this? How was he going to take care of his father and a little girl and keep his job at the post office? What did he know about raising a child? And what if Allison's daughter was like Allison? Talk about nightmares.

A shadow flitted past his living room window, and Ted froze with one foot in the air. He'd forgotten about the crows, forgotten about how they haunted Allison after she spent a summer looting their nests. He raced for the door that emptied into his garage, and saw a large ebony bird light on a fence post at the end of his driveway. How could they remember after all these years? How did they know Allison was coming? Ted shivered though whether it was from the cold or a premonition, he didn't know.

Then a large car pulled up to the curb, and Ted saw his older sister jump in her seat when she spotted the crow. "Go on, now, shoo," he said to the bird as he walked toward the street. "She's not staying but if you're here, she'll never get out of the car, and we'll never get this over with. Go on now, shoo."

The bird looked straight at him then lifted off into the gray sky. The weather forecasters were talking about another six inches of snow before morning, and Ted wanted his sister and whatever-his-name-was-this-time to be long gone before the flakes started their descent.

Just then the back door of the car popped opened, and a slender girl with an unruly mop of dark blonde hair launched herself onto the sidewalk. Without a single look at the car, she marched toward Ted, her dark brown eyes never wavering from his face. "Are you my uncle?" She paused as she hunched a grungy blanket around her shoulders.

He swallowed, and noticed the twitch of a curtain in the house across the street. Well, this story will be all over Carding before I get back in the house, he thought. "Are you my niece Suzanna?" he asked.

The girl nodded. "That's me. Can we go inside now? You have a lot of cold and snow here and I'm not used to it," she said.

A little smile tugged at one corner of Ted's mouth. I'll bet she gives Allison a hard time, he thought. How good is that? Aloud he said: "Of course. Go right in. The woodstove is going, and you'll be warm in no time. I'll be right behind you."

She started marching again. As she passed her uncle, Suzanna looked up. "She'll try to make a scene, you know," the child said.

Ted nodded. "She always does."

"Hey, Suzanna, don't you have a good-bye kiss for your mother?" Allison called. She stood uncertainly at the end of the driveway, a large blue suitcase in one hand. But Suzanna walked into her uncle's house without a backward glance.

Ted took a moment to survey his only sibling. She had thinned out to the point of being stringy. Gone were the hips and the round softness in her face that drove all the boys mad in high school. Her hair, or what he could see of it, was stick straight now, its color falling somewhere between reddish and brownish. And of course she wore heels, the only female in all of Vermont without sense enough to put something warm on her feet in winter.

"Apparently you'll have to go kiss-less," he said.

Allison looked everywhere but at her brother. "Yeah, well, you know kids," she said. "Never grateful."

"Hmph, you'd know all about that, wouldn't you?" Ted said, pitching his voice low so no one else could hear.

Allison's head snapped up. "That's not fair," she hissed.

"Is that Suzanna's suitcase?" he asked. He'd already said more than he meant to, and he didn't want to waste any more time on his sister.

"What?"

"Is that your daughter's suitcase you're holding?" Ted asked again.

"Yeah. I think it's got everything she needs," Allison said.

"You can leave it there," he said. "I'll pick it up when you're gone. I imagine you're in a hurry to leave."

"You can say that again," the man at the wheel said through the open car door. "If you two aren't planning on a family reunion, I say we get out of here. There's a casino in Connecticut with a slot machine that's got my name on it, and we could be there before midnight if we get cracking. Come on, Allison, get it over with."

"How long are you leaving your child here?" Ted asked.

Allison rested the suitcase on the snowy ground then looked down at her empty hands.

"You don't know, do you?" Ted said.

"No, I don't." She looked at the house, and then at the car. "Well, I guess I'd better get going. I'll call ya."

Ted nodded. Allison turned, took two steps then craned her head over her shoulder. "How's Dad?" she asked.

Ted felt his face twist. "Who wants to know?" he asked.

She opened her mouth then shook her head. "I don't hate anybody."

Ted waited until his sister's car drove out of sight. Then he picked up his niece's suitcase, and turned toward his house. When the curtain across the street twitched again, he waved.

THREE

QUILTLING IS THERAPY

During winter in Vermont, it takes a long time for each day's meager share of sunlight to reach into the valleys where so many of the state's towns crouch on the flat spots carved out by its rivers. That's why in early February in Carding, you don't expect the light to touch the town green until mid-morning. If you can avoid venturing outdoors until then, you do.

Back in the days when everything moved by foot or horse, Carding Green was a fenced-in common area where errant cows, sheep, and goats whiled away their hours until reclaimed by their owners. But after the Civil War, the state's farmers moved west for the chance to plow flat ground, and the need for a town animal shelter gave way to the desire for an open place crisscrossed by paths that let Carding-ites move through the center of town quickly.

After a while, a few trees moved in to fill the vegetative vacuum on the common, as trees do. Ordinarily, Carding folks wouldn't have done anything about them but business was business, and too many saplings got in the way of buyers and sellers. So instead of a center-of-town forest, which would have been the trees' preference, the townsfolk cut down all but a few sugar maples, a small tribe of white birch, and a handful of sycamores. In spring, the trees' bright green made the year-round folks in Carding smile. In summer, their shade cooled those who attended band concerts in the gazebo. In fall, tourists gushed over the red, yellow, and orange leaves, scooping them up as souvenirs. And in winter, townsfolk judged the windiness of the day by the sway of the trees' bare branches.

Vermont's landscape is usually in a hurry to go up or down, making the relative flatness of Carding Green remarkable. Around its perimeter, the oldest houses squeezed out space among the oldest businesses, and together they shared the available real estate with a community building that included the town hall, a library, and a room dedicated to Carding's history. A post office, a bakery, a few handcraft shops, a store that everyone called "the Coop" because it was owned by Andy Cooper, and the Carding Academy of Traditional Arts rounded out the town's amenities.

South of the green, the land undulated upward, its slope skeined by narrow streets. The population of houses large and small thinned out once you got past Belmont Road. In some places, the bygone hill farms had been reclaimed by a new breed of agronomist, hardworking folks who championed the merits of locally grown food. Above the farms, the Appalachian Trail meandered past long-abandoned, stone-lined cellar holes where June-blooming lilacs suggested a past of starched curtains, cookstoves, and whitewash.

To the north of the green, the land swooped down to Half Moon Lake, a big fat puddle that filled a hole carved out by the Corvus River. At the head of the lake, a thirty-foot bluff jutted out over the water, a great knobbly knee of granite that has resisted the river's erosion for time out of mind. The cliff is known in Carding as the Crowhead, and the Corvus River catapults off the top of it before coming to rest in the lake below. In summer, the setting sun sets the falls ablaze in a dancing rainbow. In winter, the water forms icy castles that freeze, crack, melt, and renew themselves from the winter solstice to the vernal equinox.

As it traveled from one end of the lake to the other, the Corvus River transformed itself from a raging torrent into a quiet stream that wound around an island then spread out in a marsh before gathering itself back together again to head east to the Connecticut River, the great dividing line between Vermont and New Hampshire. On the southeast lip of the lake, a town beach stretched itself out like a girl coated in suntan lotion. Continuing east, a neighborhood of narrow streets and small cabins known as the Campgrounds crouched on the lake's shore at the base of the Crowhead.

The Campgrounds was founded in 1857 by a traveling Methodist preacher who stopped in Carding to admire the falls, and decided to stay. A gifted orator and writer, Jeremiah Belmont attracted a wide following, and three years after settling in Carding, he played host to a monthlong religious revival on the lake. Over the years, Belmont's revivals attracted fervent followers. At first, everyone slept in tents but that got tiresome so Belmont's congregants erected wooden cabins around the main preaching grounds at the base of Crowhead.

Over the decades, the fortunes of the Campgrounds waxed and waned with wars, disillusionment, periods of renewed religious fervor, and the excesses of the common culture. By the time hippies started dancing in the parks of San Francisco, the Carding Campgrounds had quietly turned itself into a secular enclave of family-owned cabins. Indeed, half the population of Carding whiled away the hours of Vermont's annual warm spells in the Campgrounds.

On the north shore of Half Moon, tiers of granite ledge rose sharply from the water's edge making it impossible to land a canoe or swim. The rocks continued their upward climb for the next 4,000 feet to form an intimidating peak called Mount Merino, a place beloved by skiers, snowboarders, and those who made their livings serving the Spandex-clad revelers.

Though she hates the word matriarch, Edie Wolfe does serve that purpose in town because she's the woman who knows or guesses more about Carding folks than anyone else. People believe she can feel the mood of the town in her bones but Edie claims it's just arthritis. It is true that over the years, she's developed an impressive ability to figure out the connections among people, and she's rarely surprised by anything that happens in town.

"It's just studying people, knowing where they come from, something about their families," she says. "Whether we like to admit it or not, we're all products of our pasts."

Edie lives with her cocker spaniel, Nearly, in a house with a front porch overlooking the town green. Diagonally across from her living room windows, the Carding Coop's doors open and close, its modest front masking a rambling structure that offers patrons everything from morning coffee to cans of corn, AAA batteries, wool winter pants, clothes-drying racks, grass seed, and house paint. There are stories, never confirmed, about tourists who were so mesmerized by the Coop's vast hodgepodge of merchandise, they had to be rescued by a special ops team of clerks trained by Andy Cooper himself. Never one to miss a marketing opportunity, Andy keeps a jar of buttons by his cash registers that read "I was lost and found at the Carding Coop." The foliage crowds love them.

"Do you know I talked to a guy from New Jersey today who told me he saw someone wearing one of those buttons in the Tokyo airport," he told Edie over one of their regular cribbage games. "He said they had a nice chat about our little corner of the world while waiting for their flight."

Edie smiled as she arranged her cards from low to high. "Little corner of the world? I would say that the whole world is made up of little corners, wouldn't you? No matter how much we globalize—how I hate that word—we try to make something familiar out of our surroundings wherever we are." She laid down her four of clubs, and said: "Thirty."

After Andy said "Go," Edie moved her peg, and continued, "Humans are nothing if not creatures of habit and routine, and I think the need for the familiar drives a great deal of human behavior because we don't really like change. We fight it with every cell in our bodies." She laid down a ten.

Andy slapped down a five, and reached for one of his pegs. "Fifteen for two," he said. "Speaking of change, did you hear about Allison Owens leaving her daughter on Ted's doorstep?"

Edie lifted her eyes from the board. "I did. How old would you say she is, the girl I mean?"

Andy wrinkled his nose. "I'm not good at guessing ages but I'd say somewhere between nine and twelve. Definitely out of diapers but not into acne."

Edie sat back in her chair, the better to sift through her friend's words. "You don't suppose...?"

Andy met her eyes. "I do suppose, actually. We all figured that sooner or later, Allison would show up in Carding needing some sort of a favor from her brother."

"So she's dropped her child on his doorstep," Edie said. Then she sighed. "I don't suppose she gave a thought to visiting her father."

Andy shook his head. "Nope, don't expect so. After what she did, I don't see how she could look her father in the face anyway."

"That poor child." Edie shook her head. "Can you imagine what she's been through?"

"No, but I imagine you'll find out." Andy gathered up the cards then handed them to Edie. She raised an eyebrow at him.

"Are you saying it's none of my business?" she asked.

Andy smiled. "Now that would depend on your perspective, wouldn't it? You know as well as I do that you find out about everything in Carding sooner or later. People tell you things. If you ever decide to give up quilting and card playing, you could be a therapist. You'd make a bundle."

Edie dealt six cards to each of them. "Quilting *is* therapy, Andy."

"So you tell me." He fanned his cards out, calculating the odds of making a double run out of them with the right cut card.

"Do you know if Allison is still in Carding?" Edie asked. She pulled two cards out of her hand, and laid them face down in the crib. "Or did Ted run her off with a shotgun like he once threatened to?"

"You couldn't blame him if he did." He put down a card. "Six."

Edie set down a nine. "Fifteen for two." She moved her peg. "No, I wouldn't blame him though I can't see him actually doing it. Ted's just like his mother and father—solid, get-up-in-the-morning, take-care-of-yourself folks. Shooting people, no matter how much they deserve it, just isn't his style. Did anybody besides Ted see Allison?"

Andy nodded his head then gasped when Edie turned over the cards in her crib. "A double run? Well, that does me in. You win." He scooped up his cards. "The story I heard is that she came in a big car…"

"Probably driven by a boyfriend of some sort," Edie said as she put away the cribbage board. "Glass of wine?"

Andy nodded. "Yeah, thanks. Anyway, the story is that Allison showed up in this big car—with a man at the wheel—and dragged a suitcase out of the trunk. The girl jumped out of the back seat just as Ted stepped out of the house."

"Who saw this?" Edie asked as she planted a healthy glass of Andy's favorite red at his elbow then sat down with one of her own.

"Lydie Talbot and her sister Millie," Andy said.

Edie nodded. Information from that quarter was unimpeachable.

"Lydie says that when Ted stepped out into the yard, he told Allison to stop just where she was, and for once in her life, the woman did as she was told. They exchanged a few words, and then Allison called to the girl to come for a kiss. But the little one just turned her back, and marched into the house."

Edie felt a squeeze around her heart. "There's a lot of pain there. The poor kid."

Andy nodded. "I guess Allison stood there for a bit, and then her latest and greatest behind the wheel told her to get in the car, and they sped off."

The two friends stared at their empty glasses in silence for a spell, as if they'd find a solution to the little girl's problems in the last drops of wine. Then Edie roused herself.

"Well, Ted's a hardworking man, trustworthy and all that, but he's got his father to look after, and I doubt he knows the first thing about taking care of a young girl. He's going to need some help," Edie said. Then she raised her glass in his direction. "Another?"

Andy glanced at the clock. "No, I'd better be off. The skiers from away come earlier every morning which means I'm up earlier. I'll leave you to it to find out the girl's name, and all the particulars. Let me know how I can help."

FOUR

GRADE A DARK AMBER

New post on Carding Chronicle blog: February 4

Ancient Roads on Warrant at Town Meeting
by Little Crow

Good morning, Carding:

A message from our town manager, Paula Bouton: According to the rules laid out by the Vermont state legislature in Act 178, every town has to figure out what they've got for their Class 4 roads and legal pathways. These old streets and trails—everyone calls them ancient roads—are used to add up the total miles of highway in a town. This is the number the state uses to figure out how much money we get to help take care of our roads.

In other words—the more miles a town has, the more money a town gets from the state Agency of Transportation.

Like all the other towns in Vermont, Carding has a lot of roads and trails that aren't used by cars any more but may still be town roads because they were never legally discontinued by a vote at a town meeting. According to Act 178, we have to find and make a list of all these roads. Paula says it's been quite a project comparing old town maps to new town maps, and then going through the town meeting records to figure out what's still a legal road and what's not.

Paula says that so far, she's found four old roads that were never legally discontinued. I guess you could call them roads unsalted because the town doesn't plow them, sand them or apply sodium chloride to them when it snows. If voters don't legally discontinue them at town meeting next month, that means our road crews will be maintaining them.

There's a list of the ancient roads Paula's found so far posted in the town hall and the town library. Paula says she and her assistant, Lisa Foster, will continue to add old roads to this list right up until March 1 so if you have any questions or think you know of an old byway, let the folks in the town hall know so they can do the research.

Town meeting is one month from today, on Tuesday, March 4. I'll be looking for you.

Little Crow | February 4 | Categories: Local Government

Gideon Brown inhaled a lungful of the shower's hot, moist air while the water formed rivulets down his back. Damn, he thought, that was good. It's been too long. I'll bet I impressed little Lisa. He smiled as he remembered the sound of her sigh at the end. Yeah, I'll bet I impressed her.

He scooped up a thick bar of soap, and started to raise his arm when its scent hit him. Roses, he thought, his nostrils widening. And was that vanilla? Really, why would anyone buy soap that smells like that?

"Lisa," he called.

She whirled from the bed she was smoothing, startled by the unfamiliar voice coming from the bathroom. Oh, he mustn't holler like that, she thought. Then she remembered they were in the Campgrounds. No one would hear them.

Pushing the bathroom door ajar, a pillow clutched to her chest, Lisa peeped into the steamy bathroom. The man-shape standing behind the fogged shower doors was too short and too broad through the middle to be there. The line of his buttocks sat too high. It wasn't the casual, soft roundness that was one of the reasons she married Peter. Gideon's backside profile was more arrogant, somehow, as if his muscles were proud of themselves. Cheeky, she thought, and then she smiled at her own joke.

"Yes?"

"Have you got some different soap?" Gideon asked. "Something unscented?"

She dropped the pillow. "Um, no. I'm sorry. Why? Don't you like that kind?"

Gideon hesitated, wondering if he should try to entice her into the shower. But he had to be at work by nine or old Harry would miss him.

"Oh, OK. I just didn't want to smell…significant. If you know what I mean," he said, wagging the soap.

"Oh sure, I understand." Lisa turned her face away, picked up the pillow, and slipped back through the door to the bedroom. The sight of unfamiliar shoes and socks on the rug made her start. What was I thinking, she wondered. I've just had sex with my brother-in-law. No one will be on my side if I get caught. Why did I do this?

She hurried to make the bed, and heard the water stop as she bent to smooth its quilt. She hoped Gideon hadn't noticed how she'd sighed at the end. She'd tried to stifle the sound but her regrets had already started by that time, and she just couldn't keep them in. She could tell Gideon was diligent about his performance, and Lisa was old-fashioned enough to believe that a woman never disrespected a man's efforts in bed so she hoped he hadn't noticed her sigh.

She glanced at the bedside clock. Eight-oh-five. He'd said he had to be to work by nine. Good. The sooner they got out of the cabin, the better. She rushed toward the kitchen just as Gideon opened the bathroom door.

Isn't that sweet, he thought. She's shy. Probably hasn't been with anyone but Peter since they got married. I'd better reassure her that she did just fine.

He sniffed the skin of his forearm before he pulled on his shirt. Experience had taught him that it was small details like the smell of an unusual soap or walking into town from the wrong direction that would give away the presence of a new woman in his life. And in a town like Carding, secrecy was essential—and notoriously difficult to achieve.

Gideon was surprised to find Lisa standing by the back door with her coat on and her car keys in her hand when he emerged from the bedroom.

"I thought you had the morning free," he said. Lisa shifted her eyes away from his. Uh oh, he thought, I hope she's not one of those confessing types. That would be bad for business. Peter Foster was the only engineer on Brown & Sons' payroll, and Gideon's father set a lot of store by him. Dad will kill me if Peter quits because of something I've done, he thought. And he's already angry enough about what happened with Chloe.

He took a step toward Lisa, and she shied back. "Are you…are you all right?" he asked. Damn, he thought. She looks like she's going to cry. Now what do I do?

He glanced at the clock on the wall above her head. He had less than an hour to get her calmed down, and himself out the door in order to make it to work on time. The clock was a smiling black cat whose tail moved back and forth like a pendulum while its eyes moved in the opposite direction. "Hey, that clock reminds me of the dentist we had when I was a kid. Dr. Williams had one of those on his waiting room wall," he said. "Cruel man. I always thought he hated children."

"Mom found it at a yard sale years ago, before she divorced Dad." Lisa struggled to swallow. "She's always liked stuff from the fifties. I'm surprised Dad kept it, to tell you the truth."

Gideon looked at her face again, and judged that his diversion had tamped down her tears. "Are you all right?" he asked again. He had to know if she was considering telling her husband about him.

Lisa's face collapsed toward her chin. "I don't think this was the right thing for me to do," she whispered. "I think you'd better go." She pulled her coat a little closer.

Gideon checked to make sure he'd put all his clothes back on. He remembered one occasion when he'd accidentally left his watch behind, and that woman had had a lot of explaining to do to her husband. He didn't want to go through that again. He ran his hands through his pants pockets, checking on the whereabouts of his wallet, pocket knife, and comb. Then he reached for his jacket.

"I'm sorry you feel that way," he said. "I thought…"

She crossed her arms over her coat. "So did I. But I was wrong. You'd better go."

Gideon pulled his jacket on and started to zip it up. That's when his truck keys fell to the tile floor. As he bent to get them, he suddenly gasped and stopped moving.

"What's wrong?" Lisa asked.

"My back," Gideon said. "I can't straighten up."

"You're kidding!" Lisa's voice shot to its highest register. "We've got to get out of here."

"But it hurts." Gideon put his hands to his knees, panting. Lisa whirled in place. What was she going to do?

"You can't stay here," she hissed. "Can you at least get down the steps to the backyard? Where did you park your truck?"

"Over on Beach Road, at the turnoff that the ice fishermen use," Gideon said, his face pointed toward the floor.

"Why did you park so far away?" Lisa wailed. "How am I ever going to get you there? We can't be seen together."

"I didn't want anyone to spot my truck," Gideon said. "What was I supposed to do? Put a Brown & Sons pickup in the Campgrounds' winter parking lot to give folks a reason to wonder what I was doing here? The Browns don't own anything in the Campgrounds, remember?"

He tried to straighten up but immediately returned to his bent-over position. "I'm sorry," he said. "It's no use. You're going to have to help me walk."

Lisa nearly fluttered off the ground in her anxiety. Gideon needed help. She knew that. But she didn't want to touch him again. And she certainly didn't want anyone to find him bent over in a place where he wasn't supposed to be with a woman who called in sick to work so that she could...could... She shook her head in frustration.

"Can you walk if you keep your hands on your knees?" she asked.

Gideon took a step, and gasped. "It's raising my foot. It's hard to do that."

"Can you shuffle?"

Gideon slid his left foot slowly along the floor. No gasping. Then he tried the right.

"That's it," Lisa said, sounding every bit the cheerleader she was in high school. "You can do it."

"Yeah, this is great fun, isn't it?" Gideon said. The minutes dragged on as he inched his way across the floor then down the three steps to the yard.

"There now, you'll be all right, won't you?" Lisa asked.

"No. No, I won't."

"No? What do you mean?" Gideon heard the quaver in her voice, and had to remind himself that most people did not have his level of experience in matters of adultery. Part of his role here, he told himself, was educating his new conquest. He turned his head so he could see her.

"My dear Lisa," he said. "While I may be able to shuffle all the way to my truck—maybe—I will never be able to climb into it or drive. I require your help."

"Help?" She nearly squeaked. "I can't believe I called in sick for this." Then she looked down at the back of Gideon's head, and suddenly realized that the curly brown mop he sported with such pride had a prominent thin spot. And the hair around this thin spot was a bit longer than its neighbors. Lisa suddenly grinned, and a wholly inappropriate guffaw passed her lips. Gideon Brown—Carding's strutting rooster—had a comb-over.

Gideon joined in with a chuckle of his own even though he had no idea what had tickled her funny bone. This is a good sign, he thought.

She can see the humor of our situation. Relieves the tension. That means I can probably get in a couple more "visits" with her at the Cooper family cabin before winter is over. Once spring came, Gideon knew it would be easy to satisfy his needs outside of Carding. But with two months of winter still to go, it made more sense to stay as close to home as possible. Traveling could be a bear this time of year.

Lisa pressed a fist against her mouth to fight her nervous giggles. I might as well stand in front of town hall and tell everyone coming in the door that I called in sick this morning so I could flail around in bed with my sister's husband. Then it occurred to her, in a flash so strong it nearly knocked her over, that that was exactly what she ought to do.

It's not that I hate Peter, Lisa realized. In fact, I think he's one of the dearest and kindest of men to ever live. But that's the problem—he's perfect and I'm bored. Lisa glanced at the stooped-over man at her side, and had another epiphany—Gideon could be her ticket out of Carding.

"Wait here," she said aloud.

"For what?" Gideon asked.

"I'm going to get your truck, and move it to where you don't have to walk so far," Lisa said. "Give me your keys."

"But won't that be…risky?" he asked.

"What else can I do? Leave you here as a perch for the crows?" she said as she turned away.

Gideon grunted. "There is that." Then he cocked his head in order to view the movement of Lisa's backside as she stalked off. Magnificent, he thought, absolutely her best side. She thinks it's her breasts but she's never seen herself from this angle. Yes, I hope I can keep this one interested for a little while longer.

The walking path down the middle of the Campground's main road to the miniscule winter parking lot was tamped down enough for Lisa to jog to her car. That's what the problem is, she thought exultantly. I'm bored, bored, bored with seeing the same people I grew up with, bored with my job at town hall, bored with seeing the same old buildings around the same old green. Bored with my life so far.

It's not sex I want, she realized as she slipped into the driver's seat of her Toyota. One human body is pretty much like another as far as its various parts are concerned. And there's only so many ways you can fit them together. So Gideon Brown is hardly the final answer to my prayers, Lisa thought. But he might become—she hesitated over her choice of words—grateful for what I can provide in the short term.

Mom always says that grateful men are the most useful men, and a little gratitude from Gideon could go a long way toward easing my way out of this town.

Lisa didn't know exactly what she expected to see when she got back to the Cooper family cabin. She hoped that Gideon had made some effort to get a bit further down the path on his own. But she found him exactly where she left him, though a bit more upright.

He grinned when she appeared, letting his eyes touch her body as if revisiting scenes from a favorite movie. Lisa nearly laughed at the obvious technique. You have no idea what you're going to do for me, buddy boy, she thought. And you wouldn't appreciate it if you did.

"The spasm is starting to ease," Gideon said. "I'm really sorry about this. Rather embarrassing, if the truth be told."

A laugh leaked out of Lisa, and she suddenly realized she felt happy. In the time it took her to retrieve Gideon's truck, she'd made an important decision about her life. She looked at her brother-in-law with something close to real affection. How could she be angry at a man with a bad back and a bad comb-over when he was going to be her ticket out of Carding?

"Do you think you can walk down the path to the Campground Road by yourself? The snow's tamped down pretty firm," she said.

Gideon nodded. "It'll be slow but I think so…if you'll help me."

Lisa tucked one of her shoulders under Gideon's arm so he could lean on her. At first, he winced with every step, and Lisa heard him hiss between his teeth. But his movements grew easier as they moved along, and by the time Campground Road came into view, Gideon was moving slow but steady.

Just before he stepped into the road, he let his hand fall from her shoulder to her backside for a good squeeze, and Lisa giggled. Gideon squeezed again then patted her posterior with an air of possession. Yeah, throwing himself on Lisa's motherly instincts had turned the tide. They were friends again, he was sure of that. There would be no guilty confessions to her husband now, Gideon thought, not when she lets me touch her like this.

"I hope I get to see you again," he rumbled close to her ear.

Lisa pulled away and smiled. As she walked back down the path, she swayed her hips a bit more than usual because now she knew what he liked to watch. "We'll see," she said over her shoulder.

Gideon stood watching from his angled position until she was out of sight. Then he straightened, walked briskly to his pickup, and roared away. If he was lucky, he'd have enough time to get a coffee at the Crow before he had to be at work.

New post on Carding Chronicle blog: February 4

High Wind Warning from the Sky Guys
by Little Crow

Just a quick note: The weather duo of Nate and Pearly Jones on Dirt Road Radio emailed with a heads-up that the winds from a storm charging in from the coast will be making our trees do the boogie woogie by early this afternoon. Be aware of falling limbs, especially on the roads around the Wooly Mountain. (Mount Merino to those from away.) Gusts could reach upwards of 45 mph, nothing to take lightly.

Fortunately, most of the snow has crystallized into ice particles so there won't be much, if any, drifting.

Still, be careful out there.

Little Crow | February 4 | Categories: Local Weather

Peter pocketed his phone after reading Little Crow's wind warning, and hoped that the man he'd come to see about heavy equipment for Brown & Sons would hurry it up a little. He didn't relish driving back to Carding on the interstate with a headwind. Forty-five miles per hour meant you could change lanes without touching the steering wheel as you crested the Green Mountains around Montpelier.

Lisa should be up by now, he thought as he glanced at the time, rushing to get out of the house, and in a panic because she couldn't locate some frill or another in the mess in her closet. But if he didn't remind her, she'd forget about securing the latch on their garage door, and he didn't want to buy another pair of hinges. The last big blow nearly wrenched the door off because of her forgetfulness.

He waited patiently while her phone rang—Lisa never remembered where she left her cell—but no one answered. He checked the time again. She couldn't possibly be at work. That would make her—what?—five minutes early? Still... Peter punched in Lisa's work number, and Paula answered in half a ring.

"Lisa? No, sorry Peter," she said. "She called in sick. I'm assuming she's home with her phone turned off."

"Huh. OK," Peter said. "She wasn't up when I left. Thanks, Paula."

Peter tapped his phone screen while he chewed over this bit of news. Lisa's usual mode of illness was two parts not-feeling-well mixed with three parts drama. He found it hard to believe she'd miss an opportunity to milk him for sympathy before he left the house if she was sick. But then, she'd been pretty quiet lately.

Peter suddenly felt a deep chill grip his heart. Could she be pregnant? No, oh please no. The last time they'd talked about having kids, she was quite clear she had no intention of ruining her figure for any child until she turned thirty, and that was still a couple of years away.

He shuddered. Children...with Lisa.

At that moment, his phone rang. It was Harry.

"Yeah." Peter listened. "No, Harry, the grader's not worth the money he's asking. Sorry. But the backhoe is. What's your top price? I want to head back as soon as possible, and I think this guy is ready to make a deal. If we can move it along, I can make it back by nine."

Peter turned to the heavy equipment dealer as soon as he hung up, feeling a whole lot colder than what you'd expect for a day in early February in Vermont.

Ted Owens watched sunlight ooze across his kitchen table as he stirred half-and-half into his second cup of coffee. The knot of anxiety in his belly tightened as he watched his niece pour milk on her cereal. When she first arrived, Ted was inclined to think of Suzanna as "that poor kid" but the child would have none of that nonsense. In their short conversations over a Sunday-night supper of BLT's and soup—Ted's culinary skills were limited—the girl expressed no eagerness to see her mother again nor any contempt for Allison's actions. In fact, Suzanna's demeanor reminded Ted of the resignation of airline passengers who just learned their flights had been delayed...again.

He'd asked her timidly about school, and was informed that until last Thursday, she'd had a seat in a sixth-grade classroom in Las Vegas, and she expected her mother to drag her back there soon enough. So, Suzanna announced, it would be a waste of time to enroll her in Carding Elementary. Yes, a complete waste of time.

Ted felt his eyebrows rise at this pronouncement, and the hatred he harbored for Allison kindled anew. It was all well and good to ruin your own miserable life but to drag a child through your muck...

"Does your mother do this sort of thing often?" he asked. "Drag you off in the middle of the night, I mean."

The girl nodded, spooning up her milky breakfast. "Sometimes it's because she gets fired but sometimes it's because there's a new Bruno," she said.

"Bruno? You mean that man who drove you here?" Ted had never laid eyes on anyone named Bruno before. He always imagined a man with a name like that came standard issue with a broken nose, and biceps the size of full mail sacks. Ted worked in the Carding post office, and moved a lot of full mail sacks so he knew what he was talking about. But the man behind the wheel of that large black car had been skinny with a face like a tack. Bruno didn't fit the profile.

"Oh, I don't remember what that guy's real name is," Suzanna said. Ted's eyebrows reached for his thinning hairline. "I call all my mother's boyfriends Bruno because it's easier to remember that way. Can you get some Cheerios next time you're at the store? And maybe some bananas, too? I like fruit on my cereal when I can get it."

Ted winced. She calls them all Bruno because it's easier to remember? How could a mother do that to her child? Aloud he said, "Would you rather have something besides cereal? Eggs? Pancakes?"

The girl stopped spooning soggy flakes into her mouth. "Pancakes? Can I have them with maple syrup? I had some once, in a restaurant, from a bottle shaped like a leaf. Mom said it was made here in Vermont but that was before I knew where Vermont was. It was very good." She stopped moving for a moment to listen intently to a passing car.

"That's a taxi delivering Lydie Talbot," Ted said. "She's takes care of her sister, Millie Bettinger, across the street. It's not your mother."

The girl relaxed, and they exchanged their first conspiratorial look. "I kept the leaf bottle. It's in my suitcase," she said. "You can see it if you need to know what I mean by maple syrup."

Ted smiled. "No, it's OK. We see those little leaf bottles around here a lot. Andy Cooper, over at the store, he sells dozens of them." Ted stood up, opened his refrigerator then placed a small glass jug in front of the girl. Dark brown liquid filled it to a point where sugar crystals marked the line between syrup and no syrup.

Suzanna pulled the jug closer and tilted it in the light. "Are you sure this is maple syrup?" she asked.

"Yes. I helped make it, in fact," Ted said. "A friend of mine owns a sugarbush up on Belmont Hill."

"Maple syrup comes from a bush? I thought it came from a tree," the girl said.

Ted laughed. "No, though now that you point it out, I suppose bush is kind of a strange term for a place where lots of maple trees grow together and get tapped for syrup. Try pouring a little on your cereal."

Suzanna looked doubtful. "It's darker than what was in my leaf bottle. Will it taste different?"

Ted's eyebrows, which had climbed down from his hairline, now bunched up against one another. Suzanna thought they looked like two fuzzy caterpillars coming together for a kiss, and she quickly put her hand up to her mouth to scratch an itch that didn't exist in order to hide her grin. She didn't want her uncle to think she was rude. Since he was now her only friend in the world, that wouldn't do at all.

"It probably tastes even better than what you had," he said as he pulled a spoon out of the silverware drawer. "You see, there are different grades of maple syrup based on their sugar content and color." He lifted the jug, slid its spout open, and dripped a little of the brown liquid into the bowl of his spoon. "I think that the grade A dark amber is the one most worthy of pancakes." He handed the spoon to the girl. "Here, try it for yourself."

She obeyed, tasted, and then let a pent-up grin rip across her face. "I can put this on cereal?" she asked.

Ted poured a thin spiral of syrup over what remained of her breakfast. "Have at it," he said.

Suzanna dug in with relish, and Ted let himself think that maybe this uncling business had a lot going for it after all.

He stood up, and stretched his back. "I need to get to work," he said. "Since you're not going to school, you need to come with me."

Suzanna looked up, her eyes round as buttons. "Why?"

"Well, I can't leave you here all alone, now, can I?" Ted said.

"Mom does, all the time."

Ted smiled. "Well, I'm not Mom."

Suzanna scooped up the last of her cereal. "That's what I like best about being here so far."

Edie Wolfe always kept a sharp eye out for friends as she and Nearly crossed the Carding Green on their early morning walks. Nearly, an aging but still handsome cocker spaniel, trolled about the path at the far end of the leash he shared with Edie, his nose to the ground as he gathered the latest news. He preferred to keep Edie on a leash because it was easier to keep track of her that way. The woman had a bad habit of wandering off to chat at the most unexpected times. And once she got to talking, well...let's just say that the leash made it easier to pull her away.

Like most mornings, their destination was the Carding Academy of Traditional Arts. But the way they took to get there, while routine, was circuitous. First they stopped at the Coop for their newspapers. Then they headed over to the Crow Town Bakery for a morning scone (hopefully without currants because Nearly hated those berry things), and coffee. Then the post office because Edie preferred to pick up her mail instead of having it delivered to her house, and then they finally ended up at the academy. Once at the school, Nearly always cadged a healthy chunk of scone before circling his bed for a well-earned nap.

For some reason, this morning's routine didn't follow their well-worn plan. Instead of her usual vigorous step, Edie dawdled as if she had a thorn in her paw. Then she stopped beneath the naked sycamores to adjust a boot. Nearly sighed, breathing in the scents of various humans, dogs, and squirrels then shifted his large ears forward. What are we waiting for, he thought. There's nothing new to smell here.

Suddenly, Edie came over all lively, as if she'd just picked up the distinct odor of a mouse that needed killing. Nearly loved to kill mice, nasty things that got into his food dish at night unless he kept them under control. But the dog knew it was not mice Edie was smelling. Humans could barely detect the smell of a skunk if it stood right next to them.

He turned his head in the same direction as Edie's. Someone—or rather two someones—moved under the maples. He tilted his nose up to sample the air but couldn't pick anything special out of the aroma package coming his way. Then he felt a tug on his leash, and Edie murmured "C'mon boy."

Their pace, though faster, was still off their usual step. Nearly turned his head toward the people he'd spotted, wondering if they had anything to do with this strange start to their morning. Then he and Edie got closer to convergence with the two someones, and his human slowed. Nearly was right. She did mean to cross paths with them.

"Good morning, Ted," Edie called out. Oh, Nearly thought with disappointment, it's him, the human who never carries dog treats. How boring. But then Nearly caught a few molecules of something strange… mmm, hard to describe…not illness exactly. But something not exactly healthy either. Nearly put his nose to the ground, and wandered about the humans' feet.

Ted started when Edie called his name. He'd been mentally rehearsing how he'd tell his sister to get lost if she showed up to take Suzanna away. He sensed Edie's interest in the girl, and he had an impulse to throw himself in between his niece and the older woman. But then he realized that was absurd. Edie Wolfe had never liked Allison. That fact alone made her a potential ally.

"Edie," he said. "Good morning. I'd like you to meet my niece, Suzanna."

"How do you do, Suzanna," Edie said. "Are you off to help your uncle sort mail this morning?"

The child glanced up at Ted. "I'm not sure what I'm going to do," she said in a very small voice.

Nearly stopped his snuffling, and sat on the ground as close to the girl as he could get without being rude. It was his observation that courteous dogs got more treats than rude ones. And Nearly was widely acknowledged as the premier treat-cadger in town.

Ted let his hand rest on Suzanna's small shoulders. Suddenly he realized it was the first time he'd touched the child since she'd arrived. Have I become that cold, he wondered. Then in his next flash of neural activity, he realized how long it had been since he'd had a reason to touch another human being. That thought stirred up a stew of pain in the area around his heart, and he glanced down at his niece. How hard should I hope I can keep you with me, he asked himself. Then he cleared his throat.

"Suzanna's just arrived in Carding," he told Edie. The words came out in a croak, and he cleared his throat again. "I didn't have time to arrange for someone to take my place this morning so I'm afraid she'll be stuck with me in the P.O."

Nearly shifted his position, and tilted his head back to sample more air coming from the small person. She hadn't rolled in anything dead, of that he was certain. Humans routinely let those opportunities go by. No, this was something different, as if the small person had spent too much time in the presence of something not quite alive.

Nearly turned his nose to draw in air directly from the man, just to be sure he wasn't the source. The dog sensed uneasiness there, like the smell a squirrel gave off when it edged too far away from a tree in its quest for acorns. But what he smelled definitely wasn't coming from the man. No, the odor drifted from the girl.

"Why is your dog looking at me like that?" Suzanna asked.

Edie looked down at Nearly and smiled. "My old boy can't see as well as he used to," she said, stooping to caress one of the dog's large, soft ears. "You're new to him so he's trying to make a place for you in his people catalogue. That way, next time he meets you, he'll know you're all right, that you're someone who won't hurt a dog."

Nearly looked up at his designated person. *She senses it too,* he thought. *Something's not quite right with the small one.*

"He catalogues people?" Suzanna asked.

"Well, that's what I call it," Edie said. "Being so much smaller than human beings, Nearly has to know right away whether he can trust someone or not. In my experience, he only needs to meet someone once in order to do that."

Suzanne nodded slowly. "I do that, too" she said, her eyes fixed on the dog. "Do you think he trusts me?"

Edie and Ted exchanged a flashing glance, and in that instant, they formed a pact to protect the girl. "Oh, I believe he does. Nearly doesn't waste any time on people he can't trust, and he's been quite patient while we chat. He would have tugged on his leash a long time ago if he didn't want to be close to you."

"Oh." The girl uttered the syllable with the finality of a last puzzle piece falling into place. Then she looked directly into Edie's eyes, and the older woman almost gasped at the hardness she saw in the girl's face. *Was this little one going to turn out like her mother,* Edie wondered.

"What do you do with a dog besides walk with it?" Suzanna asked. She gave her tongue a deliberately sharp edge. You could tell a lot about people if you riled them. That way, you'd know whether you had to hide the next time you saw them coming.

But instead of getting starchy like Suzanna expected, the older woman laughed, and bent down to stroke the dog's ears once again. "I suppose if you ask that question in very practical terms, the answer would be 'not much,'" she said. "Nearly and I don't hunt in the brush for woodcock, which is what his ancestors were bred for. But then, people don't have pets for practical reasons."

Suzanna shifted on her feet. The woman's laughter unsettled her.

"So why do you have a dog?" she asked, more gently this time.

Nearly cocked his ears forward. He smelled fresh scones. He stood to signal that it was time to be off. Edie smiled at the girl.

"I believe the more friends we make in this world, the better," she said to Suzanna. "Nearly and I are friends. We take care of one another in our own ways. He brings a sweetness to my life that it wouldn't have otherwise, and I protect him, make sure he's healthy, feed him well. In my opinion, it's a very even trade."

Edie wound the slack of Nearly's leash around her hand. "And right now, he's letting me know it's time to get on with our morning routine—scones, coffee, the newspapers, and our mail." Edie and Nearly started to move off. "So I shall see you at the post office in a little while." With a wave and a good morning, Edie and Nearly walked off.

Suzanna stood quite still, watching them. Then she looked up at her uncle. "Does she know my mother?" she asked.

Ted nodded. "Edie knew your grandmother, too. In fact, your grandmother and Edie Wolfe were the best of friends."

Suzanna considered the implications of this bit of information. It felt very odd to think about having a grandmother, and she wondered if they would have liked one another. Then she looked up at her Uncle Ted again. "That woman doesn't like my mother, does she?"

Ted sighed. "I think that's probably true. But I want you to understand that that doesn't mean she doesn't like you. In fact, I think quite the opposite." He let his fingers rest on her shoulder again. "Do you know what I mean?"

Suzanna nodded. "I think so."

FIVE

THE IMPLICATIONS OF FINE DENTAL WORK

New post on Carding Chronicle blog: February 4

Trees Down on Mountain Road
by Little Crow

As expected, high winds are taking their toll on the trees. The electricity's been flickering off and on for the past hour in the center of Carding where Andy Cooper reports that the thermostat on the Coop's dairy case finally gave up and died so you'll find milk and eggs in the beer case for the rest of today.

There are small branches all over our roads, and two big birches came down on that tight curve on Mountain Road, blocking access to the ski resort. Town and mountain crews are cleaning up the debris and expect the road to be reopened shortly.

Snowshoeing and snowmobiling in the woods might not be a good idea unless you're wearing a helmet.
Little Crow | February 4 | Categories: Local Weather

Suzanna had never been in the back of a post office before. In fact, she couldn't remember if she'd ever been in the front of a post office before. She wondered if she should count that as two firsts or just one.

Suzanna liked to add things up. It kept the inside of her head neat and tidy while her mother messed up the rest of her life. So far, it had been a great morning for firsts—first maple syrup on cereal, first dog up close, first people she'd ever known who disliked her mother as much as she did. That was three firsts before she got to the post office. And if she added in her trip to the post office, that would be four.

She watched as her uncle whirled about in his little domain snapping on lights, and moving a chair for her to the "warmest spot in the place, until the heat kicks in." She listened to his chatter with the truck driver as they carried cloth bags and trays of mail into the building.

"You OK on your own for a while?" Ted asked after the driver left. "I've got to sort the mail."

"Sure. Can I look around?"

Ted nodded then started sorting the day's letters, magazines, and junk mail into their little boxes. Suzanna slid off her chair to wander around his desk, and look at all the posters on the walls. Then her heart seized at the sight of a magazine face up in one of the plastic tubs. "Where are they now?" a garish headline asked. And there in the middle of the cover was a picture of her mother when she was a TV star.

Suzanna looked over her shoulder at her uncle, and saw he was busy so she slid the magazine out of the tub, and started to read. As it turned out, the magazine writer knew more things about Allison Owens than her daughter did. Suzanna began to count up these new facts.

One, Allison Owens (or Alli-O as she was called on television) was born and grew up in Carding, Vermont. Two, she left town the day she graduated from high school. Three, her mother, Anna, died just a few months before Alli-O left town for fame and fortune.

Anna. The girl silently mouthed her grandmother's name.

Suddenly the back door banged open. Suzanna leaped to her feet, afraid her mother had returned, and slid the magazine back into its place. But instead of a thin and twitchy Alli-O, Suzanna was confronted with a solid slice of womanhood, someone not much taller than herself but strong enough to carry three full trays of mail.

Ted rushed to help the woman unload her burden. "Ruth, you shouldn't be carrying all of that at the same time," he said.

"Ha, I've carried much more than that, much more," the woman boomed. "Piece of cake, this is. Coffee on?"

At Ted's nod, Ruth whirled toward the steaming coffeemaker then stopped as if struck by a horseshoe during a game at the town beach in summer. She leaned forward to get a good look at Suzanna. After a moment, a grin split her face, showing off the fine dental work bestowed on her by her ex-husband, the dentist, who was now on his fourth—and youngest—wife.

Suzanna glanced nervously at her uncle who seemed completely at ease. It's OK, his expression told her. This woman's all right, too.

"You must be Allison's little girl," Ruth said in a voice that thumped against the walls. "I have to say that you do look like your grandfather." She stepped close enough to touch Suzanna if she wished. "But I'd be willing to bet you smile like your grandmother." She offered her hand.

"My name's Ruth Goodwin. Glad to meet you."

Suzanna reached out, uncertain what to expect from this strange woman. But Ruth's touch resembled her smile, warm, gentle, and oddly comforting. Suzanna liked it.

"Ah, see?" Ruth turned toward Ted. "She does smile like your mother."

Ted's eyes flicked down and back, and his mouth twitched a little. But then the expression disappeared. "She does. Suzanna's got a smile just like Mom's."

"SUZanna?" Ruth's head whipped around. "Really? Interesting choice of name."

"Why? What's so interesting about my name?"

Ruth considered for a moment as she brought her second hand up to engulf the girl's fingers. "Your grandmother's name was Anna. Did you know that?"

Suzanna nodded. "I just found out today. Before…before I got here, I didn't know anything about any family but my mother and her Brunos," she said.

"Brunos?" Ruth looked from Ted to the girl and back.

Ted cleared his throat. "Suzanna told me this morning that she calls all of Allison's…companions…Bruno because it's easier to remember just the one name."

Suzanna took careful note of the expression of deep disapproval that pinched up Ruth's face. "Bruno, is it?" She shook her head while squeezing Suzanna's fingers. "Bruno."

The girl hesitated because there was this peculiar feeling pressing against her breast bone. With an internal start of surprise, Suzanna realized that she wanted to confide in this woman. Until that moment, she'd never bothered to tell anyone about her hurts because it was no use telling adults anything.

"One of the Brunos called me Zee, not Suzanna," she said in her smallest voice. Ruth inched forward so she wouldn't miss a syllable.

"Zee? Why? If I was going to shorten your name, I'd call you Anna, not Zee," Ruth said. Poor little kid, she thought.

"He said he called me Zee because I was always the last thing my mother thought of."

Ruth's eyes turned hard, and Suzanna would have run if the older woman had left her any room to move. "Zee. Really," Ruth said. She looked up to hold a quick, silent conversation with Ted. "Well, young lady, you will never be the last thing I think of. And I'll bet I can say the same for your uncle, and lots of other folks here in Carding." She shook her head, and muttered "Zee."

Edie grunted as she struggled to find her academy keys while juggling coffee, scone, and newspaper. One of these days, she told herself, I'll remember to put them in my pocket before I leave the house. Nearly gazed up and down the street, waiting, just as he did every morning.

With a carefully chosen oath, Edie finally pushed the heavy door aside, stepped onto the mat, and flicked on the overhead lights.

"One of these days, Nearly, one of these days," she said as she nudged the door closed with her foot.

She flipped on more lights as they walked down the hall, checked the thermostat, and then straightened a small study of a Carding house painted by Joseph Stillman Croft, circa 1905, that tilted to the left every time someone opened the door. Then, as she did every day, she cringed in anticipation of crossing the foyer. No matter how she tried, Edie never mastered the trick of ignoring the domineering oil painting that frowned over that space.

Renowned the world over for his stylized, folk-art depictions of rural Vermont, Joseph Stillman Croft, 1867–1942, kept his darker works hidden in his Carding home while he lived in it. The largest of these, *Thieves of Fire*, claimed prominence of place on the wall next to the wide staircase because of a peculiarity in Croft's will that had bequeathed his home to the Carding Academy of Traditional Arts as long as no one removed or substantially changed the location of any artwork or piece of furniture in the building's foyer. To do so would nullify the academy's right to use his home as a school.

On paper, it seemed like such a small price to pay. But in fact, the glowering oil felt like a threat. The young woman on the right of the painting, her face turned slightly away from the viewer—was she weeping? In mourning? Turning away in fear or shame? Across the canvas, a crow watched from the highest branches of a bare tree, a stubbled field between them. The thing always gave Edie the shivers, and she wondered for the umpteenth time if covering it up permanently would violate the terms of Croft's will.

As soon as Edie opened her office door, she spread her scone across its waxed-paper wrapping, broke it into pieces, and handed Nearly the largest fragment before wandering off to do something more important than eating. Nearly didn't understand why humans shared food. A dog, faced with something tasty and edible, protected it from all comers while scarfing it down in as few bites as possible. But his designated human never acted that way which made Nearly proud and grateful.

After he swallowed his portion, Nearly smelled the uneaten pieces of scone on Edie's desk, their fading fragrance mingling with book dust, turpentine, the scent trails of human traffic, and just the faintest whiff of mouse. In order to resist the temptation to clean up after her, Nearly moved to a position on the opposite side of the desk where she'd parked one of the three beds reserved for his use at the academy. Back when he was a very young dog, he thought he'd be helpful and eat left-over food before it got stale. But after a particularly memorable scolding from Edie, he'd refrained from making those efforts in the interests of maintaining canine/human harmony.

The front door rattled open. "Edie, anything to go out in the mail?" Nearly picked up his head. He liked the human called Ruth. He liked her dog, R.G., too. When they were younger (the dogs, that is) Nearly and R.G. enjoyed nothing more than snuffling off together in the woods. Nearly, it was widely acknowledged among Carding's canines, possessed the keener nose. But no dog in Carding had a finer voice than R.G. Fortunately, Nearly had a deep appreciation for the finer points of the canine voice, and he felt that R.G.'s accompaniment fostered admiration for the talents of both of them so there was no inter-canine jealousy.

"Good morning, Ruth," Edie called. "Just a couple of catalogs, that's all."

Ruth craned her head around the door then walked over to scratch behind Nearly's ears while he nosed her pant legs for messages from R.G. Nothing much beyond the usual "Good morning. How are you?"

Then the small human, the one who smelled so strange to Nearly, tiptoed into the room.

"Edie, have you met Suzanna?" Ruth asked.

Edie smiled. "Just briefly, this morning on the green." Suzanna's face looked both expectant and apprehensive. "So, are you delivering mail with Ruth this morning?"

"Ted thought it would be more interesting to drive around with me than watch him sort envelopes and packages," Ruth said. "Suzanna's never been to Carding before so I thought I'd show her around the lake, and the falls, and the mountain."

"I've never seen a ski mountain before," Suzanna said softly, her eyes sweeping the walls covered by student quilts, paintings, and drawings. She tugged on Ruth's sleeve. "Can I ask a question?"

"Of course," the two older women chimed together.

"Do you like that big painting, out there?" She pointed toward the foyer.

"No, not at all," Edie said. "But we're kind of stuck with it, I'm afraid. The man who built this place left it to the academy in his will providing we never move anything in the foyer. I'd take it down in a heartbeat if I could. Creepy, isn't it?"

"At Christmas, we drape strings of lights over it, and that helps," Ruth said. "But otherwise, we all try to ignore it as much as we can." She took a small stack of envelopes from Edie. "How come you're not closing the road this morning?" she asked.

"Oh no," Edie raced out of her office. "I forgot."

Together, the two women opened the front doors, grabbed two signs, and dragged them toward the street. Nearly, who had followed because he loved to watch humans in a hurry, suddenly caught a funny smell, and his nose bobbed in the air. His movement caught Edie's eye. "Something's got his attention," she said. Then it drifted her way too, and she breathed in. "Roses."

Ruth sniffed. "And vanilla," she said.

"Morning, ladies." Gideon Brown smiled as he hurried past on the way to Brown & Sons, a tall cup of coffee clutched in his hand. "Closing Academy Road again, I see."

The two women exchanged glances behind his back. There was only one reason for Gideon Brown to smell like a scented candle. "He's on the hunt again," Ruth whispered, and Edie nodded.

While the two women placed the "Road Closed" signs in their proper places, Suzanna examined Carding Green in minute detail. Tourists in colorful Spandex and tasseled hats loped from shop to shop. The doors of the Carding Coop flapped open and closed like bird wings as people moved in and out, in and out. The smells of cinnamon and baking bread wafted past her nose.

"Ah, smells like Diana's got that fan of hers going again," Ruth said as she walked up to stand by the girl.

"Fan?" Suzanna asked.

Ruth pointed across the green. "You see that brick building with the big doors and white sign?" Suzanna nodded. "Well, that's the Crow

Town Bakery, and the woman who owns it is pretty smart, just like her mother," Ruth said as she nodded in Edie's direction. "Every time Diana pulls something good out of the oven, she turns on a fan that's in the window above the door so all the good smells get out onto the green. Claims her sales have gone up by 30 percent since she started doing that. Folks smell that cinnamon and they just come running."

Suzanna swallowed. "It does smell good."

Ruth looked down at the girl, and all the motherly instincts she thought she'd put away when her two kids moved out on their own surged up again. Once a mother, always a mother, she thought.

"Tell me, what did Ted feed you for breakfast?" she asked, crossing her arms over her chest. "I'm assuming he did feed you."

Suzanna nodded. "Flakes and milk," she said. "I don't really like flakes because they're all soggy by the time you get to the third spoonful. He didn't have any bananas, which is at least something when all you've got is flakes. But he did have maple syrup, and that was really good."

Ruth pulled out her cellphone, and punched two numbers. "Hey Diana, Ruth here. I'm on the other side of the green, and those cinnamon buns sure smell good. Could you put a couple aside? And some juice and chocolate milk." She looked down at Suzanna. "You do like chocolate milk, right?" The girl nodded. "Coffee for me. We'll be there in just a few minutes."

Suzanna wondered why these grownups were so eager to please her. And as she thought about the possible answers, she kept count of the people going in and out of the bakery, just for something to do. She could tell by the way they moved that most of them had smiles—or something close to a smile—on their faces. You could tell by the way folks walked if they were smiling or not. Smiling people moved in an easier way.

But then this strange blot appeared in the crowd. Suzanna narrowed her eyes. It was a man, a man with stiff, almost jerky movements. As he stalked up the sidewalk, the crowd parted in front of him then closed behind him as if touching him would contaminate their days. He cut off the corner of the green instead of following the sidewalk, picking up his pace in a trajectory that would bring him face to face with Suzanna. She didn't like that so she plucked at Ruth's sleeve.

"Please...er...what should I call you?" she asked.

"Would Aunt Ruth suit you?"

Suzanna jumped. "Aunt? I can do that? I've always wanted an aunt."

Ruth beamed. "Oh believe me, Suzanna, you'll have a bunch of aunts here in Carding in no time at all."

"OK then, Aunt Ruth, who is that man?" she pointed, "and why is he so mad?"

Ruth followed the girl's finger then swung her head over her shoulder. "Hey Edie, it's old Harry, and he's in a tear."

Edie stepped up, Nearly at her heels. "So what else is new?" she asked. The dog pitched in with a low, almost inaudible growl that made Suzanna look down to see how close he was to her leg, just in case. But his eyes were locked in the same direction as Edie's.

"Edith Wolfe," the man roared as he crossed the street toward them. "Why are you closing Academy Road again? You did the same thing yesterday. Just who do you think you are?"

Suzanna leaned against Ruth. She hated loud voices, particularly if they were male. Her new aunt pulled her close.

Edie smiled. "Why, good morning, Mr. Brown. How nice to see you. You're looking well. For your information, we have a tour bus of quilt students due here in an hour. That's why the road is *temporarily* closed."

The man stopped. "How dare you good morning me?" he hissed. "You and that foul school of yours, always blocking the road to my trucks, making us go around the long way just because you don't want to inconvenience any of your artsy-fartsy students. I've told you before, this detour of yours adds a half a mile to every trip one of my trucks makes. Do you have any idea how much a gallon of diesel costs?"

"Hmmm." Edie cocked her head in a thinking pose, tapping her cheek with a forefinger. "Let's see, I know I'm just a woman but I bet even I could figure that out."

Harry jerked his head a little, and Suzanna sensed his whole body tighten. Then Edie smiled, big and broad. "Oh, of course, that must be what that sign means down at the Mini-Market on the highway. I saw it only yesterday but if I try really hard, I know I can recall what it said. Hmmm..." She tapped her toe on the sidewalk.

"Four dollars and fifteen cents." Harry's voice escaped in one long, strained hiss. "And do you know how many miles I get to a gallon of diesel in one of my trucks?"

"Five," Edie answered. "Unless that has changed since we had this conversation yesterday."

"So every time you close that road—which I have just as much right to use as anyone else—you cost me money." Harry clenched every muscle in his face. This pulled on his scalp, making the short hairs on the back of his head bristle. Suzanna gawked, fascinated, and this made Harry notice her.

"Who's the brat?" he yelled at Ruth.

Ruth hugged Suzanna. "I'd love to waste more of our morning listening to the sweet way you have with words, Mr. Brown, but some of us got work to do." She glanced down at the girl. "Ready?"

At Suzanna's nod, the two walked to the packed Jeep waiting at the curb, and drove off with a wave for Edie. As they pulled onto Main Street, Suzanna let out a long sigh. "How can Mrs. Wolfe not yell back at that man? He's awful. My mother would have been screaming."

Ruth negotiated a right onto Meetinghouse Road, picking her way among the tourists. "First of all, it's not Mrs. Wolfe. That's Edie's birth name not her married name. She took Wolfe back as her last name when she got divorced. I've known Edie for years, and she'd much rather you call her something like Aunt Edie or Aunt E or Mrs. Edie." Ruth pulled up in front of the Crow Town Bakery, and set the emergency brake. "And old Harry Brown is good at twisting people up tight so they say and do stupid things. That's how he controls them, and Edie refuses to be controlled by that blowhard."

"So Mrs....um...Edie stays calm so that that man can't control her?" Suzanna asked.

Ruth laughed. "Yep. I think she kind of enjoys tweaking him," Ruth said. "Come on, let's get those cinnamon rolls while they're still warm."

Suzanna inhaled as deep as she could as they walked into the Crow Town Bakery. "Oh, this is heaven," she said as she peered into the glass case where Diana displayed her shop's wares—fat muffins bristling with currants and cranberries, spirals of cinnamoned dough bulging under trickles of icing, chubby bagels shouldering their way out of their bins as if eager to be eaten.

"Ruth." A woman's voice boomed over the friendly din. "Got your order right here." Diana Bennett plucked two paper bags from behind the counter.

"Do you make these?" Suzanna asked, pointing to the cookies, muffins, rolls, and bagels.

"You bet we do, my husband and I." Diana hooked a finger over her shoulder at a dark-haired man bustling around the cash register. "That's Stephen. It's a family thing, you know?"

She leaned over the counter, her dark eyes gleaming, as Ruth extracted money from her wallet. "Old Harry was in here earlier, in a nasty mood," Diana said quietly.

Ruth nodded. "Yeah, he was lighting into your mother when we left. You don't suppose Louisa's threatened to divorce him again, do you?"

"Hmph, wouldn't blame her if she did, the way he treats her," Diana said. "But he just bought her a new car so she's all smiles at the moment."

The two women shook their heads in unison. "No accounting for taste," Ruth said. "By the way, I'd like to introduce you to Ted's niece. This is Suzanna Owens. She's come to stay in Carding. Suzanna, this is Diana Bennett, the best baker in town."

"So you're...um...related to Mrs. Edie?" Suzanna asked, eyeing the bags in Ruth's hands.

"Ah, I see you've met my mother already," Diana said, reaching over the counter to shake Suzanna's hand. "I'm not surprised. Welcome to Carding. I hope you like it here."

"Well, this day has been very interesting so far," Suzanna said.

Ruth waggled the two bags. "Guaranteed these will make it even more interesting. See ya, Diana."

Suzanna dove into her cinnamon roll as soon as they got into Ruth's Jeep. For a while, all Ruth could hear was chewing punctuated by the slurp of orange juice. Ruth had insisted on juice first, chocolate milk second. "Vitamins," she'd explained, suspicious that Ted wouldn't feed the child right.

After the initial cinnamon rush subsided, Suzanna paused long enough to ask a question. "Aunt Ruth." The two words felt so unfamiliar, the child stumbled over them. "How does Edie know that stuff about...what do you call him? Old Harry?

"Harry Brown," Ruth said, rolling down her window to stuff a mailbox with a sheaf of envelopes and magazines. "You mean how does she know that smiling and being polite makes him even madder?"

"Yeah, that."

"Well, wives learn all sorts of things about their husbands over time," Ruth said, stuffing the latest L.L. Bean catalog into the next box.

Suzanna choked on her orange juice. "Married? Edie is married to that awful man?"

"*Was* married," Ruth corrected, patting her on the back. "And it was a very long time ago."

"But they don't go together at all," Suzanna said as she coughed.

Ruth laughed. "I'll have to remember to tell Edie you said that. It will please her to no end." She stopped again, stuffed three mailboxes, then moved on. "They very definitely didn't go together at all. Which is why Edie left him before they were married a year."

"So is he that baker lady's father?" Suzanna asked.

"No, Diana's father isn't Harry," Ruth said. "In fact, no one but Edie's absolutely sure who the father of her children is. You see, when Edie left Harry, she went to live in Europe, Paris actually. And she met someone there, fell in love, and they had twins. Diana's got a brother named Daniel who lives in New York City."

Suzanna leaned back in her seat, a big smile stretched across her face. "Wow. Carding is way better than any TV show."

six

AMERICANA

As students filed through the academy's front doors, Edie smiled, directed, answered questions, and then smiled some more. When Chloe Brown bobbed through the crowd trailing streamers of fabric in blue and orange, a clutch of women followed in her wake oohing over her color selection. J.C. Davis, the woodworking teacher, clanked as he walked by, a can of small chisels in his hand. Joanne Lendaro struggled down the corridor to her machine quilting studio, lugging a heaped basket of fabric and batting destined to become practice pieces for her students.

Then a comfortable hum settled into the old building, like a hive of human bees happily making honey. Sometimes that honey was a new design based on an ancient quilt or a new way to turn a wooden bowl or weave a rug. Other times, it was simply the sound of people making something that didn't exist before just for the sheer pleasure of making it. Edie counted the hum among her favorite sounds, and she sighed contentedly as she returned to her office.

She sighed again, this time without much contentment, when she spotted a handwritten note perched on top of the papers in her inbox. "Edie," it read, "you promised you'd rewrite the academy's brochure before we had to print more. We're down to our last 100 copies. Please?" It was signed by Agnes Findley, the academy's board president.

When Edie plopped down in her chair, Nearly looked up, hoping for more scone. "Sorry, boy," she murmured. "We finished it about an hour ago." She tipped her coffee cup. Empty. Well, it's the longest job that's never started, she told herself, and she picked up the brochure.

"I wonder how people would react if we told the whole truth about Joseph Stillman Croft and the academy," she said to Nearly as she rattled the paper open. He yawned, turned counterclockwise on his bed, and settled down for his second morning nap.

"Yeah, that's what I think, too," Edie said, and then she began to read while she twirled a red pencil in her hand.

The Carding Academy of Traditional Arts

In the final years of the nineteenth century, a painter named Joseph Stillman Croft discovered the beauty of Carding, Vermont—the roll of its hills to the Corvus River, a deep pool called Half Moon Lake, and Mount Merino in the distance.

Croft stayed for two months during his first visit, taking rooms at the local tavern. The painter left when the snows started, going back to his studio in New York where he showed his paintings and sketches of the moody Vermont countryside to everyone who stood still long enough. ("Moody," Edie snorted. "What makes bare trees and snow moody? It's just winter, plain and simple.")

When he returned with the lilacs in 1897, Croft brought with him a small entourage that included Hansen Willis, the author of the popular Damien Hawke mysteries, and Hansen's wife, Emily. (I never did understand what the Willises saw in Croft, Edie thought. They were so warm and kind while Croft was so cold and nasty.)

Croft and the Willises returned like spring robins for four more years until Croft built a house in Carding in 1901, and moved here permanently. The Croft house, which is now the center of the Carding Academy of Traditional Arts, is situated on a slope above the town center.

For the first couple of years, Croft was sociable. ("Only because he needed people in town to do things for him," Edie muttered.) But he changed over time and eventually became something of a recluse. From 1904 until the artist left town in 1930, no one but a few servants saw the inside of "Croft's Palace" as the house was known to the locals. ("Croft's Pile is more like," Edie said. "And that was probably the nicest thing they called it.")

For the Carding Academy of Traditional Arts, it is Emily Willis who matters most. Born into a New York family of old money, Emily could have lounged about in fashionable dresses, content to be a decorative planet in her famous husband's orbit. But Emily detested that sort of uselessness, so while Hansen worked on his books, Emily traveled the Vermont countryside, sometimes in a carriage but often on horseback—wearing pants! ("Shocking that women had legs back then," Edie said.)

Emily kept meticulous journals of her travels, complete with hand-drawn maps marking every view, every tavern, every farmer with meat or produce to sell. Then she started bringing home what her husband called "curios," and her passion for collecting "Americana" was born.

(Edie loathed the term "Americana" and she drew a line through it. So inexact.)

In 1908, Emily persuaded Hansen to buy a rambling house with an attached barn just up the hill from the Croft house so they could spend their summers in the cool of Vermont instead of the heat of the city. That house is now a guest house for students who travel to the academy for classes.

For twenty years, Emily and Hansen's May arrival in Carding was a signature event. Unlike the reclusive Croft, the Willises loved company. As their three children were born, their household expanded to include a motley crew of cousins who welcomed the neighborhood children into their raucous games, picnics, and outings at Half Moon Lake.

With Emily's encouragement, Half Moon Lake's tiny beach—a bare spot left by a spring flood—was expanded. She encouraged the town to build a bandstand on the green, and local music makers filled the summer air with jigs, reels, Sousa marches, and new songs that Emily brought from New York.

Emily and Hansen Willis breathed life into the whole Corvus River valley. Because they were "from away," they saw this beautiful place with a different eye, a different perspective. They were among the first to recognize the importance of American creativity: art didn't have to come from Europe to be good.

Emily worked to preserve traditional arts such as quilting, knitting, woodworking, weaving, lacemaking, and sewing. Her collecting became more avid and soon filled the Willis's barn. She bought quilts, handmade dolls, cigar store figurines, glass witch balls, stone carvings, and pottery fired in wood-burning kilns. She copied patterns from local knitters, hunted for lace makers, and bought several of George Eastman's new Kodak cameras to record the curios that were too big to drag back to the city.

In 1912, Emily dropped a huge pebble in the cultural pond when she opened the first floor of her New York home during the week before Christmas so others could view her collection of "American art." As she expected, the critics tut-tutted and pooh-poohed. But their harumphing only made Emily's smile bigger because the eager women who crowded her parlor—many with their children in tow—adored the display. By the time Emily closed her first exhibit, just about all the curios she'd collected had found new homes.

The uproar over the first "Carding Exhibition," as it came to be known, was a cause célèbre in the pages of the town newspaper, the *Carding Chronicle*, for several weeks, and it sparked an idea in Kitty Wolfe's head. Kitty not only helped her husband Oscar set type for their newspaper, she raised five children, bred some of the best hunting dogs in the valley, and was an avid quilter. She and Emily Willis kept up a lively correspondence over that winter, so folks suspected that the two women had something planned.

It started with quilting and knitting patterns published in the *Chronicle*. Kitty sent extras of the patterns to Emily, who distributed them among her friends. Pretty soon, Joseph Pulitzer's *New York World* caught wind of this "new trend for women," and started reprinting the *Chronicle's* patterns.

With the money that the patterns earned, Emily and Kitty converted Emily's parlor into a schoolroom, and the Carding Academy's first students arrived in 1914. They stayed at the inn, and walked across the green to their classes.

Edie yawned as she tossed the academy's brochure to one side. "Oh, I don't think I can take any more of this marketing hype," she said to Nearly. As much as she would like to tell the whole truth about how Croft's house became the Carding Academy of Traditional Arts, she knew it wouldn't help the school or its fundraising. After all, the legend of Joseph Stillman Croft still beckoned art lovers to Carding's hills, much to the satisfaction of its inn owners, shopkeepers, and tour guides. People loved the painter's folk-art style so much, they came to Vermont expecting to find it just the way Croft first saw it.

Edie opened her email, and wrote: Agnes, I took a stab at rewriting the brochure but discovered you are right. Its precarious hold on the truth serves our purposes just fine. Order more copies of it as is. Edie.

Dark thoughts still clouded old Harry Brown's mind as he stomped to the top of the hill where the Brown & Sons garage sprawled. As always, he turned around to look down on the green, just because he could. Harry Brown knew he was the best businessman in Carding—sharp-eyed and smart, a guy who almost always kept his word—and no woman could take that away from him.

Harry sighed, and checked his watch. Peter must be back by now, he thought as he pushed open the garage door, and headed up the stairs to the little kitchen on the second floor. He emptied what was left of his coffee into the sink and poured some new in its place. As he sipped, he stood at the window overlooking the vast garage floor where his crew was buzzing. As always, Harry's youngest son, Jacob, stood off to one side, his thumbs flying over the keypad of his cell phone. Harry's insides cinched up when he saw that. Gawd how he hated those things, those phones. They had their uses—handy for getting through to a crew on the road or when you needed help. But this texting stuff! How could anyone type on those little gadgets?

Then he spotted Noah, his middle son, lounging against the side of a truck. As his father watched, Noah yawned, his mouth gaping, then he stuffed his hands deeper into the pockets of his jacket, and settled his tousled head deeper into his shoulders. Noah always complained about the cold, claimed he was sensitive to it. Harry figured it was because he never moved, and if you never move, you got cold. Harry's wife, Louisa, claimed that Noah had "my constitution," and she hauled him off to Florida whenever she could. Harry figured she was shopping him around to prospective Southern wives so he'd have an excuse to live permanently in that godforsaken place.

Well, good riddance to him if he does, Harry thought.

He looked around for Gideon, his single hope for Brown & Sons' immortality. The boy had his faults, many of them too much like Harry's for the old man's comfort. Gideon worked hard on-site, knew how to do a concrete pour so it was done right, and seemed to understand some of how Brown & Sons had to be run.

But Gideon's lust for everything female outstripped his father's, and when he was on the prowl, any common sense the boy had went on vacation. That's why Gideon ran into that academy student. It was the reason why he slept in his basement instead of next to his wife, Chloe. It was the reason why Harry didn't have any grandchildren. He kept hoping that Gideon would somehow make it up to his wife, and took some solace in the fact that Chloe hadn't moved out of their house yet. Harry dreaded the day when she did because that would make some folks in Carding remember how Edie left him.

Peter showed up while Harry bent his mind on locating his eldest son, and finally spotted Gideon pacing in the deepest shadows of the garage. Something uncomfortable writhed in Harry's chest as he examined his son's behavior. Gideon had his head down, his eyes turned away from everyone else. But on closer examination, Harry thought he detected a smile on his eldest son's face.

Just then, Peter shouted across to Gideon, and Harry watched his son start, glance up at the kitchen, and then look away just as quickly. In that moment, Harry knew as sure as he knew the exact balance in his checking account why Gideon smiled.

Harry cursed, then sauntered down the steps toward his eldest son. Gideon shrank away, backing toward the trucks. But Harry stopped him with a shake of his head. The two stood side by side in silence while the crew saddled up for their morning's work. Harry considered then rejected several ways to confront Gideon. He wished his son was still small enough to wallop. Just then, a strange flowery scent wafted his way. Harry sniffed, sniffed again, and then glared at Gideon. "Never use scented soap," he said.

Then he stalked away.

New post on Carding Chronicle blog: February 4

Trees Cleared from Mountain Road and Roast Beef Supper
by Little Crow

The Carding road crew and a crew from the Mount Merino Resort report that the trees down on the Mountain Road by the entrance to Wooly Mountain have been cleared. The town dispatcher says there's about two cords of wood up there for the taking though he cautions that it's birch so it will burn quick.

Father Lloyd over at the Episcopal Church wants me to remind everyone that the final roast beef supper of the season is this Saturday night. Three seatings. Homemade pies for dessert, and if you don't show up, that means there's more for me.

Can I get away with calling this the Last Supper?

High winds are forecast through the night so be careful if you're out and about.

I'll be looking for you.

Little Crow | February 4 | Categories: Local Road Conditions

Everyone in town knew Ruth Goodwin loved Carding, Vermont. Since her life became "dentist-free," as she called it, Ruth had served on nearly every board or committee in town, and every time she showed up, things got done. When she served on the conservation committee, she hiked every trail, dirt road, and path in town, mapping the local flora and counting birds. Then she persuaded the state to declare Half Moon Lake and the Corvus River's marsh and falls a nature preserve. A year later, she and Edie led the charge that prevented Harry Brown from installing 200 condos and a golf course on the flanks of Mount Merino. Oh, Ruth was proud of that fight. Old Harry got so mad at town meeting, Ruth thought he would tear himself in two like Rumpelstiltskin.

To use Harry's favorite phrase, it was a "triple-a-plus-plus" victory for Ruth and Edie.

After that battle, Ruth retired from town politics and took a place on the board of Carding Academy because Edie was its executive director. Even though she'd never done anything remotely crafty in her life, Ruth thought the academy board would make a nice change from the verbal wrestling of town politics. Then under Edie's tutelage, she surprised herself by becoming an avid quilter. She'd always liked puzzles, she explained to her mystified kids, and that's what a quilt is, a puzzle made of fabric.

"But Mom," her daughter wailed when she heard the news, "you wouldn't sew on buttons when I was little."

"Well," Ruth huffed, a little embarrassed, "anyone can change."

So Suzanna Owens couldn't have had a better guide to Carding than its principal mail carrier.

"You see that house up there." Ruth pointed to an oversized log cabin perched at the top of a steep driveway. "Owned by a guy named

Yancy. He started some sort of tech company or another. Only here for a few weeks a year to watch bird migrations."

"Bird migrations?" Suzanna asked as she peered through the trees. "I've seen stuff on TV about birds flying south for the winter but I've never lived in a place where that happened for real. Why does Mr. Yancy want to watch birds so much?"

Ruth's heart tumbled over in her chest. "Your mother never brought you to a place where you could see wild critters? Not even a zoo?"

Suzanna shook her head as she concentrated on opening a small bottle of apple cider, one of two that Ruth had bought. She had had apple juice before, and it was OK once in a while. Well, it was kind of boring, actually. Which is why Suzanna was skeptical about something Ruth described as "apple juice before they take the apple out of it."

But one swallow of cider changed her mind. "Oh, that's awesome," Suzanna said as she wiped her hand across her mouth. "Mom doesn't like being outdoors at all. Do you have a lot of wild animals around here? They're not going to bite me, are they?"

"Yeah, we do have a lot of wild animals around here but only the mosquitoes and black flies bite, and we don't have to deal with them for another couple of months." Ruth pulled up to a row of mailboxes attached to a fence section leaning decidedly to the right. She made a point of pushing on them in order to judge the structure's sturdiness. One more smash by the town snow plow ought to do it, she judged.

Suzanna carefully replaced the cap on her cider before asking: "Whose mail goes in those boxes?"

"Only the Lindstroms at this time of year. They use this road in the winter because the other way out of their place in the woods doesn't get plowed," Ruth explained. "So I leave their mail here in the Coopers' Campground box because no one lives in the Campground in the winter. It's more convenient for the Lindstroms to stop here than for me to drive to their place."

"How come nobody lives here in the winter?" Suzanna asked as she finished her cider, wishing for more.

"Those little cabins have no insulation at all which means that keeping them warm in winter is impossible. So folks just close them up in the fall then reopen them in the spring." Ruth rolled down the Jeep's window to shovel mail into the wobbling boxes, and sniffed the air. Wood smoke. She scanned the horizon in the direction of the Campground. A fire down there at this time of year would destroy the century-old structures. Finally, she spotted a wisp of smoke rising from the direction of the Coopers' camp.

"Huh, that's odd," she said.

"What's odd?" Suzanna asked, trying to see something besides snow.

Ruth shook her head as she eased back onto the road. Maybe Charlie or Andy loaned the cabin out to some hunter or fisherman, she thought. I'll check with them later. "Just thought I saw something but it's OK. Now we've got to move along to pick up packages in the next town. You settle back, and enjoy the show. This is one of the prettiest roads in the valley. I've heard there's been a lot of deer spotted along here lately so keep your eyes sharp."

Suzanna wriggled under her seat belt, trying to remember all of the firsts she'd experienced that morning because the list was getting hard to remember—maple syrup, cider, delivering mail in a Jeep, getting an aunt, and eating the best cinnamon roll in the world. And now she might see a deer. She sighed, and Ruth noticed a contented smile creep over the child's face.

As the two travelers swept around Mount Merino, Suzanna oohed and aahed over the way the sun sparked the snow, how long fingers of ice stretched from the roof to the ground on a hunter's cabin, and how the shadows cast by a flock of crows swooped over the snow as they flew down the valley. She leaned forward to watch as long as she could, her elongated "Wow" a proper salute to the birds. And then a sweep of open field appeared, and Ruth slowed. "There's some wild apple trees along the edge of this pasture," she said, "and sometimes you can spot deer browsing there."

She and Suzanna stared, and then suddenly the little girl squealed. "There! There! Ooh, look at that," Suzanna said as the animals sprang away, saluting their audience with the white flags of their tails. "Oh wow. That's amazing."

Ruth laughed, and the two travelers chattered all the way back to the Carding post office. But the wood smoke she saw hovering over the Campgrounds niggled away at the back of Ruth's mind. Who would light the woodstove in the Cooper family camp at this time of year?

After the Brown & Sons crew dispersed, Peter Foster made a point of disappearing from the garage. He didn't like the look of Harry Brown, and as his grandmother used to say: "Who needs that at the breakfast table?"

Besides, if he timed it just right, he might run into Chloe as she walked across the green for coffee.

Peter worried about his attraction to Gideon's wife, and hers to him. Peter liked his life as regular as the plans he drew. Regularity meant less worry, less stress, more symmetry. That's why Peter played bass in his band, Thieves of Fire, to provide the regular beat that whirled dancers around the floor. The bass is the heartbeat, he'd tried to explain to his wife. But for Lisa, glitz was the reason for living so she remained disappointed when Peter refused to take up the fiddle or sing lead. "No one notices the bass," she complained.

Chloe, however, appreciated his playing. At the Winter Solstice Dance, she'd made a point of directing her applause at him, smiling as though the two of them shared a secret. That night had stirred Peter's heart in the most disturbing way. Next to her flashy sister, Chloe was a quiet star, her luminous beauty—now that he was awake to it—far more compelling than Lisa's. Now it infused his life, interfered with his thinking, and hovered over his heart.

Now Peter divided his life in two parts—B.S.D. (Before the Solstice Dance) and A.S.D. (After the Solstice Dance). Before, he had bragged about his orderly life—music, a decent (if boring) job, a house in his beloved home town, a pretty wife. But after he heard Chloe's laugh, watched her whirl about the dance floor with her hair streaming and that green dress swirling about her legs, Peter saw no one else but her. Everything about Chloe pleased his eye, and pierced his heart. In that moment, standing on the stage watching her dance, Peter knew he'd married the wrong Cooper sister. And that knowledge made him ache.

After that, Peter watched Gideon with close attention, finding nothing in the man to make Peter believe him worthy of Chloe's affections. Oh, Gideon could drive a truck, and worked harder on-site than either of his two useless brothers. He also had a knack for estimating jobs accurately. But Gideon shared his father's loathsome opinion of women, and Peter hated that about the Browns.

So why had Gideon Brown married Chloe Cooper? Peter didn't know for sure but he'd bet it had a lot to do with old Harry because everything Gideon did or did not do had a lot to do with old Harry. The father craved respect or barring that, fear, and unfortunately, Gideon treasured his father's good opinion. So when Harry decided that Gideon needed to settle down, he chose Chloe because marrying a very young and pretty woman gave father and son something to strut about.

But what was in the match for Chloe? Money? Gideon did all right financially but so did Chloe. Her quilt designs, her books, and her classes at the academy all sold well. Besides, she wasn't the type to marry for money. Lisa was, Peter reflected. He knew his wife well enough now to understand that.

Sex? Peter got stomach cramps every time he considered this scenario. Given how Gideon treated women in public, Peter figured he was too selfish to care how he made a woman feel in private. So why did Chloe Cooper marry Gideon Brown? Peter believed that a lot of what happened in life was timing, like music. If you play the right notes in the right sequence at the right time, you get something good to listen to. But one note out of place, and all you get is noise.

Chloe married Gideon within a year of her return to Carding from college. Her parents, Charlie and Angela Cooper, had divorced soon after she left for school so she had no real home to come back to. Shy and hesitant about putting herself forward, Peter figured Chloe welcomed Gideon's charm and attention. For his part, Gideon had found someone that Harry approved of.

Even though the folks of Carding wished the young couple well, they also figured that sooner or later Gideon would go back to his old ways. Unfortunately, they turned out to be right. After a couple of years of sleeping with the same woman, Gideon returned to satisfying his craving for variety in all its female forms. Chloe discovered this truth the hard way when she returned home early from a conference to find her bed occupied by Gideon and another woman.

Peter felt justified in assuming these things because of the trajectory of his own marriage. After he'd returned to Carding for the job at Brown & Sons, Lisa picked him out for special attention. Flattered, he asked her to marry him after a few nights of high energy intimacy. Since she liked him well enough, Lisa agreed. But Peter knew she'd grown bored with the regularity of their life together, and truth to tell, he'd grown tired of her.

As he opened the back door of the Brown & Sons garage, Peter glanced over his shoulder at father and son, Gideon with his hands jammed deep in his pockets, Harry looking like a grenade with its pin pulled. Despite the way Gideon treated Chloe, Peter pitied him. He doubted that Harry ever bestowed a kind word or a morsel of praise on his eldest son. Maybe that was why Gideon jumped from woman to woman, looking for approval.

So what am I going to do about this, Peter wondered as turned up the collar of his jacket, and headed toward the bakery. Divorce Lisa? Ask her to go to a marriage counselor? Yeah right, that will go over well. According to Lisa, only other people had problems.

"Penny for your thoughts, Peter." He started, then smiled with all his soul as Chloe strolled up beside him. "Where are you headed?"

"Um, uh, to the bakery." She looked amazing, a vibrant multi-colored scarf wrapped around the collar of her jet black coat. Neither of them moved.

"Well, how do you like it?" Chloe wriggled her shoulders.

He stared at her face for a moment then reluctantly let his eyes rove down to her boots. "Um, sorry, I'm not much good at this sort of thing. What am I supposed to like?"

"The scarf. I just finished it last night." She grasped one end and flipped it up. "What do you think? I'm teaching a class at the Academy on how to make them next week."

He stared again then finally shook himself. "It's...um...different." Each colorful piece of the scarf jutted off in its own direction, and beads sprouted up in the most unlikely places.

Chloe laughed. "I don't expect you to wear it, Peter, just tell me how it strikes you. The word different doesn't give me much of a clue."

"Ahem, OK." Peter stepped back in order to survey the scarf's aesthetic qualities. "I like that the colors are in small pieces because every time you move, the scarf changes." He crinkled up the place between his eyebrows. "But I have to say I'm not crazy about the beads. Strikes me as overkill."

Chloe laughed again, and Peter swore he saw the sound sparkle in the air. "That's much better. News I can use, you might say. I thought that might be the case but I can't see it on myself so I have to rely on someone else to tell me how it works. You have a good eye for color."

Peter knew that the grin on his face had turned from happy to dopey, and his voice crawled off to hide somewhere, leaving him momentarily speechless. Chloe seemed to be waiting for him to speak so he tried to kickstart his tongue but dredged up only a small "umm" in return for his efforts as they turned to walk together.

"Good morning, Peter. Good morning, Chloe," Edie called as she tried to pull the academy's "Open" flag from its holder by the front door. But the wind had other plans.

The pair turned as one, and Edie spotted Peter's flushed face right off. "Here, let me get that before it ends up in New Hampshire," he said, furling the fabric while Edie pulled.

Then Peter and Chloe walked off, cutting across the green.

Edie chewed this little interlude over in her mind as she fetched Nearly and his leash. She'd noticed that appearances of Peter and Chloe together had increased significantly. On one level, that pleased her. She'd long thought that Peter's easy ways suited Chloe much better than Gideon's ego and bluster. But what if their emotional attraction dripped over into the physical? She knew that the blowback to an affair between Chloe Cooper Brown and Peter Foster would be formidable. The males of the Brown family didn't take abandonment lightly. That's why, when Edie left Harry, her parents spirited her away to Europe.

"It's better to go off and wait until the talk dies down," her father had counseled all those years ago. "If you give Harry the space to bellow like the wounded bull he is, folks will get tired of him, and then you can come back."

Of course, no one figured Edie would meet the love of her life in Paris so it was a long time—and two children—before she returned to her home town.

She sighed. All relationships come with consequences, she thought, and when relationships change, alliances change. What would an affair between Chloe and Peter mean for the delicate balance among the various factions in Carding? The possibilities made Edie uneasy.

SEVEN

THE GENOS AND
THE SMALLS

New post on Carding Chronicle blog: February 6

Fire Closes Fiorello's Pizza
by Little Crow

Got a text from a friend last night who told me that he went out for pizza and found Fiorello's on Route 37 closed. We thought we'd make inquiries, and learned that Carding's favorite pizza joint will remain closed for the rest of this week to repair damage to the kitchen after a fire in the brick oven.

An upgraded sprinkler system is also slated for installation.

Now, the good news is that Fiorello's bar will be open for drinks (and light snacks) tonight, Friday night and Saturday night this week. Thieves of Fire will do their weekly music gig on Saturday starting at 8 p.m. for all you dancing fools.

In the meantime, the Crow Town Bakery is open for breakfast and lunch. The Old Mill at Merino Resort is open for dinner every night and brunch on Sundays. But if you really crave sauce and toppings on a crust, you'll have a hike because the closest pizza place is a 12-mile ride from Carding.

The manager of Fiorello's promises that the closing will be short, and he'll let the Chronicle know first so you can read it right here.

I'll be looking for you.
Little Crow | February 6 | Categories: Local Food

Two days passed before Gideon dared to speak to Lisa again. He knew his father suspected that he'd taken up with the engineer's wife—the old man had spent too many hours in the henhouse not to recognize the signs. Gideon also knew that Harry disapproved. Good civil engineers were hard to find, and if Peter figured out that his wife and Gideon… well, Peter would probably quit working for Brown & Sons.

Who could blame him?

After his crack about the scented soap, old Harry doubled down on the situation by getting real friendly with Peter, treating the engineer like a prodigal son. Even Gideon's brothers noticed. What was the old man up to, they whispered to their older brother. He wasn't thinking about changing his will, was he? Noah's anxiety was particularly keen on this point. He had big plans for setting himself up in Florida once Harry died, plans that even their mother didn't know about.

As much as Harry's newfound affection for Peter Foster raised the collective eyebrows on his sons' faces, Gideon's fears around Chloe outweighed all that. She'd started humming again. He'd heard her upstairs when he muted a commercial during a Bruins hockey game. It was a light, meandering sound floating above the clack of her sewing machine.

No one ever credited Gideon with much discernment when it came to women but he prided himself on his mastery of female sounds. For example, he could still gauge Candy Croft's mood by the quality of a single sigh overheard in the Coop. And he hadn't rolled around with Candy in the back seat of a car since high school. Gideon had catalogued his wife's sounds so he knew what Chloe's hum meant. She was happy.

Happy with him living in their basement.

Happy without him in her bed.

Happy living a life over which Gideon had no control or influence.

And with that thought, Gideon suddenly understood why his father still hated Edie Wolfe after all these years. By her actions, Chloe held Gideon up to ridicule the same way that Edie's flight to Europe made his father a laughingstock so many years ago. Gideon Brown, the guy that every girl in high school wanted to date, couldn't hold onto his own wife? Couldn't sleep in his own bed?

If—when?—Chloe left him, Gideon knew his father would take the repudiation personally, and Gideon would pay for it.

But in the meantime, a man has needs, Gideon told himself as he snagged a prime parking spot across from the town hall. Turning his radio on, he cocked his head in an attitude of intense listening, as if news about the never-ending Presidential campaign mattered to him. The pose gave him time to review the excuse he would use for dropping in on Lisa at work. She'd know why he was there, of course, but Lisa's boss was no fool, and Gideon didn't feel that the value of his dalliance with his sister-in-law outweighed the consequences of getting found out by Paula Bouton. Lisa was fun, and she had potential but he didn't want to be saddled with her for the long term.

Gideon sighed as he flipped off the radio. The sound of bleating politicians made him nauseous. Then he pocketed his keys, checked the rearview mirror to make sure his hair still covered that annoying thin place, and stepped across the street.

When Gideon walked in the door, he thought the town manager's office looked as though a paper bomb had exploded. Town maps covered every available surface—floors, tables, chairs, walls, the tops of file cabinets. Paula Bouton stood in the middle of the mess, a sheaf of papers in one hand, a pencil in the other. Even though they'd both graduated in the same class from Carding Regional High School, Gideon had never practiced his wiles on Paula even though she was well-built and attractive. There was something about the woman that commanded deference, not flights of male fantasy. Generally, folks in Carding described Paula as a no-nonsense female equally at home fishing on Half Moon Lake as she was schmoozing at the capital in Montpelier.

"Odd choice for office decorations, isn't it?" Gideon asked as he carefully stepped through the door.

Paula laughed. "Not exactly streamers and balloons, that's for sure." She waved her hand about the office. "Trying to finish up what the legislature requires on this ancient road project, and figure out what we need to put on the warrant for a town vote."

At the sound of his voice, Lisa poked her head out of the room-sized vault where all the deeds to Carding's property resided. Her quick smile in Gideon's direction was all the encouragement he needed. When she disappeared, he looked over at Paula. "Any problem with me helping myself in some deed research?"

Paula waved her hand over her shoulder. "Lisa can help if you need it," she said, and Gideon ducked around the counter.

Lisa's smile was still in place as she asked Gideon if he knew the number of the deed book he wanted.

"Not sure," he said, moving as close to her as office protocol allowed.

"Do you know the name of the property owner?" she asked, motioning him with her eyes toward the card catalog.

She opened a drawer between them, laid a piece of scrap paper on top of the cabinet, and wrote: "Saturday night? Peter's at Fiorello's."

Gideon nodded. This was much easier than he expected. Maybe he should consider making this affair last a little bit longer. He took her pencil and wrote. "Cabin? 7:00? I'll buy the soap."

Lisa giggled, slapped her hand over her mouth, and then shook her head while she held up eight fingers.

Gideon grinned, nodded, and then tiptoed to the door to check on Paula's whereabouts. Satisfied that the town manager had eyes only for her maps, he scuttled back to Lisa's side for a quick squeeze to her backside, and a shared, knowing look. Then aloud he said: "Thanks for finding that." Lisa's eyes narrowed to slits as she reached down, planted her hand on top of his, and moved her bottom suggestively. If I'm going to do this, she told herself, I'm going to do it right. Gideon suddenly felt very warm. And grateful.

"Any time," Lisa said. Then she reached for the note they'd written, and tore it into small bits before dropping it into a wastebasket. Ah, Gideon thought, she is coming along nicely, getting into the "other woman" mode. I won't have to fake back spasms next time.

As he emerged from the vault, Gideon stopped to admire the maps Paula had taped to the wall. He loved maps of Carding and its surrounding towns, the older the better. They gave him a sense of belonging to history because he could point to a spot and say: "Here, right here—I've fished here, logged here, built roads here, here, and here."

He had to take a closer look.

"What's this all about?" he asked. "Why do you need a map from 1810 to find anything? Haven't we got satellites to take care of this stuff?"

Paula sighed. "If only. These old roads and property rights-of-way cause more headaches than anything else you can name. Remember that standoff about those old maples over in Worcester a few years back?"

"The guy who nearly got tarred and feathered because he wanted to cut them down?" Gideon asked.

"Yeah. The folks who stopped the cutting claimed the trees lined an ancient road, and they turned out to be right," Paula said. "We've already had a couple of fights over ancient roads here in Carding, and I'm trying to make sure we don't have any more."

Gideon's eyebrows curled into one another. "I don't remember any fights over old roads here. Where did that happen?"

"Up here." Paula jabbed a finger at the top right corner of the 1810 map. As she did, Gideon caught a whiff of something warm and spicy and cocked an eye in her direction. She did keep herself nicely fit.

Paula spotted his interest out of the corner of her eye and nearly laughed. These Browns. Where did they get off thinking that the half of humanity blessed with two X chromosomes in every gene had nothing better to do than get all excited by their attention?

She jabbed at the map again, barely resisting the urge to bring the heel of her right foot down on the toes of his left. "Up here," she repeated in her best school teacher's voice. Gideon backed up a fraction of an inch, and turned his thermostat down. What was he thinking?

"This is where the Genos and the Smalls fought over a path up to the Campgrounds," Paula continued. "According to the Genos, the path was the remains of an ancient road that connected their property to the Campgrounds so they had the right to cross the Smalls' land whenever they wanted. The heirs of the Small estate vehemently disagreed. We got that one settled quickly by checking the ancient road claim against the town reports."

Gideon followed the direction of Paula's finger. "Oh yeah, I remember my father talking about that. I used to hunt up that way when I was a kid. But why did you have to check the town reports?"

"Because the only way you can officially abandon a public road is through a formal vote at town meeting. The logic goes like this: The town makes the roads, the town maintains the roads, the town owns the roads, so the voters, who are the town, have to make the official decision about whether to abandon a road or not." Paula walked over to another map pinned to the wall, and pointed to the same area. "See here? If you compare this 1905 map to the 1810 map, you'll notice the markings for the Small Road disappear. And if you check the town report for 1900, you'll discover that the town officially discontinued it by a vote at town meeting that year."

"Advantage to the Smalls, right?" Gideon heard movement behind him, and pictured Lisa posing in the vault door.

Paula peered over her glasses at the eldest Brown son, and couldn't help but notice Lisa lounging in the background in a way that emphasized her upper curves and lower willingness. Great, Paula thought. That's all I need. Sexual tangles make life so much harder than it needs to be, and I don't get paid enough to referee Lisa Foster's love life. It's hard enough to monitor her work life. Paula turned her attention back to Gideon.

"When you multiply what happened between the Genos and the Smalls by the number of towns in Vermont," she began.

"Two fifty-one," Gideon said.

"What?"

"Two hundred and fifty-one, the number of towns in Vermont," Gideon said again.

"Ah, yes." Paula cleared her throat, a tiny ahem sound barely audible to the human ear, an ephemeral rebuke of Gideon's interruption. He heard it, understood it, and in that moment, he crossed Paula Bouton off his list of possibilities forever. If she'd known, she would have been very pleased.

"The state legislature is tired of these problems because they tie up the state courts, so they've directed all towns to make inventories of their ancient roads," Paula said. "We've done that. Now we're rooting through the town records to see which of them have been officially abandoned because if a road has been legally abandoned, we don't have to worry about it any more. Plus, we'll settle a lot of potential disputes before they can start."

"Like the Smalls," Gideon said.

"Exactly. The Genos' claim had no merit once we checked the records," Paula said.

"So what about ancient roads that haven't been officially abandoned?" Gideon asked, crowding in close to the 1810 map.

"That's what we're doing now, trying to figure out if there are roads that the town stopped maintaining long ago but never officially abandoned so we can take a vote on all of them at town meeting next month," Paula said. "If the town decides to abandon them, we can leave them just as they are—roads unsalted, unplowed, and unmowed. But if the voters decide to keep a road, that means grading it, maintaining it, and plowing and salting it in winter. Depending on how the vote goes, that could add a lot to our road budget."

"What if someone built a structure on a road that's no longer used but has never been officially abandoned?" Gideon asked.

"If voters decide the town should keep a road like that, then we'd have a building on a public road," Paula said.

"So what would happen to the building?"

Paula sighed. "That would be a terrible mess but I suppose, in the end, the building would have to be moved or torn down. I hope we don't find anything like that. That kind of fight can split a town so bad, the wounds last for generations."

Gideon nodded. "Yeah, I imagine so." He reached in his pockets for his gloves, and Paula saw a small smirk flit over his face. "You have a good day, Paula. You too, Lisa." He winked in her direction. "Thanks for your help."

Well he's not much, Lisa thought as she watched Gideon strut down the hall, his little bald spot glowing under the fluorescent lights. But at least he's willing to play with me, and that's better than being home alone while Peter's off with his stupid band.

Paula didn't move for several long moments after Gideon left, and Lisa returned to doing whatever she did that resembled work. While Paula regarded Gideon's need for serial seductions as yet another example of male foolishness, it did not necessarily follow that Gideon Brown was a fool. The man had as good a nose for land opportunities as his father, and that's what made Paula suspect that he'd spotted something on the old map that she'd missed. She turned back to it, replicated the tilt of Gideon's head then shut her eyes for a moment. When she opened them, she tried to see the map for the very first time. Then she gasped.

"Lisa," she called, "would you help me get this map down from the wall? I think we might have another one for the ancient roads list."

Gideon snatched up a copy of the Carding Academy brochure as he sped through the lobby of the community building, reading as he walked past the library then down a narrow hall to the town's historical society office. He wanted to gallop. He wanted to skip. He wanted to pump his fist and yell "Woohoo!" But he did none of those things. Surprise is essential, he kept telling himself, and I have to be absolutely certain before I say anything to anyone.

Gideon had to shoulder open the historical society's door. All the money we pay in taxes, he grumbled to himself, and this damn door never works right. He blinked as he tumbled through the opening because the windows were covered by thick blinds.

"Doesn't anyone in this place believe in electric lights?" he asked as he groped for a switch.

"Light doesn't do the paper any good." A female voice soared toward him out of the gloom. "Breaks it down, makes it yellow faster."

A feeble lamp cast shadows about the woman as she hunched over a large, open book spread across her lap. Though the quaver of her voice pegged her age as somewhere over seventy, her shape and hair gave nothing else away.

"What do you want?" she asked.

Gideon advanced, carefully toeing the floor ahead of him in hopes of not tripping over an invisible pile of books or a rucked-up rug.

"What do you want?" the woman asked again. Gideon thought he detected a note of alarm. "And who are you?"

"Gideon Brown," he said. "And you are…?"

"Millie Bittinger," she said. "What do you want?"

Gideon cranked up his memory, searching his internal archives to place the woman's name. "Ah," he said. "You live across from Ted Owens' place, am I right?"

"So?"

"So I just remembered who you are, that's all," he said. "How are you, Mrs. Bittinger?"

"Miss, thank you very much," she said with an audible sniff. "Now what do you want?" She tugged her book deeper into her lap, and spread her hands across its pages.

"What is it, Millie?" A creaky male voice from the other end of the room made Gideon jump.

"It's Harry Brown's eldest son, I think. Name of Gideon," she said in a raised voice. "Heckuva name for a boy but then his mother always had fancies." She turned toward Gideon. "You woke him up. Armand always takes his nap at this time of day."

"I didn't know," Gideon said. "Sorry."

"Hmph."

"What does he want, Millie?" the old man said.

"I don't know yet because he's taking such a long time about it," she said. "What do you want, young man?"

"Town reports," he said.

"Well, there's a lot of them in here," Armand said. "Could you be more specific?"

Gideon consulted the brochure. "The early 1900s, 1901 through 1930, I think."

"What for?" Millie asked.

"Do I need a reason?" Gideon said. "I'm a resident of the town. I pay my taxes. I want to see these town reports, that's all."

The chair cradling the old man grumbled as he pushed himself upright. "All right, all right, keep your shorts on. I'll show you where they are," Armand said.

"Just point me in the right direction," Gideon said.

"Hmph, you can't let just anybody come in here and rummage around in Carding's archives," Millie said. "You need to be supervised."

"Do you work here?" Gideon asked. "I don't remember seeing anything in the town budget about paying someone to work at the historical society."

"That's the problem," Armand said. "That's why Millie and I come here. We care about this stuff and want to make sure it's preserved." He coughed, fumbling in his pocket for a handkerchief. "It's our way of giving back to the community, as they say."

"There's a box of tissues right there," Gideon said, pointing.

"Never touch them," Armand said, unfolding the largest square of cloth Gideon had ever seen used on a single nose. "Tissues cost money." He shuffled toward a cabinet in the corner of the room, and started to bend at the waist.

"Remember your sciatica," Millie shrilled.

"Oh. Yes. You're right," Armand said, and he smoothed out the little bends in his knees. Then he pointed toward the bottom drawer and made a motion with his head in Gideon's direction. "You'll find what you're looking for in there. Make sure you don't rearrange anything or take anything."

Gideon bent down to coax the indicated drawer open. "Is there a copy machine in here?" he asked.

"Eh?"

"A machine that makes copies of the reports I want," Gideon said.

The two older people looked at one another for an elongated moment. "That might be it," the woman finally said, pointing to a heap of books slopping over the top of something that Gideon identified as having been manufactured since the turn of the century.

"Yeah, maybe." he sighed, unable to see into the open drawer at his feet. "Would you please point me in the direction of a light switch? Or would you prefer I find a candle?"

Forty-seven minutes later, Gideon Brown's feet barely touched the snow-covered ground as he strode across the town green. When he reached the sycamores in its center, he turned to look at the headquarters of the Carding Academy of Traditional Arts, and examine the contours of the slope on which it squatted.

"Well, I'll be," he whispered. He'd built enough roads, and graded enough slopes to pick out the telltale signs of human intervention on a landscape. That funny little jog in Academy Road wasn't just a local eccentricity. Nope, now that the ground lay bare of greenery, Gideon could see the reason why the folks of Carding in the early 20th century hated Joseph Stillman Croft so much. He had built his home right on top of Academy Road so he would have the best view in town. And Gideon guessed that the wily artist paid some of the local officials to look the other way while he did it.

But what was more important to Gideon was that there was never a vote at any town meeting to formally abandon the section of Academy Road under Croft's house. That meant that the Carding Academy of Traditional Arts was sitting on a public road owned by the town of Carding, Vermont, and if he and his father could persuade enough people to vote to keep that section of road public, then the old Croft building would have to go.

And when that happened, the 89 acres of land behind the building owned by Harry Brown would be wide open for development. Carding could have fast-food restaurants, big box stores, and maybe a fitness center, Gideon thought. People with money will fall all over themselves to buy second homes up here, homes built and sold by Brown & Sons.

Gideon rubbed his hands together with glee as he marched toward his car. His little trip to town hall had given him something to get his father off his back, and as an extra-added bonus, the promise of a little fun on Saturday night with the pink, curvy, and willing Lisa Foster.

Yes, it had been a very good day.

And we drove around the outside of a mountain, and I could barely see its top," Suzanna prattled on as she and her Uncle Ted walked to the Coop. They made quite a pair, the rather tall, shambling man with his steady pace, and the skipping, excited child. But the companions made an easy fit with one another.

"Did you see any skiers coming down the slope?" he asked.

"Oh yes. They looked like little drips of color running down a mound of vanilla ice cream," she said. "But then one of them fell, and Ruth stopped so we could watch to see if he was OK."

"And was he?"

Suzanna squinched up her face. "After a while. A bunch of other skiers rushed over, and got him back up. Ruth said it was a good thing he didn't lose a ski cuz it's a long walk to the bottom of the mountain. I guess it's pretty slippery up there, huh?"

Ted nodded. "Sure can be."

"Do you ski, Uncle Ted?"

He nodded again. "I do, though I haven't been on the slopes for quite a while." He looked down at the bouncing girl. "Would you like to try it? I could teach you, if you like."

Suzanna's eyes grew wide. "Really?" She stopped walking, and swallowed. "That mountain's awful big."

"It is," Ted agreed. "But we can start you out in our backyard. There's a little slope where you can get the feel of the skis on your feet, and start off slow. That's how I learned."

"So if I fall down…" she said.

"You won't hurt yourself, and you won't have far to walk." Ted pushed the door of the Coop open. "How's that for a plan?"

"Oh yes oh yes oh yes oh yes."

"So, what else did you see besides the skiers?" Ted said as he picked up a shopping basket.

Suzanna held up her hand so she could count on her fingers. "We saw a lot of crows flying over the road. We came to a place where the river wasn't frozen but steaming up like a pan of water on the stove. Some of the steam was frozen on the branches of the trees, and the sun made it sparkle like diamonds."

Ted smiled. "The kettle hole. The water moves so fast there, it doesn't freeze very often, and the mist coats everything." He stopped at the meat counter. "Do you like baked chicken? I thought we'd make that for supper."

When she nodded, Ted picked out a package of thighs. "What else did you see?"

"A woman on the roof of a house shoveling snow off of it." Ted heard the amazement in Suzanna's voice. "I had no idea people shoveled roofs. And then there was a place on the lake—Ruth says the water's slow there—where there's all these small buildings on the ice."

"They're called bobhouses. They're used for ice fishing."

"Yeah, and two of them had smoke coming out of their tops. I thought that was amazing, that you could make fires on top of ice and not melt through." Suzanna stopped to draw breath, and then spotted someone she knew. "Oh…hi…Mrs., um, Edie. Aunt Ruth said I could call you Mrs. Edie. Is that all right? Where's your dog?"

The older woman laughed. One day with Ruth Goodwin had done the child a world of good. "I would love it if you call me Mrs. Edie," she said. "How was your day?"

"I saw people skiing, and Uncle Ted said he'll teach me how to do that if I want him to, and I do."

"Indeed," Edie said, and she airlifted one eyebrow in the postmaster's direction. "Well, I might have some equipment to get you started. It's older but in great condition, good enough to practice on, and then if you like it, we can get you some stuff of your own."

Suzanna whirled around in place, her arms outstretched, singing "Yes oh yes oh yes." Ted and Edie laughed, and that sound made Andy Cooper peer around the end of an aisle.

"I didn't know the price of chicken was that exciting," he said, eyeing the girl. Suzanna stopped so quickly, she stumbled over her own feet, and just managed to catch herself on a pedestal display of bananas.

"Skiing," she gasped, a dreamy expression on her face.

Andy grinned at her but his eyes cut over to see Ted's face. "I see she's caught the bug from you already," he said.

"What bug?" Suzanna asked.

Ted shuffled his feet, his gaze locked onto the Coop's wide plank floor. "She didn't catch it from me, Andy. She rode the postal route with Ruth today, and saw folks coming down Mount Merino, the ZigZag Trail, I think."

Andy nodded then stretched his hand out to the girl. "I'm Andy Cooper, and you must be Suzanna, Ted's niece."

She accepted the older man's hand with great solemnity. Unless he smiled, Andy's face fell in formal folds about his mouth, folds that reminded her of a statue she'd once seen from a car window when a Bruno drove her and her mother through New York City one night. The statue, half in shadow, half in light, looked lonely to Suzanna, like this man shaking her hand. But then Andy smiled, dispelling the illusion.

Funny, she thought, how a face can change from light to dark and back again. "What bug?" she asked again.

Andy eyeballed Ted who still had his eyes on the floor. "Well, if you won't tell her, I will," he growled. Then he settled his gaze on the girl. Looks just like her grandfather, he thought. Spitting image. "Come on, I'll show you."

Andy took Suzanna's hand, pulled it through the crook of his arm, and walked her toward the store's coffee corner, now nearly deserted. Ted and Edie followed, Ted's face covered by a rosy flush, Edie's expression a bit apprehensive.

"You see these pictures?" Andy pointed to a row of black and white photographs on the wall. Suzanna nodded. "See anyone you recognize? Wait a minute, let's boost you up so you can really see." Andy picked her up, and put her on a chair.

Suzanna leaned close to the pictures, most of them featuring a man with great dark eyes. In one picture, the man was by himself, carrying a pair of skis on his shoulder. But in all the other pictures, he stood surrounded by children, and the kids were all on skis.

Suzanne examined the man's face in minute detail, her forehead scrunched up. After a moment, she turned to her uncle. "He looks like you but not quite. Is he your father?"

Ted nodded. "Your grandfather, Robert Owens."

"The best ski coach in America at the time," Andy said. "Some of the kids he taught went on to compete on the state and national teams. And nobody beat Carding Regional High on the slopes when Rob was coach. He was a marvel."

Suzanna reached out to touch the photograph with the tip of a finger, tracing the details of her grandfather's smile, the line of his hair, and the skis he carried on his shoulders. Suddenly, tears spilled over her cheeks. "I never knew I belonged to so many people," she whispered. Ted and Edie sniffled. Andy began to blink rapidly.

"What happened to him?" Suzanna asked. "Did he die like my grandmother?"

Ted shuffled away, and put his grocery basket down to grab a paper napkin from a dispenser. "No," he said, struggling to overcome the enormous obstacle in his throat. "No, your grandfather is still alive."

"Where is he?"

Ted drew in several enormous breaths then held up a hand to stop Edie from comforting him. "I'll wail like a baby if you do that," he said, a smile wobbling across his mouth. She stopped, and they all waited as Ted breathed, cleared his throat, tried to speak, and breathed again. Suzanna turned her head from one adult to the other, trying to understand. Finally, her uncle turned to face her.

"Your grandfather lives in assisted living over in Woodstock," he said. "He has Parkinson's disease which makes it very difficult for him to move around. But he's still as sharp as ever, and I know he'll be excited to meet you. I try to visit him at least twice a week but I haven't been there since you've come to…to Carding."

"What's assisted living?" Suzanna asked. "It's not like a casino, is it? I don't like those places."

Ted laughed with relief. "No, believe me, it's nothing like a casino. This place is called Woodstock Gardens, and it's a lot of very small apartments for people who have diseases like Parkinson's that make it hard for them to get around. There's someone to cook meals for them, nurses when you need them, people to visit with, a bus service so folks don't have to drive, and it's all on one floor so they don't have to deal with stairs. That's what finally made your grandfather decide he wanted to move there. He couldn't get in and out of our house because of the stairs, and he couldn't drive any more which made him crazy because I was at work all day, and he didn't have anyone to talk to."

He's still trying to justify it, Edie thought, even though the assisted living had been Rob's idea.

"Can I go see him?" Suzanna asked. "Is that allowed?"

Ted grinned from ear to ear. "Not only allowed, it's encouraged. Dad will be tickled to meet you. We can go on Friday night, if you like. I'll call ahead so we can eat supper with him."

Suzanna nodded in her most serious manner, feeling almost dizzy with all this new stuff coming into her life at the same time. "Do they have maple syrup and cider there?"

"Dad always has a bottle of maple syrup handy, and we can bring the cider," Ted said. "OK?"

"OK." Now it was her turn to sigh. "A new grandfather. What do you think about that?"

Andy reached over Suzanna's shoulder to point to a boy in a photograph standing near her "new grandfather." The child's face beamed out of the picture, his hair sticking up all over his head. "This is your Uncle Ted, the day he won the slalom event at the New England regionals. Believe me, Suzanna, you come from a long line of people who know their way down a hill of snow. Rob will be so proud to know that you want to learn to ski."

"Really? That's you, Uncle Ted?" The girl's excitement infected both of the men, which Edie noted with more than a little bit of interest. Ted Owens talking about skiing again, she thought. Wonders will never cease. Then, remembering that Nearly was waiting for her, she turned away with a wave.

"Let me know if you need equipment for Suzanna," she told Ted. "Diana had to buy Faye new boots and skis this year, and I believe she still has last year's. They should fit." As she walked away, Gideon Brown skidded around a corner, and they almost collided. As the two made their polite excuse mes, Edie noticed two things—Gideon had nothing in his hands but a bar of Ivory soap, and he avoided looking her in the eye as he backed away.

Now what was that all about, Edie wondered.

EIGHT

JUST SO MUCH CUTTING

New post on Carding Chronicle blog: February 7

Fiorello's Pizza Reopening with Music and Dance
by Little Crow

The Creative Dance Collective will be on hand for the Grand Reopening of Fiorello's Pizza tomorrow night. They'll be demonstrating some Québecois step dancing as well as teaching some contradances so that everyone can join in the fun when Pete Foster and the Thieves of Fire turn up the music at 8 p.m.

Fiorello's manager reports that repairs on the oven and the sprinkler installation went much faster than anyone expected.

"We had a lot of help," he said. "People didn't want us closed for the weekend so they came by to make it all happen. The kitchen's even got a new coat of paint."

To celebrate, Fiorello's will have dollar slices and dollar beers available for Saturday night only.

The music and dancing start at 8:00, dance demonstrations will begin at 9:00. Should be fun.

I'll be looking for you.
Little Crow | February 7 | Categories: Local Entertainment

By Friday morning, Suzanna had learned the rhythms of work at the post office. She greeted the truck driver when he showed up with the early morning delivery, chattering to him while carrying smaller packages into the building. Then she made cocoa for herself and coffee for her uncle. By eight, when Ruth showed up, Suzanna was ready to roll through Carding in the Jeep with her new aunt.

First stop was always the Crow Town Bakery where Diana handed them bags stuffed with cinnamon rolls, orange juice, coffee, and chocolate milk. Though Suzanna never noticed, she and Ruth left a trail of grinning people in their wake as they delivered the mail, both of them talking as fast as they could. When the bird watcher, Mr. Yancy, turned up on Friday morning for a spot of wintertime reconnaissance in Half Moon Lake's marshy area, Suzanna stories were the first ones he heard when he stopped at the Coop for supplies.

"She's never been in a place where she could watch birds?" he asked Andy, horrified.

"That's what Ruth says," Andy assured him. "Seems old Alli-O didn't even tell Suzanna that she had an uncle or a grandfather before she dropped her in Carding, much less talk to her about birds. Can you imagine?"

Yancy hurried to his house with a few minutes to spare before the mail Jeep arrived. When Ruth and Suzanna spotted the raised flag that indicated outgoing mail, they found a present for the girl—a set of small binoculars.

After Ruth and Suzanna left on their mail route, Ted took a deep breath and dialed his father. "Sorry I haven't called sooner, Dad," he said. "But I think you'll understand why when I tell you the news."

Ordinarily, Ted dreaded his visits to Woodstock Gardens. Oh, it was a nice enough place, clean, well-attended, reasonably good food. His father played on a crackerjack cribbage team, made full use of the library's many audiobooks, and walked (with an attendant) to lunch and back every day. But his father's housing choice felt like a personal rebuke to Ted. I should have done more to keep him at home, he always told himself when he drove into the parking lot. And now that Suzanna had come to live with him, he felt more strongly than ever that all the members of his family should be together.

Mixing generations is a good thing, Ted told himself. Besides, he missed his Dad. Ever since his Mom died and Allison fled town without a backward glance, they had been the world to one another, and the house felt cavernous without the old man. Maybe the presence of his granddaughter would be enough to tempt him home.

Suzanna stayed oddly quiet during their drive, her grip on their jug of cider firm, her eyes fixed on the road.

"Are you feeling OK?" Ted asked as they drove through the center of town then turned south on Route 12. "You're awfully quiet."

"I'm all right," Suzanna said. "I'm just not sure how to talk to a grandfather, and I'm trying to figure it out. I want him to like me."

Ted reached over to pat her clenched hands. "Dad loves to talk, and he's no different than Ruth or Edie or Diana or anyone else you've met since you came to Carding."

"What if he asks me about my mother?" Suzanna said in her smallest possible voice.

"Ah, I see," Ted said. "Do you feel there are things you shouldn't say about your mother?"

"Well, since he is her father," Suzanna pointed out, "he might not like to hear some of the things I think about Mom. Nobody ever does."

Ted thought about that as he parked the car. "Would you rather not talk about your mother at all? If you tell Dad that, I know he won't ask."

"No, it's not that," Suzanna said, unclipping her seat belt. "I just don't like my mother, and I don't want to hurt his feelings if I say that."

"You know, I think you're both going to feel awkward so why don't you just let the conversation take its course," Ted said. "This visit, he's just going to want to get to know you. You'll figure the rest of it out as you go along."

Robert Owens stood as straight and tall as he could in the lobby of the Gardens, waiting anxiously for his first glimpse of his only grandchild. Ted had told him Suzanna smiled like his dear wife, an expression he had more difficulty remembering with every passing day. Robert wanted a refresher, wanted to see something of his Anna again in this little girl.

When he spotted them through the glass doors, Robert's shaky hold on his stature nearly failed him, and he strained to remain upright.

"Are you OK, Mr. Owens?" his attendant asked. She was the nice one, he remembered, though he couldn't recollect her name.

"I'm all right," he murmured. "I just don't want her to see me the first time sitting in a wheelchair."

Robert sensed an ache deep inside himself as soon as the girl walked in the door. He could see the outlines of the young woman she would become, and her resemblance to his long-gone wife felt uncanny. She's not Anna, he reminded himself as they drew near. She is herself.

"Hello Suzanna," he said, stretching out his hand, glad to see that his tremor medication had actually worked for once. "I am your grandfather, Robert."

She reached out, her eyes never wavering from his, drinking him in as if she was recovering from an ancient thirst. "Hello…sir."

The old man's mouth and eyebrows moved up. "Sir?" he said. "You can call me that if you want but I'd rather, when you're comfortable, that you call me Grampa. Sir is far more formal a word than we need between us, I hope."

"Oh," she said, pulling back a little. The old man's hand was warm, and strangely soft. She liked his smile. "I saw that in a movie once so I thought…"

His eyes joined his mouth in the smile. "I see. This is a little strange, meeting like this, isn't it? What would you like me to call you?"

"Suzanna's OK," she said. She pointed at the jug Ted held in his hand. "We brought you some cider."

"And I've made arrangements for us to have dessert in my room, a little apple crisp that we can drizzle maple syrup on," Robert said. "Ted tells me you're quite fond of it." He turned to his son. "I think I'd like to sit down now, if you don't mind."

Suzanna watched as her uncle and the attendant helped her grandfather lower himself into a wheelchair. He sighed as he laboriously lifted one foot and then the other off the floor onto little platforms. Then he reached out a hand to her. "Come here, child. My eyes are not what they used to be, and I'd like to see how pretty you are close up. I hope you don't mind."

She stepped closer, sniffing the air. Her mother always said that old people smelled bad but Suzanna thought her grandfather smelled nice, like spicy soap. They stared at one another for a long moment, and then she smiled. His heart dissolved. "Your uncle is right. You do have a smile like your grandmother. I'm so glad." He reached up to squeeze his son's hand. "Let's get into the dining room, shall we, before all the salmon is gone."

It took a while but with a little coaxing, Robert and Suzanna eventually fell into an easy back and forth. Though he was loath to admit it, Robert sensed that his stand in the lobby had cost him, and he was afraid the oncoming fatigue would cut his time with his granddaughter short. But when she skipped off to find a bathroom, Ted reassured him. "This isn't the only time I'm going to bring her here, Dad. Don't feel you have to push yourself," he said. "We'll go right after dessert, OK? But we'll be back."

Robert glanced around. "I wanted to ask her…about Allison. But I don't dare. Do you know how long she's going to stay?"

"No idea, from Allison's point of view," Ted said. "From my point of view, Suzanna belongs in Carding."

Robert smiled at his son. "You have such a great heart," he said. "Make sure it doesn't get broken. Your sister is not…"

"Grampa," Suzanna said as she bounced back to her chair, "I saw a picture of you on skis at the grocery store. Did Uncle Ted tell you?"

"Really? Andy Cooper still has those old photographs up on the wall?" She called me Grampa, Robert marveled.

"Yeah, and guess what? I'm going to learn how to ski," Suzanna said, a big yawn taking over her face. "Uncle Ted said he would teach me, and Mrs. Edie said she knows of some skis and boots I can use. Can we have dessert now?"

As his quiet son and his chattering granddaughter wheeled him back to his apartment, Robert felt the power of speech leave him. Ted was going to teach the girl how to ski? Ted? Oh, his son was so right. This little girl belonged to Carding.

"Are you sure about this?" Harry breathed. "Tell me what you saw again."

Gideon drew back a little from his father. The man had never learned to respect anyone's personal space, hunching so close that part of Gideon's inhale included his father's exhale. As his brother Noah once observed: "Why the man thinks anyone wants his used oxygen is beyond me."

Gideon groaned, and rose to his feet, his hands on the small of his back. "Tweaked it," he said to his father's questioning look.

"Yeah, what were ya doing when ya tweaked it?" Harry asked.

Gideon glared. "Road work. For you. Remember?"

Harry glared back then let it go. If his suspicions about his son and Peter Foster's wife turned out to be true, he'd deal with that later. Right now, he needed to know what his good-for-not-much son saw on that old map in Paula Bouton's office.

"Stick some frozen peas in your belt," he said. "The cold will numb it enough that it won't hurt."

Gideon moved his chin in the direction of the small refrigerator under his microwave oven. "Nothing in there but milk for my coffee," he said.

Harry raised his eyes to the floor above. Both men clearly heard Chloe's humming above the clack of her sewing machine. "Any signs of a thaw in that business with your wife?" he asked.

Gideon shook his head, and his body tensed, waiting for his father's inevitable lecture, as if the old hypocrite had a right to lecture anyone about husbands cheating on their wives. But hypocrisy had never bothered Harry Brown. As Chloe once waspishly pointed out, hypocrisy was what passed for religion in old Harry's life.

"Maybe if I talked to her," Harry suggested. Gideon nearly laughed. He might not understand much about his estranged wife but he knew for certain that Chloe hated her father-in-law.

"Nah, I don't think so," he said. "I don't think she's in the mood for listening."

"Hmph, wives should always listen to their husbands," Harry said. "Saves a lot of time and trouble. So what was on that old map?"

Gideon laid a piece of paper on the table between them. "You know that big jog that Academy Road makes around the old Croft place?" he asked, sketching.

"Yeah. Been that way as long as I can remember," Harry said.

Gideon drew lines to indicate the full meander of the narrow road that twisted through the center of the academy's campus, and then added a square to represent the Croft house. "Ever wonder why the road bends so sharp there?" he asked.

"To get around the old Croft place," Harry said.

"Not exactly." Gideon drew a dotted line through the square. "In 1901, Croft started building his house, and he chose to put it right on top of the main road coming into town."

"So that's why everyone in town hated him," Harry said. "Makes sense to me."

"Actually, no one seemed to be upset about where he built his house at the time," Gideon said. "I figure he spread a lot of money around so people just shut up."

Harry nodded. "That's just triple-A-plus-plus business. Anyone else with the smarts would do the same."

"It wasn't until after the house was built that folks in Carding started hating Croft," Gideon said.

"Yeah, I gather people liked his paintings but they didn't like him," Harry said.

"That's because after he finished his house, Croft tried to cut down the trees on the green so he'd have a clear view of Half Moon Lake and Merino. Said he wanted to be able to paint nature from his front porch,"

Gideon said. "I guess he paid a couple of kids to do it in the middle of the night but they got caught as soon as the first maple came down. After that failed, Croft tried to buy votes to get folks to agree at town meeting to clear the green. Might have done it, too, if it wasn't for Emily Willis and the *Chronicle* going up against him."

Harry shook his head. "I always figured that Willis woman was an interfering busybody. So she turned the town against Croft, eh?"

"Sure did. In fact, at town meeting of 1921, they voted to charge him a road assessment because he kept demanding extra grading on that jog," Gideon said. "That was the first year women could vote at town meeting, and they hated Croft."

"Bet he didn't pay it." Harry grinned. "I know I wouldn't have."

"You're right. And that's where the whole thing stood until Croft moved out of Carding in 1930, and left his old house to Emily Willis and Kitty Wolfe for their academy," Gideon said. "Though why he did that…"

"…is still a mystery to everyone in Carding," Harry finished. "I know all that. What I don't know is what this road stuff means. What's this ancient road thing that Paula Bouton's all excited about got to do with the land I own behind the old Croft place?" Harry was getting impatient, and the metal folding chair that passed for furniture in his son's basement wasn't doing his backside any good.

"The state legislature passed a law that says every town's got to account for its ancient roads, roads that were originally built by the town but have fallen into disuse," Gideon explained. "Unless a town officially abandons an ancient road, it's still a public right of way. No vote was ever taken at a town meeting in Carding to abandon the part of Academy Road that's sitting under Croft's house."

Harry stared at his son. "Are you trying to tell me that the town still legally owns the land under the main Carding Academy building?" His eyes started to gleam.

"When I looked at that 1810 map, I noticed how the road used to go straight downhill to the corner around the green with no jog. But the jog is there in the 1912 map." Gideon leaned back in his chair. "I looked at Paula's list, and saw that she didn't have anything about Academy Road on it. So I stopped at the historical society to look through all the town reports from 1901 to 1945. That old road under the Croft place is still legally owned by the town, and you can see the remains of it if you stand in the center of the Green and look toward the Croft place."

"So that means that the town meeting we're going to have next month has got to do what to benefit us, exactly?" Harry asked.

"Paula's making a list of all the ancient roads that need to be voted on at town meeting. If the town votes to abandon a road, its ownership goes to the closest landowner. If the town votes to keep a road, that means we have to maintain it—plow it, salt it, grade it, the whole she-bang—so everybody can use it," Gideon said.

Harry drummed his fingers on his chin. "Let's say that the town decides to keep a road but there's a building on it. What happens to the building?"

"Well, Paula says it would be a fight to force someone to take a building down but that only delays the inevitable." Gideon fixed his eyes on his father's face. "Can't have a building blocking a public road-way now, can we?"

Upstairs in her divided house, Chloe looked up from the fabric she was cutting, startled by a loud bellowing from downstairs. The sound reminded her of a coyote pack she'd once watched corner a deer. It rip-pled uncomfortably through her heart, and she laid her scissors down to cover her ears.

Her father was right, staying in her marriage with Gideon was a cruel joke that she'd played on herself. She saw that clearly now. It was time to move on, she realized. Finally.

Chloe picked up her scissors, a tiny smile now hovering on her mouth. She ran her eyes over the pieces of fabric clinging to her design wall. Getting out of her marriage was just like making a quilt, she decided. Once you figure out where you want to end up, all the rest is just so much cutting. She'd call her father in the morning, and ask him to get the legal ball rolling. She knew he'd be thrilled.

Downstairs, the two men opened beers and clinked their bottles together. "Not a word of this to anyone until Monday," Harry said. "I want to make sure we prepare the ground before it's common knowl-edge. We've got to make sure the vote goes our way. I don't suppose we can rescind the right of women to vote before then, can we?"

Gideon's eyebrows rose, and old Harry tilted his bottle upright with a grin. "Just kidding. I think the vote will go our way once we've explained a few facts of life to the right people. It doesn't take too many votes in a small town like this to sway a town meeting in one direction or the other."

About three inches of powdery snow fell on Friday night, just enough to refresh the scenery and give the guys who owned plows an excuse to get out of the house early on Saturday morning. Suzanna bounced out of bed as soon as the morning light shifted from dark to not-so-dark. Ted found her wrapped in a blanket at the kitchen window, staring at the backyard.

"Suzanna, your feet must be freezing," he said. She nodded as she hopped up and down.

"Does the new snow make the hill more slippery?" she whispered.

He shook his head as he fished around in the bottom drawer of an old bureau. "Here, put these on," he said, handing her a pair of slippers knitted long ago by his mother. She'd be pleased with this girl, he thought. Just not pleased with how she got here.

"A little loose snow on the top is good when you're learning because it gives your skis something to push against when you want to stop." He opened the door of the woodstove, and stirred up the night's ashes to reveal a small clutch of orange embers. Then he added kindling to restart the blaze. "And we're going to have a good, warm breakfast before we head out. Your grandfather," Ted felt a glow as he said those words, "always made us eat oatmeal before a meet because it stuck with us longer than cold cereal. Do you like oatmeal?"

Suzanna examined her nose print on the cold glass. "Does it come with maple syrup?"

"It can."

"Then I'll like it," she said.

As Ted measured and stirred, located the raisins, and checked the milk, Suzanna moved from window to window, admiring the transformation snow brought to the landscape.

"Come eat while it's hot," Ted finally called, and she reluctantly took her place at the table, uncertain about this oatmeal stuff.

But it turned out OK. Not her favorite but OK. Just as she reached the bottom of the bowl, they heard the slam of a car door, and Suzanna nearly levitated from her seat. Ted leaned back in his chair to see the driveway.

"It's all right," he said. "It's Edie—and she's got skis!"

The girl rushed to open the door, jumping and clapping as Edie walked in with a pair of ski boots, a bulging bag, and a pair of shortish skis. "My dear child," Edie laughed as she crossed the threshold. "those slippers will do you a lot more good if you keep them on your feet. If you can manage to get some boots on, I have something else for you in my car."

Together, the two adults managed to corral the girl long enough to get her arms in a jacket and her feet in rubber boots then sent her out to retrieve three pairs of ski poles from Edie's car.

"You have your hands full." She grinned as she looked at Ted's face. "In the most wonderful way."

Like most folks in Carding, Edie regretted the fact that Ted gave up the slopes after his mother died in a skiing accident. She understood the man's grief-stricken decision. But Anna Owens would not have approved of her son's sacrifice.

Ted sensed the drift of her thoughts. "Mom would like this little one," he said. "I just hope I haven't lost my touch on skis."

Edie reached up to grasp his shoulders. "Ted, it's way past time for you to reclaim yourself. I know your heart froze up when your Mom died. No, don't look away from me." He turned his face back to look her in the eye. "You know as well as I do how your mother glowed when she saw you race. There's a lot of Anna in that little girl, and you're the best person to put her on skis. It certainly isn't going to happen with your sister."

Ted sighed—big, loud, and deep. "No argument there. I've felt the ski stirrings for a while now, even before Suzanna showed up." His mouth tightened up. "I just wish my sister…"

"We all wish that," Edie whispered. Ted's eyes widened. It was rare in Carding for anyone to voice an opinion about Allison when he was in the same room. It was as if she'd died.

"I'm not going to let Allison take Suzanna away," Ted said. "I'm a better mother than she is. From what little I can gather, the poor kid's been dumped more places than either you or I can imagine. I can't let Allison do that."

"Have you talked to her about it?" Edie nodded toward the window where they could see Nearly greeting the girl.

Ted watched the golden cocker jump around Suzanna as though he had springs for legs. "How old is Nearly now?"

"Almost ten," Edie said. She watched as the child launched a snowball then raced the dog to fetch it. "He'll need a long afternoon nap after this."

"So, is all this equipment from your granddaughter?" Ted asked.

"Yes, Faye's never been able to use the same ski equipment two years in a row because she grows so fast. Diana swears she times her growth spurts with Christmas," Edie said. "I just bought that jacket for her last year. I'm afraid there are no mittens or gloves, however. Faye manages to lose every pair Diana buys for her. I swear half the kids on Mount Merino keep their hands warm with my granddaughter's lost gloves."

Ted laughed. "I used to do that all the time. It got so bad, Dad trained the ski team to watch where I put my gloves, and gave prizes to the first person to find them when I couldn't. It got so embarrassing, I finally started paying attention for myself. Which, I suppose, was Dad's point."

"How is your father doing? Did you go see him last night?"

"We did. He loved Suzanna as soon as she walked through the door, and I think she felt the same way about him," Ted shook his head. "He tells me they're upping his medication again to control his tremors, the second time in as many months. All in all, I thought he was pretty good last night. I know he put a lot of effort into looking as well as he could for her. He thinks Suzanna needs to stay here, too."

"But have you talked to her about that?" Edie asked. "Do you know how she feels about staying here? If you're going to set yourself up to fight for that little girl, you need to make sure you know she wants to live here."

Ted nodded as girl and dog clattered through the back door. "I'll talk to her today," he whispered. "I promise."

"Oof." Suzanna fell on her backside. Ted watched her flop around, her feet tangled in skis, while he pulled on his gloves. Then he reached down.

"Here you go." He pulled her upright. "It's always good to get your first fall over with right away. Now you don't have to worry about it."

Suzanna's feet moved in opposite directions, and she clenched her leg muscles to keep from landing in the snow a second time. "Wow, these things really are slippery. Are you sure I'm going to be able to ski?"

Ted nodded. "Oh yeah, I have no doubt at all. Now, pull your feet together slowly. I've got you." She did, and then Ted backed away until he was holding only her hands. "Let's get you over to the porch where you'll have something to hold onto while I set up the ropes."

When he felt Suzanna's whole body resist movement, he put a hand on each side of her waist. "Put your hands on my shoulders," he said, and she did. "OK, now slide your feet forward one at a time."

When they reached the porch, Ted placed her hands on a pair of brackets that held a brimming planterbox in summer. "OK, while I'm setting up a couple of ropes down the slope, I want you to get used to the way it feels to slide on snow. Hold onto the bracket with your hands, and push your skis back and forth, just a little to start."

"Like this?" Suzanna jerked her legs back and forth, looking for all the world like an uncertain stork.

"Hmm, I think we can do better. Don't move." Ted darted off.

"Don't worry," Suzanna whispered.

Ted was back in a moment with the ski poles they'd chosen for her. Then he scooped her up under her arms to set her closer to the house, her skis more or less parallel with the building. "Now take hold of the bracket with your left hand, and a pole in your right." She did. "Slide your feet back and forth." Suzanna wobbled. "Slowly, slowly. Good. Now do that a few times until you feel comfortable. Then try picking your feet up just a little, as if you were walking. The idea is to get used to moving with two slidy sticks attached to your feet."

He watched for a moment, decided she'd get the hang of it better if he wasn't looking then disappeared over the edge of his backyard slope with a coil of rope over one shoulder, his heart pouding a little more than usual.

Suzanna moved her feet in small steps, tramping down the snow. She discovered that if she looked at something besides her feet, she did a lot better so she tilted her head up to examine a wispy cloud that had come to play with the sun. When the cloud slid off, the golden orb blazed across the snowy landscape, and the unspoiled white made her gasp. Ted looked up, glad to see she'd already picked up her pace.

As she waited for her uncle, Suzanna imagined herself on Mount Merino, passing other skiers with the speed of light, dazzling them with her footwork. Before she knew it, she'd won a place on the Olympic ski team, and…and…

"Wow, you've really picked up some speed there." Suzanna started out of her fantasy. She'd never even seen Ted return. "Ready for the slope?"

Her fiery cheeks bunched up with her smile. "Yes. No. I guess so."

Ted handed her a second ski pole, and demonstrated how to coordinate them with her newly acquired ski walk. Slowly, teacher and student made their way to the top of the Owens backyard slope.

The family homestead, built in the early 1970s, sat on five acres of land. The house snugged up close to the road because Ted's mother refused to spend her free time keeping a front yard in shape for the sake of their neighbors when there were so many interesting things to do in the backyard. So Ted's father eliminated the front lawn by putting a wide stone walkway from the front door to the driveway that he edged in with a fence along the road. Anna took care of the rest of it by planting a lilac hedge that they let run wild.

Behind the house, the land started off in a relatively flat manner then undulated in a series of three slopes, each one steeper than the one before it. When his mother was still alive, the flat acreage held a kitchen garden, a clothesline, and a picnic table in summer. In winter, it served as the staging area for one of the best sledding hills in town.

The first slope, the baby slope, is where Robert Owens had taught Ted how to ski by sliding downhill then using the rope to steady himself while he learned to make herring bone tracks in the snow to come back up. Ted smiled down at his niece. "Ready?"

Suzanna swallowed, looking down the gentle hill. "It looks a lot steeper from here than it does from the back window."

Ted laughed. "Yeah, funny how that happens, isn't it? Believe me, you'll be fine. First I'm going to teach you how to do a snowplow, and how to get up by yourself after you fall." He grinned at her sharp look. "Every skier falls now and then, and you've got to get yourself back up."

For the next hour, Ted showed Suzanna how to turn the back of her skis out to make a V in the snow, how to dig her edges in so she could get back up when she fell, and how to use the rope to steady herself for the climb up so she could go down the slope again. Though he didn't say it out loud, Ted noticed that she glided more easily every time she went down the hill, and used the rope less every time she went up. Then just as his stomach made its first lunch-time growl, Suzanna took off, and glided all the way down the slope without a falter. At the bottom, she whipped around, poles in the air.

"I did it! I did it!" she whooped. He applauded, she bowed, and then "oof." Ted skied down to help her up, both of them laughing.

"OK, ready to try the next step?" he asked.

"Oh yes." Suzanna gripped the rope with soaking wet mittens. "This is the most fun I've ever had, ever."

So Ted taught her how to control the trajectory of her skis by shifting her weight from one foot to the other. Together, they made small, curved paths down the slope until Suzanna suddenly stopped, grabbing her belly.

"Whoa, I am really hungry," she said. "I could eat mountains of food."

"Me too. I'll tell you what, let's pack our gear in the truck, and go get lunch at the Crow. How's that?"

Suzanna put on the brakes. "Are we going to the mountain next, Uncle Ted?"

He shook his head. "Not yet. I have some place else I think you'll like better. It's a bit steeper and longer than my backyard but not quite the mountain. Come on, you need dry mittens."

Once inside, Ted made Suzanna drink a glass of water while he peeled an orange for her. "People don't think about it in the cold but you can get just as dehydrated as on a hot day," he said. "And the orange helps with that too."

Suzanna proved her hunger by downing the fruit before he located a second pair of mittens. Then he stirred up the fire, and stuffed the stove with more wood. "There, that'll last the afternoon," he said. "Come on, let's get to the diner before all of Diana's chicken chili stew is gone."

Suzanna liked the way that people nodded and waved at her uncle once they got into town. No one ever knew anyone in the places her mother took her, unless you counted the silly girls with their batwing eyelashes who crowded around Alli-O looking for autographs because she'd been on a TV show. And Suzanna didn't count them for anything at all.

"Hey Ted, long time since we've seen you in here on a Saturday," Diana called as they walked through the Crow Town door. She looked at Suzanna. "Those skis of Faye's fit you all right?"

"Oh yes. Thank you." Suzanna nodded gravely. "I got all the way down the hill and back lots of times, didn't I, Uncle Ted?"

Diana laughed. "Good for you. Off to the mountain this afternoon? Judging by the crowd in here this morning, there will be long lines at the ski lift."

"No, not the mountain, not yet." Ted looked squarely at his friend. "I thought I'd bring Suzanna over to the cabin."

Diana's eyes flew open, and then she said very slowly. "Good for you. It's about time." She picked up her pad and pencil. "Now what'll it be?"

Once they ordered, uncle and niece slid into one of the booths in the bakery's front window. Suzanna leaned forward on her elbows, her eyes focused on her hands. "Uncle Ted," she asked softly, "can I ask you something?"

"Of course. Ask away."

"Why does Harry Brown hate Edie Wolfe so much?" Suzanna looked up as a waitress slid bowls of chicken chili stew under their noses, suddenly afraid that her question had been heard.

"Thanks, Hillary," Ted said, reaching for the grated cheese. He took a mouthful of the stew, savored it, and then looked across the table at his niece. "Harry and Edie go way back," he said, sprinkling more grated cheese. "The two of them were married once upon a time, and Edie caught him..." He squirmed before he went on. "Well, let's say there were some serious marital differences."

Suzanna nodded. "She caught him in bed with someone else, right?"

Ted looked up, his lower jaw sagging.

"I don't know what that means, exactly, but I do know that the same thing happened in one of the television shows Mom did. I guess for grownups, sleeping in the same bed is not the same thing as a sleepover, is it?" she asked.

Ted laughed. "No, not exactly. Anyway, Edie left Carding that same day. We found out later that her father helped her get out of the country, and she ended up in France. Old Harry has a temper," he said when Suzanna's face scrunched up in a question mark, "and I think she was afraid of what he might do to make her come back to Carding."

"But he couldn't make her come back if she didn't want to, right?"

"Probably not in the long run but if she'd stayed in the States, he would have found her and made her life miserable. Edie's father, he was Senator Wolfe then, knew that Harry didn't have a passport so he couldn't follow Edie overseas." Ted cleaned his bowl. "My Dad told me that Harry was more angry than anyone had ever seen him. He wasn't used to people who wouldn't do what he wanted. He said a lot of very stupid things, even threatened the Senator. Anyway, Edie filed for divorce, and Harry finally had to agree to it. He was humiliated by the Wolfes, and he's never forgiven Edie for that. He hates the way that folks welcomed her when she came back with her two children." He nodded toward the Crow's counter. "Diana has a twin named Daniel who lives in New York City."

Suzanna nodded as she finished up her own bowl. "So when Harry gets mad at Edie, it's sort of a a revenge thing," she said.

"Yep, more or less. So, how about we get some of Diana's ginger cookies, and head on out?"

As Ted turned out of town, Suzanna asked, "Are we heading toward Half Moon Lake?"

"Yes we are," Ted said. She remained silent as he negotiated a series of roads, each one more narrow than the one before. Then the roads ended in a small parking lot carved out of the snow by the town plows.

"So what are we doing here?" Suzanna asked as she unbuckled her seat belt, and stuffed the last bit of her cookie in her mouth.

Ted unloaded skis and poles from the back of his truck. "My parents bought one of the cabins in Carding Campground when the Methodists decided they weren't going to use this as a retreat any more." He handed Suzanna her poles then knotted the laces of her ski boots together. "They don't plow the roads in the campgrounds in the winter because no one lives there, and the roads are really narrow, more like paths, really. So we have to walk in. It's easier to carry your boots if you sling them over your shoulder like this." He showed her how.

As Suzanna nodded, a dark green truck pulled in behind theirs. Charlie Cooper's face lit up when he spotted Ted, his niece, and the ski equipment. He grinned as he shook Ted's hand. Like everyone else in his generation in Carding, Charlie had fond memories of Anna and Robert Owens. Seeing Ted re-embrace his heritage was a very good thing.

"So, are you taking Carding's newest skier over to the rope tow?" he asked.

"Thought I'd give it a try," Ted said. He sensed the older man's barely contained excitement but tried to ignore it. "Hope it doesn't take too much to get it going."

"Shouldn't," Charlie said as the three of them filed down the narrow path tramped in the snow to the Campground beyond. "Andy and I cleaned and oiled it back in November. Ran it for a while, too. Just as good as the day your Dad put it together."

A shadow slipped over Ted's face at the mention of his father. But then he glanced at Suzanna, skipping far ahead, and he set his jaw. "Time to let the ghosts rest in peace, son," Charlie said quietly.

Ted nodded. "Yeah, I've been thinking maybe I should have done that a while ago."

Charlie chewed on the younger man's words as the trail took a deep bend toward the northeast. As they turned, the trees stopped, and they could see the whole campground tucked into the folds of the sloping land, the frozen surface of Half Moon Lake and then Mount Merino rising up on the opposite shore. It was, everyone in town agreed, one of the most beautiful views in all of Vermont.

Suzanna turned around. "Uncle Ted, how come there aren't any trees growing here?"

"By general consensus, the folks who own the cabins keep the field open so that everyone has a view of the lake and the mountain. Seems only fair."

"It looks like a ghost town," Suzanna said.

"It's a whole different place in the summer," Charlie said. "Most of these cabins are owned by families, and they come here to swim, for cookouts, family reunions, that kind of thing." He stopped, eyeing some depressions in the snow heading off to their right. "Hmph, looks like something kinda big roamed through here recently. Wonder if it was a bear."

"A bear? Really, you have bears up here?" Suzanna squeaked.

"Yeah, we do, though you don't see them very often, especially this time of year." He shrugged. "Oh well, I'm going to check our cabin, and then I'll be along to help you with the rope tow, OK?"

"Oh, you don't have to do that," Ted said. Then he caught his friend's expression.

"If I run the tow, you and Suzanna can ski together," Charlie said. "It'll be fun." He turned away with a wave.

"So what is this rope tow thing?" Suzanna asked.

Ted pointed at a little camp with a deep front porch, and a steep backyard. "That's the Owens' family camp," he said. "Dad picked this one out..."

"...because of the slope," Suzanna finished. "He sure must have loved to ski before he got that Parkinson's stuff."

"He did. Anyway, that's where we're headed."

Suzanna's pupils had shrunk so much because of the glare off the snow, she couldn't see anything when she first entered the lean-to attached to the back of the camp. But after blinking for a few moments, she spotted an engine that looked as though it had reared up on its backside. Metal tools and a couple of shovels leaned against the back wall. A large coil of thumb-thick rope hung from the ceiling.

"What is this?" she asked.

Ted slapped the top of the engine with an affectionate hand. "This, my dear niece, is probably the finest little rope tow you'll ever see that's not on a ski mountain." He pointed down to the bottom of the hill where a thick post stuck up out of the ground at the edge of Half-Moon Lake.

"I'm going to attach a bull wheel to that post down there to match the one up here." Ted pointed to a large metal wheel with a groove cut into its outside edge. "Then we undo all that rope except for the last loop, drag the other end downhill, get it around the second wheel, and hopefully, when we turn on this engine, we can just grab hold of the rope at the bottom of the hill, and it will bring us back up to the top."

"Just like on the mountain?" Suzanna asked, gazing across the lake to Mount Merino where small dots of color zipped across the snow.

"Just like the mountain except here, you can practice without a lot of other people around, and we can stop it and start it as many times as we want," he said.

Suzanna laughed. "You mean I can fall down a lot?"

Ted reached up to unwind the rope. "Yeah, that too."

Suzanna grew thoughtful. "Uncle Ted, did my mother ever come to this place?"

"In the summer, always. Your mother loves the sun." He bent down to snap his skis to his boots. "And when she was little, our Mom brought her here in the winter. But Allison..."

"...hates the snow," Suzanna said, and her mouth turned down. "Yeah, I've heard her say that a jillion times."

Ted bent down so they could see one another face to face. "You get to choose, you know," he said. "You get to choose who you want to be. Do you understand? If you don't want to be like your mother, you don't have to be."

Suzanna's eyes glistened with tears. "But I don't get to choose where I live, do I?" She spoke the words in such a low voice, Ted almost missed her question.

"Would you like to stay here, in Carding?" he asked. "With me?"

Suzanna's eyes flew open, and Ted realized she was frightened. Could she be scared of me, he thought.

"Do you...really want me?" she asked.

No, she's not scared of me, he corrected himself. She's been disappointed too often to trust what I say, what anyone says.

"I will become a teenager, you know," Suzanna said. "And my mother says they are all monsters."

"Hmph, well your mother certainly was, that's for sure," Ted muttered. "But I wasn't, and I daresay that most of the other kids in Carding weren't either. We got stupid from time to time. But we weren't monsters, and I find it very hard to believe that you'll be a monster either."

Uncle and niece gazed at one another. "It will take some doing," Ted said, "and your mother may make a show of fighting me, maybe in court. But if you could stay here in Carding, would you like that?"

Two tears tipped over the edge of Suzanna's eyes to trail down her cheeks, and then she launched herself at Ted, nearly knocking him over. He hugged her back, and awkwardly patted her hair.

"All right, then, that's settled," he said, holding her at arm's length. "But staying in Carding means going to school, mind. Carding Elementary was a good school back when I was a kid, and I hear that it still is. Are we agreed?"

The little girl stuck out her hand, and they shook. "Well, that's settled," Suzanna said.

"What's settled?" Charlie asked as his bulk blocked the light streaming in the open side of the hut.

"That I'm going to stay here, in Carding, with my Uncle Ted," Suzanna said. "And I'm not going to be a monster teenager."

"Well then," Charlie said, "if you're going to live in Carding, you've got to ski. Let's get this thing working."

Later, as the two men watched Suzanna make her first solo run down "Camp Hill," Charlie turned to his friend, and said: "Are you sure about this? Allison may not go along with it, you know."

Ted nodded. "I'm sure about keeping Suzanna in Carding. It may sound strange, but I think she belongs here. It's as if the town has laid claim to her."

"Allison won't understand that at all," Charlie said. "She couldn't wait to get out of here. Besides, your sister likes the image of herself as a mother."

"Yeah, maybe, but I think that extends only to the next picture of her in *People* magazine," Ted said. "Remember, the older Suzanna gets, the older Allison looks, and for women in TV and the movies, it's all about age. At least that's what I've heard."

Charlie stepped forward so he could watch Suzanna arrive at the bottom of the hill. "Look," he said out of the side of his mouth. "She didn't fall."

"Good for you, Suzanna," Ted called. Then he turned toward Charlie. "I have reason to believe Allison's finances are tight, very tight, and I might be able to buy her off. I'm pretty sure that's the reason she left Suzanna here in the first place."

Charlie snorted. "You figure your sister will leave her only child here for a price?" When Ted nodded, Charlie snorted again. "Your sister really is a piece of work."

"Yeah, never known anyone as self-centered as my sister. She beats Donald Trump in the narcissism department hands down."

Charlie clapped Ted on the shoulder. "Well, I can guarantee one thing for sure—you're going to need a lawyer before this is over so let me know what you need, OK?"

Just at that moment, a beaming Suzanna cleared the crest of the slope. She let go of the rope, raised her hands in triumph, and then her skis slid out from under her.

"Woohoo! I made it," she yelled, raising her fists to the sky. Charlie and Ted started to laugh, and tried to help her up but collapsed in the snow next to her. Finally, Suzanna sat up. "Again?"

Ted got up, reached out one hand to Charlie and the other to his niece. "You bet."

For the next hour, Charlie ran the rope tow while Ted joined Suzanna on the little slope to teach the girl more and more about skiing. Finally, he rejoined his friend in the shed. "She's a natural," he said, beaming.

"Just like her uncle." Charlie smiled then but let the comment drop. He'd been waiting a long time to see Ted on the snow again, and he didn't want to stir up too many ghosts. "Oh, I forgot to ask—did you check inside your cabin when you got here?"

"No. Why?"

"I'm not sure, but I think someone's been in ours, so I wondered if we've got someone making the rounds of the campground, helping themselves to the facilities," Charlie said.

"Anything missing?"

"No and nothing out of place except a towel in the bathroom," Charlie said. "And I wouldn't have noticed that if it wasn't for the smell."

"Smell? Of what?"

"Well, if I didn't know better, I'd say it was roses."

NINE

An Industrious Spider

New post on Carding Chronicle blog: February 8

Pothole Repair Update on Route 37
by Little Crow

The road crew worked all day to patch the worst of the holes on Route 37 so no one will lose a muffler or blow out a tire when they drive to Fiorello's Pizza tonight to hear the Thieves of Fire, eat dollar pizza slices, and enjoy some great dancing.

Come early. Stay late.

I'll be looking for you.

Little Crow | February 8 | Categories: Local Roads

"I promised I'd help decorate at Fiorello's so I'll eat supper there," Peter said as he laid his bass in its case. "And I'll be home late. I'll try not to wake you when I come home."

Lisa yawned. I'm having sex with my sister's husband tonight, she thought as she watched Peter pack up his gear. Imagine that. I wonder if Chloe will mind much when she finds out. Lisa sipped her coffee as she watched Peter bustle about in his precise way.

"What time do you think you'll be home?" she asked.

"Well, Fiorello's got special permission for us to play until one, and then everyone who helped get it ready to reopen is invited to stay after that for a little celebration. So I don't figure I'll be back until three or so. You sure you don't want to come?" Peter asked, hoping she would still say no.

Judging by the expression on her face, Lisa hadn't heard him. He looked at her with something approaching disgust as she sprawled over his favorite chair wearing nothing but that satiny robe thing she favored on what she called her "lazy Saturdays." He couldn't imagine Chloe wearing something so silly.

Chloe. No, that won't do, Peter reminded himself. That won't do at all. I'm married to Lisa, sickness and health, the whole routine. That's what I promised. Lisa put her empty cup down on the arm of the chair where he knew it would stay until he picked it up later. Peter shifted his gaze as she stood so he couldn't see how her robe opened up at the top.

"Of course I don't mind," she said. "I'm planning a long, hot bath, and a full manicure with this new polish I got." She purred as she spoke. "I think I'll make myself something to eat. You sure you don't want anything?"

"Mmm, no thanks." Peter said as he watched her leave the room, his mouth slack. He rarely saw his wife exhibit this much ambition on a weekend. He started to ask if she was really planning nothing more than a bath and manicure for the evening but stopped himself just in time because he realized he didn't care enough to know the answer.

Peter pondered his attitude toward his wife while he checked to make sure he'd packed everything he needed for the Fiorello gig. He tried to stir up some feelings for Lisa—good or bad—but all he came up with was indifference. With a sigh, he picked up his bass and headed toward the garage.

When Lisa first moved in, she asked Peter if she could use his garage for her collection of exercise equipment. It's only temporary, she'd reassured him. So he moved his latest fix-it-up project, a 1972 yellow Super Beetle, to the barn behind the house, parked his pickup in the driveway, and it had been that way ever since. Try as he might, Peter couldn't remember if Lisa had ever used the treadmill in the time they'd been married. And the magnificent web woven by an industrious spider between the handlebars of her stationary bike had had time to collect lots of dust.

Lisa toggled her fingers at him as he backed down the driveway. His mouth jerked in an automatic response as he waggled back. He felt vaguely disturbed by her refusal to come to Fiorello's because she always complained when she had to stay home by herself at night. What had changed?

As soon as Peter's car disappeared around the corner, Lisa picked up her phone to send a text to her evening's entertainment. "Peter gone," she wrote. "Meet me at the cabin in an hour. Be ready to party."

Though she couldn't explain it, Edie felt a lingering unquiet after her short encounter with Gideon at the Coop on Friday. No matter how ugly his father had been to her, Gideon had always been polite, and they'd passed many a pleasant minute in easy conversation when their paths crossed. Now he wouldn't look at her. Why?

Years ago, when she returned to Carding with her five-year old twins, Edie often questioned the wisdom of her move. But her parents, to whom she owed so much, needed help as they aged, and since the beloved father of her children had disappeared, Edie had no reason to stay in Paris.

As soon as she got back, old Harry started acting like the ass he was. At first, he bragged Edie had come back for him, just like he said she would. When Edie openly laughed at this, Harry made a spirited show of mock horror over the illegitimacy of her children. Then he tried to claim he was their father. But that was a non-starter because, as Edie's father pointed out, "The folks of Carding are good at counting to nine."

If Harry had stopped before that last boast, his opinion of Edie might have swayed a few of the weaker minds in town. Instead, his bragging made him the butt of a number of cruel jokes. Embarrassed, he tried to blame Edie for "the confusion," as he called it. But his protestations just made the jokes multiply.

Harry finally fell silent because, as Edie learned much later, his long-suffering girlfriend, Louisa Day, was pregnant, and her father threatened to sue if Harry didn't shut up and do the right thing. Once they were married, Harry tried to poison his young wife against Edie but the two women became friendly acquaintances, exchanging kindly smiles in the Coop and pleasantries at church when Edie accompanied her parents there. In spite of Harry, Louisa taught her children to be polite to Edie. So when Gideon avoided looking at her, Edie felt uneasy.

When he passed her on the street smelling of roses and vanilla, Gideon had looked her straight in the eye. Two days later, he studiously avoided making eye contact. Edie chewed it all over while heating up leftover chicken and dumplings for supper. Nearly watched her closely, making silent but strident appeals for some of the same.

Edie looked down, and chuckled. "I see you," she said, reaching for his food bowl. "Just chicken and sauce, right? None of that green pepper or broccoli stuff."

Nearly sighed when she finally put a bowl on the floor for him. She had just poured herself a small glass of wine when the motion sensor light overlooking her driveway clicked on. She pulled back the curtain to see the vehicle. Ruth's Jeep. Of course, Saturday night. How could she forget? Edie set a second plate, silverware and glass on the table before her friend knocked.

Ruth stood in the doorway, her latest quilt project folded in her arms. "I think Gideon's definitely on the loose again," Edie said as her friend shed her boots in the mud room.

"Anyone we know?" Ruth asked.

"I have no idea," Edie said as she poured wine in the second glass. "But why would he sail by us one day looking like the Cheshire cat and smelling of roses, and then two days later, he won't look at me when I run into him at the Coop? He's never done that before."

"Hmm, well, I have another puzzle for you. Remember when I gave Ted's niece that first ride around on my route?" When Edie nodded, Ruth went on. "When we dropped off the Lindstrom's mail at the Campgrounds, there was smoke coming from the chimney of the Cooper family camp," Ruth said. "When I saw Charlie later that day, I asked if anyone had rented cabins for the winter in the Campground. He's president of the association this year so I figured he'd know, but he told me there are no rentals."

"So who's got a key to the Cooper place?" Edie asked.

"Well, Charlie and Andy, of course. And Agnes. Does Chloe?"

Edie nodded. "I believe so but she was at the academy from Tuesday morning until we closed in the afternoon so it couldn't be her." Then her fork stopped in mid-air. "No, it couldn't be," she said. "Lisa and Gideon? Lisa wouldn't do that to her own sister. Would she?"

Ruth shook her head. "They're so different. Chloe's all sparkle while Lisa never gets enthusiastic about anything—her job, her life…"

"Or her husband," Edie said.

"But she wouldn't be bored enough to have an affair with her sister's husband, would she?" Ruth said. Then she corrected herself, "Estranged husband. Gideon and Lisa wouldn't do that to Chloe, would they?"

Edie refilled their glasses. "Well, Lisa's bored, and Gideon's woman-less at the moment. Under those circumstances, I think they would. But it may be more complicated than that."

"How so?"

"Peter and Chloe have been paying a lot of attention to one another lately," Edie said.

"You think?"

"No, I don't think they're having an affair." Edie shook her head.

"But there is an emotional attachment there." The two friends looked at one another while Nearly tried to stare more chicken into his bowl.

"Well, this is going to get interesting," Ruth said. "Brownie? I made a batch just before I came over."

Edie nodded. "Make it two."

Lisa rolled over with a sigh to lift her champagne glass from the bedside table. Of all the nights she'd spent in the Cooper family cabin as a girl, she'd never once slept in the corner room reserved for the grownups.

"I'm in the grownup bed," she giggled as she wrapped her arms around her body. "Doing grownup things."

Gideon had surprised her. He'd arrived on snowshoe hefting a backpack full of champagne, chocolates, toys to enhance their evening's entertainment, and a bar of Ivory soap. Lisa laughed when she saw the soap then suggested they begin with champagne and a friendly shower. From that point on, the two of them engaged in an escalating challenge as to place, timing, and position. For Lisa, the best part was when Gideon told her he couldn't remember when he'd had a better time.

"Not even on your honeymoon?" she asked, gratified to see him shake his head.

Gotcha there, Chloe, she thought. You might be our father's favorite but your husband enjoys me in bed more than he does you.

Suddenly full of energy, Lisa got up to cook bacon and eggs while Gideon dressed. Intimate recreation always gave her an appetite. She was careful to keep the splatter screen on the bacon pan so she wouldn't leave any telltale grime behind. Gideon encouraged her to think this way. "We get along so well, it would be nice to meet here for as long as we can," he said as he fondled his favorite Lisa parts. "And I know your father checks on the cabin. It wouldn't do to leave anything behind to make him suspicious now, would it?"

They ate in friendly silence, each of them savoring their favorite scenes of the evening in the privacy of their own minds. At one point, she caught him looking at her with a serious regard.

"Penny for your thoughts," she said.

He laughed, and leaned over to kiss her. "I'll give you a whole dollar's worth," he said. "I think you're terrific. When can I see you again?"

She sighed. "Peter doesn't have a lot of gigs in winter," she said. "I know there's one on the 15th, and another on the 22nd but they're local so we'll have to watch the time. But then on March 1, he does the big Mud Season Gala over in Montpelier, and he'll stay the whole night for that one."

They looked at one another, each face echoing the glee they saw on the other's.

"We have to plan something extra special for that night," he said.

"Oh, I think so," she said. "In fact, I've been thinking about a little enhancement I'd like to try on you."

"Oh? What's that?"

"Oh, something I saw online," she said. "But I can't use my credit card for it. Peter would see the charge, and ask me about it." Lisa reached over to let her finger trace a line around the open neck of Gideon's shirt. Then she unfastened his top button.

"What are you thinking?" he asked, his smile widening. They both glanced at the clock.

"Do you think we have time?" she asked.

"Oh, I think we can make time for whatever you have in mind," he said.

"So, could you help me with my enhancement?" Lisa asked as she unfastened a second button.

"Oh, I think that could be arranged," Gideon said with a deep, satisfied sigh as he pulled his wallet out of his pocket. "If you can find a pen and something to write on, I'll put down my credit card information so you can order your...enhancement. OK?"

Lisa giggled as she pulled him to his feet. "Oh, this is going to be so much fun."

Later, after Gideon left, Lisa made the bed carefully, adjusting the quilt over the top so its big star was centered. She looked at it with disgust as she smoothed it into place. She didn't understand all the fuss her sister ("the great designer") made about fabric. To Lisa, cloth was for clothes, and that was it.

It seemed like the only woman who'd ever escaped Carding's crafty curse was Allison Owens. Lisa suddenly wondered if Alli-O and Gideon ever made it together in high school. After all, he had played football and she had been a cheerleader. Maybe he'll introduce me to her the next time Alli-O's in town, Lisa thought. I mean, she has to show up to see her kid sometime, right? And maybe Allison can get me a gig on TV. I sure have a face and a body worth looking at, and as far as I can tell, that's all you need to be a star. She wondered how grateful she could make Gideon.

As she walked out of the Campground following the trail blazed by her flashlight, Lisa thought about the order she planned to place with Cherries Jubilee when she got home. She wondered what kind of limit there was on Gideon's credit card. Not that she had any intention of maxing it out. Just that it would be nice to know. After all, she was worth a nice present or two from time to time, right?

TEN

JOEYS

Harry drummed his fingers on his chest while he waited for the sun to creep out of its Sunday morning bed. He disliked waiting for dawn as much as he disliked waiting for anything. If he'd had the ordering of the world, the sun would rise and set at the same time every day. He was a man who liked a schedule.

Back in the days when he was wooing her, he'd told Edie how he wished he could have regular sunrises and sunsets, and she laughed. At the time, he thought it was because she found the idea amusing. But now that Harry saw the past clearly, he realized that Edie always laughed at him. Back then, of course, he'd been blinded by her beautiful smile and well-constructed figure. Yeah, Edie Wolfe was quite the catch, a woman a husband could show off with pride. And it sure didn't hurt that her father was Senator Daniel Wolfe.

He remembered each and every one of her curves. That's what blinded me, Harry told himself. I couldn't see her faults—her pride, her arrogance, her unwillingness to stay in her place, to tolerate my needs. All men have needs, Harry reassured himself. Edie knew that when she married me.

Louisa fidgeted in her sleep, and Harry turned to look at his second wife. Lately, she'd taken to wearing pajamas instead of the silky night-gowns he bought her every Christmas. Then there was that filmy scarf thing she wound around her head every night to preserve her hairdo. Hardly conducive to intimacy, Harry thought. Why bother to sleep together if you're going to wear more clothes at night than you do during the day?

He turned his face away, resumed drumming, and let his mind drift back to his new favorite subject—dismantling the old Croft house, and covering the eighty-nine acres he owned behind it with condos. What should he name the development? Crow Valley Condos? Carding Hills Estates? He liked the word estates. It had a grand ring about it. Crow

Valley Estates? Wouldn't people be turned off by the association with crows? With their high intelligence and taste for road kill, the birds did have a mixed reputation.

Harry stopped drumming as a picture of the land came into his head—late fall, just past the foliage show put on by the maples, the moment when the burnished oaks got their time in the spotlight. He loved their reddish brown, the color of cinnamon. Harry grinned. That was it, Cinnamon Hill Estates. Perfect.

Of course, the oak trees would be the first things to go once construction started.

Harry rolled out of bed, eager to plan his campaign to pack the town meeting with people sure to vote his way. Chuckling, he strolled to his bathroom, grinning at the mirrors he passed. You've still got it, Harry. Yes indeed, you've still got it. Cinnamon Hill Estates. Let Edie Wolfe choke on that one.

Every morning before work, the Brown & Sons' drivers coagulated around the tailgate of Bruce Elliot's pickup in the far corner of the parking lot. They reminded Peter of a sculpture, each figure posed in a way that captured his character. Fred always stood on the left, one foot on the truck's bumper, knee flexed, a coffee mug gripped in his two hands, the box of pudgy muffins from the Crow Town Bakery within easy reach. Sam Willis, the one everybody in town called Sam the Younger, stood just behind Fred's right shoulder as befitted his place as the group's principle listener. Head bowed as he doggedly worked his way through his three muffins a day, Sam rarely spoke, which made everyone listen to every word he did utter.

Bruce Elliot always stood in the center of the group, his mouth full of stories both fair and foul, his hands in motion as he made gestures to punctuate his material. Good nature flowed from the man like water from a faucet. To Peter, Bruce lived the perfect life—snug little house, a wife who adored him as much as he adored her, children to play with, ice fishing in winter, fly fishing in summer. Peter felt reassured by the crew's presence because he could rely on them to do a thorough job without much supervision. He also trusted that they'd let him know about problems on a job site before telling Harry. That arrangement made all of their lives easier.

Even though they never expressed it in so many words, all the guys who worked for Brown & Sons thought Peter Foster was the best thing that ever happened to the company. He stood like a wall between them and the volatile Harry Brown.

"Mornin' Peter," Bruce called out as soon as he parked his truck. "Muffin? Diana made ginger ones this morning."

"Yeah, thanks." But just as Peter raised one of Diana's specials to his mouth, Harry and Gideon pulled into the lot. Sam the Younger let out a low, almost inaudible whistle while Bruce muttered something profane under his breath. The crew counted on a full quarter-hour alone with Peter before any of the Browns showed up, and they didn't take kindly to any interruptions of their daily routine.

"Mornin' boys," Harry said in a hearty voice that made the hair on the backs of all their necks bristle. Fred dropped his elevated foot to the pavement as Harry reached into his truck for a box. "Why don't you all come inside from the cold for some muffins with Gideon and me? We got something we'd like to talk over with you."

Harry stalked into the garage, snapping on the overhead lights. Once inside, he set the large box on a table, and turned to his audience. As agreed, Gideon stayed at the back of the pack.

"Now you all know we've had a problem with that school closing Academy Road whenever they like so that we have to drive all the way around the green to get out of our own parking lot, right?" A couple of heads nodded. "Well, I think I've found a solution to our problem."

Not let Gideon drive, Peter thought, slanting his eyes sideways at the younger Brown. Gideon saw the look, and smirked. He'd never liked the way the drivers looked up to the engineer. Real men pour cement, Gideon thought. They don't sit at a desk working on a computer.

Not only that, I'll bet Peter's never made his wife laugh during sex, Gideon thought. I have, and that's got to count for something.

"What's your solution, Harry?" Peter asked.

"We're going to tear the academy down," Harry said. He scanned their faces for the excitement he expected to be there. But not so much as a single muscle fluttered among them.

"How's that?" Bruce asked.

"You know that funny twist in Academy Road that we all cuss in the winter? Well, that's not the way the original road was laid out," Harry said. "It seems that old Joseph Stillman Croft built his pile of a house smack dab on the existing road, and the town still owns that portion of it. That means the academy's main building is sitting on a public road, and you can't have a building on a public road."

"Wait a minute," Peter said. "The Croft place has been there for a hundred years. Why does it matter what part of Academy Road's the original and what isn't?"

"Any of you ever hear of ancient roads?" Harry asked.

"Yeah. Paula Bouton's been making a list of them to be voted on at town meeting," Peter said. Then he paused. "Do you mean to tell me that the town's never abandoned the part of Academy Road that's under the school?"

"That's exactly what I'm telling you," Harry said. "And it's coming up for a vote in this town meeting."

"So if the town keeps that road public, you figure Croft's old house will have to be torn down?" Peter asked.

"Yep, it's like I said, you can't have a building on a public road," Harry said. "It's the opportunity I've been waiting for. I'm going to tear that old place down, put in a good road, and build condos all the way up Academy Hill with a clubhouse at the top where you can watch the sun set over Merino. Skiing in winter, golf in summer, and great foliage in the fall. And with all the artsy fartsy stuff in Carding, who wouldn't want to have a second home here? I'm going to call it Cinnamon Hill Estates. What do you think?"

Peter was the first to clear his throat. "Um, Harry, the reason that Carding is such a famous arts community is because of the academy. People come here to…"

"I know that," Harry growled. "But there's not an artist in the world who can resist money. So what if they're teaching rich people who don't know any better how to make little cloth thingies? The important thing is the starving artists will stay right here in Carding because where else are they going to go in this economy?" He scanned their faces, astonished by their silence. "Anybody else?"

Bruce squirmed. His wife Cate volunteered at the academy three days a week, and the Carding Fair, which the academy put on every Labor Day, was the highlight of her summer. "What about the fair?" he asked.

"Hmph, that thing's old and tired," Harry said.

"The crowds still come," Peter said. Harry's face took on a glacial expression, and Peter saw white anger flicker in the back of his eyes.

"You, Mr. Foster, you above all others should know what this means," Harry said, his voice flat.

Peter crossed his arms over his chest and leaned against the office wall, reminding himself that he still had a comfortable balance in his savings account and folks were still hiring civil engineers. "Yeah, why me in particular?"

"Because you see the job orders come in," Harry said, stretching his mouth out in a weasely smile, "and you know they are slowing down. How much longer do you think I can keep Brown & Sons going in this economy? I would think a smart man like you would recognize what an opportunity this is for himself, and," Harry scanned the faces of his rapt audience, "all of his friends."

Peter hesitated. Putting his own job on the line by opposing Harry was one thing. Endangering someone else's was quite another. "I hadn't realized that was your thinking," he ventured.

"Well, now you know," Harry said. He sensed some of the starch leaching out of Peter's spine. He knew the engineer's best asset was the twin of his greatest weakness. The drivers at Brown & Sons instinctively followed Peter Foster because they trusted him. He was loyal to them, and they were loyal to him. But the drivers' trust was also a trap because Harry knew Peter wouldn't betray it, even if it meant injuring himself. Harry Brown's catalog of faults ran to several pages but loyalty wasn't one of them so he felt free to exploit it in others. Loyalty, as he told his wife every time she caught him where he didn't belong, was for dogs.

"Now I've gone to every town meeting in Carding since I could vote," old Harry said, smiling as he chose the biggest muffin from the box, and stripped it of its paper. "And I've made something of a study in how town meetings work. Would you like to know what I've learned?"

Harry liked what he saw now, the look that chickens get when they spot a fox in the henhouse. "Well, I'll tell you what I've learned," he said. "Not many people show up at town meetings any more, and those that do are the ones who get to make the rules. In other words, it doesn't take many people voting the right way to get whatever they want out of a town meeting. Understand?"

Peter tasted metal in his mouth and realized he'd chewed the inside of one cheek raw. "So we either vote your way on the ancient road question or we lose our jobs. Is that right?" he asked.

"Oh, I'm not telling anyone how to vote, Peter," Harry cooed. "That would be illegal. I'm just making my position very plain. And I'm going to hold you personally responsible for making sure that idea stays clear in everyone's mind." He picked up the box of muffins and held it out to the engineer. "Now, I'd like you to have one of these before they go stale. There's no money—or time—to waste."

Peter crushed the ginger muffin and hurled it into a wastebasket on his way out the door.

"Do you think you can count on him?" Gideon asked his father as they watched the engineer leave.

Harry nodded. "Yeah. He believes he's responsible for the other guys, and he can't let them down," he said. "He's stuck, and no one knows it better than him."

"Would you really fire the guys if the vote went the wrong way?" Gideon asked.

Harry shrugged. "Doesn't matter what I'd do. It only matters what Peter Foster believes."

Peter flew down the Brown & Sons driveway, his strides growing longer and longer. "Damn the man," he said. "Damn, damn, damn."

He whipped around the corner, heading he knew not where. Chloe works at the academy, he thought. She loves that school. This will destroy it, destroy her.

Destroy us.

Us? The thought punched Peter in the gut. Us. Is that how I feel about Chloe? He whirled to go back...to what? He didn't trust himself near Harry Brown or that smug ape of a son of his.

Suddenly a car's horn blared close to his ear, and Peter realized he'd stopped in the middle of the road. He jumped out of the way as a tourist in a too-big car swept by, its driver obviously distraught that someone would delay his fun by the millisecond it took to steer clear of a man in the road. "Joeys," Peter muttered. "Damned Joeys."

Long ago, when they worked on the Mount Merino ski patrol together, his friend Ted Owens had nicknamed skiers who came from New Jersey "Joeys" because of the motherly screeches one heard all over the hills when the packing-up started on Sunday afternoons. "Joey! Joey! Come inside this minute. We've gotta go now!"

The nickname stuck and quietly seeped through Carding's local bloodstream. Soon double-parked SUVs with out-of-state license plates became "Joey-mobiles." A particularly high-powered coffee at the Crow showed up on the menu as "Joey java," an inside joke that no one bothered to explain when asked by someone "from away." And the quiet that settled on the town around seven o'clock every Sunday evening in winter was called the "Joey hour" by everyone who enjoyed it.

Ted, that's who I've got to talk to, Peter thought. Ted.

He whirled in the direction of the post office only to discover he was standing right in front of it.

"Well, hello, Peter," Edie called as soon as he walked through the door. Then her smile faded, and Nearly whined. "Why, what's the matter? Is someone hurt?"

Peter winced. How do you tell someone that her life's work may soon be destroyed? "It's Harry," he said. And then he shot a pleading look in Ted's direction.

"What's that old buffoon got cooked up this time?" Edie asked. "Claiming mineral rights under the Croft building?"

"Not mineral rights, exactly. Ancient road rights," Peter said.

"What?"

"Seems that Joseph Croft built his house on top of the original Academy Road. When he was alive, the town refused to declare it abandoned. And after he died, no one cared enough to make it happen," Peter said. "It's going to be on the warrant at town meeting, whether the town wants to keep it a public road or not. And if they vote to keep it public, any buildings on it will have to come down."

Edie clutched the counter. "Are you sure? Very sure?"

"I'm afraid so," Peter said.

"Whew." Ted glanced at Edie to make sure she was all right only to find her standing straight, her eyes so hot he felt scorched.

"This is going to come up at town meeting, you say?" Edie said. "There will be a vote so that doesn't mean Harry will get his way."

"He's threatened to fire everyone who works for him if they and their families don't vote the way he wants," Peter said. "And he's made me responsible for those votes."

"You? Why you?" Ted asked.

"Because the guys listen to me," Peter said. "And there's more."

"More? Isn't that enough?" Edie asked.

"Harry plans to build condos on the land behind the academy, and that's a project with the promise of a lot of money for the people who work on it," Peter said. "Carpenters, framers, sheetrock workers, plumbers, electricians. All those people who got put out of work by the stupidity on Wall Street. Harry's promising them jobs."

"Well." Edie drew the word out in a single, long breath. "How very interesting. Harry's timing is impeccable, as always."

"What do you mean?" Peter asked.

"Well, I've been aware for some time that we need to renovate that old pile, and I've been dreading it. In spite of the way it looks on the outside, the Croft house's innards aren't the best," Edie said. "If Harry wins, it will make a decision to move the school to another town easier."

"Does that mean you're not fighting this?" Peter and Ted asked together.

"Oh, don't be silly," Edie said. "I'll fight that old coot with everything I've got. Carding Academy should be in Carding, after all. But I don't want that man to think for a minute that he can get the better of me." She looked down at Nearly. "Come on, boy, we've got to get home. I have some thinking to do."

Ted knew no one would believe him but he swore he felt the earth wobble under the post office.

Edie sped home across the green. She needed a place to indulge the fury surging through her bloodstream. Unexpressed anger would just get in the way of what she needed to do, so it was best to get it over with as soon as possible.

She tried to regulate her breathing on her short walk home but failed to calm the twitch in her hands. "I think this one calls for the bat," she muttered to Nearly. He cocked his ears forward, and then sighed. His entire morning routine had been disrupted.

Before she cancelled her cable subscription because everything on TV bored her, Edie saw part of a show in which a beautiful but mismatched couple jousted one another with a pair of foam bats. Not long after, she visited a sporting goods store with her grandson Wil, and spotted a display of the very same bats. When she picked one up, Wil asked: "Is that for when you get mad at old Harry Brown?"

"Out of the mouths of babes," she said. "Actually, there are times I'd like to take a real one to Harry."

"That's illegal, Gram." Wil hesitated. "At least I'm pretty sure it is." He picked up one of the foam bats for himself, hefting it in one hand. "Still, it would be a lot of fun."

Edie bought two, gave one to Wil then kept the second for herself, nicknaming it the Old Harry Bat.

As soon as she got home, Edie added wood to her stove then fed Nearly a small second breakfast. With the house warm, and her dog occupied, Edie pulled on an old hat and gloves, grabbed the Old Harry Bat, and headed out to her back porch.

Whack! "You pinheaded old goat!" she screamed as she hit a door post. Whack! "You sewage encrusted vermin!"

Bang! Whack! Whack! Whack! "You nasty...bitter...old...man!"

Edie liberally salted her tirade with expletives, and threw in some of the French curses she'd learned from the father of her children. Her anger ebbed quickly but swinging the bat did nothing to assuage her sorrow. To lose the academy, Carding's heart, the incubator for so many creative people. How could she bear that?

At last the bat felt heavy, and Edie leaned against the porch wall, panting in the cold. She would fight this, of course she would. But too many families worried about feeding themselves, and that fear gave Harry's promise of good-paying jobs extra weight. As Bruce Elliot once observed: "If folks are hungry and cold, who cares about yarn and scraps of cloth?" And that from the husband of a quilter.

Edie returned to her kitchen when she started to shiver. I can't give into this, she told herself as she dropped into her favorite chair. Nearly watched her from the doorway to the living room and gave his tail a tentative wag. A small tap at the back door made Edie jump. Nearly barked but didn't move, a combination of signals that meant a friend had come to visit.

"Why Faye, whatever are you doing here? I thought you'd be spending school vacation playing with your friends." Edie looked down at her granddaughter, the brightest light in her personal sky.

"It's all over town, Gram, what that awful Mr. Brown wants to do to the academy," she said. "It's all anybody's talking about at the Crow. Wil had to stay—he's helping Mom and Dad at the counter—but we thought you shouldn't be alone at a time like this. Can I come in?"

"Yes, of course, sorry. You really caught me by surprise."

Faye slowly removed her gloves as she entered the kitchen, and acknowledged Nearly's presence with a solemn nod. Edie had to clamp down on her mouth muscles. She could see that she had become the object of Faye's latest effort to right the world. "Shall I make us some tea while we talk?" the girl asked.

"That would be lovely, dear. May I hang up your coat?"

Faye filled the kettle, put it on the stove then set their favorite mugs on the counter. Edie traced the expressions of her long-ago lover, Faye's grandfather, in the lines of the child's serious face. How he would have loved this girl.

"Now Gram, what are you going to do if that horrid Mr. Brown gets his way?" the girl asked as they settled at the kitchen table.

"I'm not sure, yet," Edie said. "What do you think I should do?"

"Well, it's simple, really. If you can't do one thing, you have to do another. Could you move the school? I've heard you complain about that old Croft place forever, how that man's will keeps you from fixing it up the way it needs. Cookie?" Faye pulled a bag from the bakery from her coat pocket, and set it on the table. "Mom sent them. She says carbs are good for times like this."

Edie nodded, a grin stretching across her face. "I do have a place in mind that would be a lovely school building, to tell you the truth, over in White River Junction. But leaving Carding would be a wrench—the green, the river, Half Moon Lake, the mountain. I can't replicate that landscape anywhere else, and it's half of what folks come here for."

Faye carefully placed her head in one hand, striking the new contemplative pose she'd been practicing in her mirror at home. "It would be different, that's for sure. Do you think Mr. Brown will win?"

"I certainly think it's possible, my dear. Folks need to work, and I can't employ them all at the academy. Harry's talking about building condos on the land he owns behind the school, and there would be a lot of work there, at least for the short term." She sipped her tea.

A knock on the back door made both of them jump. When Faye opened it, Peter Foster stepped in.

"Why Peter, whatever are you doing here? Won't Harry object?" Edie had to turn her head up to see the young man's face. "Aren't I enemy number one on his list?"

"Edie, please let me explain."

"Of course," she said, stepping back from the opening.

But before Peter took a step, a red van pulled into the driveway. Edie heard Peter gasp as Chloe got out, and stalked to the back door. "You," the young woman hollered, pointing at Peter. "I thought you were different, a better man than my pitiful excuse for a husband and his nasty father. I thought you had some decency, maybe even some backbone. But you're just like them, aren't you? Aren't you?"

Edie felt Faye come up beside her, and she laid a hand on the girl's shoulder. Chloe stood right in front of Peter, her entire body one taut , vibrating wire.

"I ran into Sam the Younger at the gas station, and he told me how my idiot husband figured out a way for his father to destroy the academy, and that you're all going to vote for it at town meeting." Chloe gripped the railing on the stairs, her face white. Faye, mesmerized by this display of unseemly adult behavior, thought she detected tears in the young woman's eyes.

"Chloe, I…" Peter started.

"Are you really going to vote for a plan that will destroy the oldest and best-known handcraft school in the country? Do you have any idea how many artists and designers got their start here?" Chloe demanded. "Do you have any idea how hard we've all worked to make Carding's reputation what it is?" She inched closer, until the top of her head nearly brushed his chin. "Do…you…have…any idea at all…what…you… are…doing?"

She may love him after all, Edie thought. You never fight with this much abandon with someone you don't care about.

"Chloe, please, this was not my idea," Peter said. Faye inched closer to her grandmother, trying not to miss a thing. Maybe her brother Wil was right: watching the goings-on in Carding was better than television.

"Harry's threatened to fire everyone if they don't vote his way, and he's made me responsible for their votes. You know what the job market is like now, a hundred people for every opening. I can't let all those guys be fired." Peter bent his head toward Chloe, and Edie swore she could see their yearning for one another become visible in the air.

"My dears," she said in a voice that surprised her with its calm. "There is no need to argue. There will be enough of that throughout town all the way up to town meeting. We must all do what we must do."

Chloe looked at her, and tears fell across her cheeks. "Don't you care about this, Edie?"

"More than I can measure, I assure you. And I promise you I will fight Harry Brown with every fiber of my being," Edie said.

"I don't think you can beat him at town meeting, Edie," Peter said. "That's what I came to warn you about. He controls too many wallets in Carding. The academy just doesn't employ as many locals as he does, and—forgive me—you can't pay the wages he does."

Chloe snorted, and Faye nearly giggled. Of all the younger-than-her-grandmother people she knew in Carding, she liked Chloe Brown the best. There was something about the way the young woman dressed and moved that she found compelling to watch. Wil explained that Chloe had style, the real kind that comes from doing what she liked no matter what anyone else thought or did. Faye had had no idea that style included snorting. She'd have to practice that at home.

"That may be true on an individual basis, Peter," Edie said. "We don't pay the same wages that folks like Bruce Elliot make. But the academy is an economic engine in Carding in a way that Brown & Sons can't be. We draw more people to Carding than Mount Merino, and those people spend money at the inn, the shops, the gas station, everywhere in the Corvus Valley."

Peter looked from Chloe's angry face to Edie's anxious one. "I think people are too scared of Harry Brown to openly vote against him."

Edie considered for a moment. "You may be right. The folks in this village may be too scared to vote for their own self-interest because they're blinded by someone else's. But I'd be willing to bet that the folks in White River Junction won't be scared of Harry Brown."

"White River Junction? What's White River got to do with Carding Academy?"

Edie smiled, and made sure she locked eyes with the young man before she spoke because she knew he'd carry her message far and wide. "Imagine the kind of economic engine that the academy could be in another community, especially a town as well situated as White River Junction—two interstates cross there, there's a train station for Amtrak, and a very active bus station. Not to mention the airport just across the Connecticut River in New Hampshire. All in all, I'd say White River Junction would make a great choice if Harry drives us out."

"You'd move the school from Carding? Really?" Peter spluttered. "But it's called Carding Academy."

"So? Norwich University started in Norwich but moved to Northfield decades ago. And they still call it Norwich University," Edie said. "Vermonters are flexible, and the university is doing just fine, last time I checked. Besides, if Harry wins this fight, and razes the main academy building to the ground, what choice do I have? Just let the school die? I don't think so."

Chloe gasped. "I think that's brilliant. When do we pack?"

Edie beamed at her. Nothing like a little support to drill her message home. "Why don't you come in, Chloe? I think Faye will make us another cup of tea. And Peter, perhaps you'd best get back to work."

He closed his mouth with a snap. With one last, stricken look at Chloe, he shuffled off to his truck.

"Poor man," Edie murmured as she watched him back his truck out of her driveway.

"Poor man, nothing," Chloe said. "He has choices to make, just like all the rest of us. He can take a different direction any time he chooses."

Edie regarded her prize teacher with a steady, knowing gaze. "In my experience, there's a heavy price to pay when you swim upstream. You do gain in the long run if you follow your own muse but there is a cost. There's a great comfort in the familiar even when it's not good for us."

Chloe felt her cheeks burn. Is that why she stayed in the same house as Gideon? The comfort of the familiar?

Ted listened to Suzanna's report of her day with only half an ear while he locked up the post office. "Are you OK, Uncle Ted?" she finally asked.

"Yeah, I'm fine. I just heard some news today that set me back on my heels." But then he smiled. "But it's not your worry. How do you feel about hamburgers? Andy's got ground beef on sale at the Coop."

She smiled. How nice that a grownup didn't burden her with something she didn't want to understand. "Cool," she said.

Ted kept his eyes on his own business as he walked through the store. He knew the ancient roads question would burn through town, and since he had to serve everyone regardless of political opinion, he figured it was a good idea to keep his head down. Then he saw Andy Cooper.

"How is old Harry's latest declaration of war playing at the Coop?" Ted asked.

"This one's going to be damn bloody," Andy said with a shake of his head. "Diana's son, Wil, has been blasting out those blog things of his one after the other, stirring people up. I don't know where he's getting his information but I kinda wish he'd let it rest for a while. The latest is that somebody in the town office in White River said that they'd welcome the academy there any time that Carding doesn't want it."

Ted gave a low whistle. "I really hope it doesn't come to that. I hate to think about Carding without the school. My Mom loved the academy, said it was a home away from home." He sighed. "But I can't blame Edie for thinking that way. She's got to protect the school, not to mention all the artists who work there."

"Yeah, moving it would change Carding forever, and getting a bunch of condos in return doesn't seem like a good trade," Andy said. "I guess Harry's really het up about this one because he figures he'll finally get one over on Edie. Says he'll close Brown & Sons, and throw everyone out in the street if the vote doesn't go his way. And he's holding Peter responsible for making sure that the crew does what Harry wants."

"Yeah, I know. Have you seen Peter's face? I've never seen him so wound up." Ted sighed. "Well, keep your head down."

ELEVEN

PUSHMI-PULLYU

New post on Carding Chronicle blog: February 14

Could Carding's Loss Be White River's Gain?
by Little Crow

The Carding Academy of Traditional Arts moving to White River Junction? Could this be true? Edie Wolfe, executive director of the academy, says that it's a possibility.

"No matter how people vote on the ancient roads question at town meeting, my first obligation is to protect the school," Wolfe said when we emailed her. "If Carding votes to keep that old road under the Croft building public, then I would say that the academy's days are numbered in this town. We have to consider an alternative location."

But White River Junction? That seems a world away from here.

"There's some very interesting buildings in White River," Wolfe said, "and a thriving arts community already in place. I think the academy could be a very good fit for that village."

Are there any concrete plans in the works, the *Chronicle* asked.

"Not as of yet," Wolfe said, "though I have started preliminary investigations into available properties. We have to be prepared. To do otherwise would be negligent."

The academy's future has made the question about ancient roads on the town meeting ballot the hottest topic in town, and opinions range widely. If the town votes to keep the section of Academy Road that's under the school public, then Harry Brown of Brown & Sons will be the biggest winner since he owns 89 acres of land behind the school, acreage that he can't really get to right now because of the school on one side, and wetlands on the other.

Brown is rumored to be considering building a large condominium project on that land if the Joseph Stillman Croft house is razed. When contacted by the *Chronicle*, Brown would only say: "People should vote to keep that road public if they want to do what's right for the town." He would neither confirm nor deny the condo project rumors.

Big changes could be in store for Carding after town meeting.

I'll be looking for you.

Little Crow | February 14 | Categories: Local Politics

Conversations overheard at the Carding Coop:

"Did you hear that Edie Wolfe's going to move the academy out of Carding? You know, she's always thought herself too good for this town, and this proves it. Couldn't birth her children here, could she? Oh no, had to have them in Europe."

"Did you hear that old Harry's planning to put a thousand condos on that land he owns behind the academy once he gets rid of the Croft building? A thousand. And he'll pay top dollar for workers. My grandson knows Harry's son, Gideon, so he's sure to get one of those jobs."

"I hear that everyone working for old Harry is bringing their families to town meeting. The man will get what he wants this time for sure. Edie Wolfe is done."

"Did you hear what happened at the quilt guild meeting yesterday? That Candy Croft kept bragging on how she's buying the first condo in Harry Brown's new project. Said she couldn't wait to look down the hill, and not see that ugly old Croft building. Made that little Chloe Brown so upset, she started to cry."

"Well, you gotta wonder how Chloe's feeling, still being married to Gideon and all, and him working so hard to get rid of the school. Remember when he hit that woman crossing Academy Road because he was too busy flirting with someone to pay attention? I hear Gideon's been sleeping in the basement of his own house ever since."

"I heard he was flirting with Candy Croft when he hit that woman. That isn't true?"

"No, it was somebody else, somebody from out of town. Gideon and Candy had a thing before he married Chloe, and even though Candy always believed he'd marry her in the end, everybody knew Gideon just used her. But it won't be long before Candy's hanging around him again, just waiting for her chance."

"Well, I feel sorry for Chloe. Gideon has always acted like a bull moose in rutting season. No morals, that man."

"But everybody in town knew it so what did Chloe expect when she married him? That he was going to change?"

"She was young, just out of college, and didn't know any better, I guess. I think she was too young to know that leopards don't change their spots."

"Tch, tch, tch, I never would have let my daughter marry someone like Gideon Brown. Where were her parents?"

"Listen, Chloe Cooper, that's who she was then, was twenty-four at the time, hardly a little kid. She didn't need to ask anyone's permission to do anything. Though I have heard that her father—you know the lawyer, Charlie Cooper, don't you?—kept trying to talk her out of it all the way to the church. But Chloe's mother, Angela…"

"One of the pushiest women in the world, in my opinion."

"That's for sure. Anyway, I heard that Angela engineered the whole thing, right down to where the newlyweds spent their honeymoon. I understand that since Chloe caught Gideon in their bed with another woman and made him live in the basement, Angela won't talk to her."

"Well, that's Chloe's gain, in my opinion. I never did see much of her mother in her. She's really her father's daughter. Where's Angela living now?"

"Out in California, last time I heard. Passing herself off as some sort of spiritualist healer. Can you imagine?"

"I can, as a matter of fact. Remember when she tried acting? Only thing she was ever good at, pretending to be something she's not."

"Still and all, losing the academy will make the town feel different. No more Solstice Dance or Carding Fair."

"No more music on the green in the summer. I love to set up a chair near the old sycamores, and listen as the sun sets."

"No more community Thanksgiving dinner or holiday cookie swap. I'll miss those, too."

"That's progress for you."

"Well, I don't think it's progress at all. When Harry Brown is done building up his Cinnamon Hill Estates, or whatever he's calling it, we'll all be nothing but the servants of a bunch of rich folks from away who come here for only two weeks out of the year, and don't care about the valley. We'll just be one of the local attractions they point out to their friends. I'm voting to abandon that old part of the road under the school. I want the academy to stay right where it is."

"How could Edie Wolfe even think about moving the school? Something named Carding Academy has to be in Carding."

"She doesn't want to move it. But if voters agree to keep the ancient road under the old Croft building public, then the building will have to come down, and that will give Harry Brown the access he needs to develop his land up there. Believe me, that school means too much to Edie Wolfe for her to just sit back and let it close. She'll move it before she closes it."

"So that's the way it is. Then I'm voting to abandon the road. I want the school to stay here."

"You'll be voting against jobs then, and there's a lot of people hurting here in town that could use a job. I can't believe you'd vote against them."

"Well, how's Peter Foster going to vote? He's a levelheaded guy. What does he think?"

"Peter's all for the town keeping that ancient road public. Says change will be good for the town, increase our tax rolls, put more money in the Carding coffers. A project like the one Harry's planning will take years to build, and there will be plenty of work that whole time."

"If Peter says it's OK, then it must be. I've liked him since he was a boy."

"Have you seen him lately?"

"Can't say I have. Why?"

"Looking awful pale and thin, walking like an old man carrying a great weight."

"I do imagine that working for Harry Brown could be an awful strain. And isn't he married to Chloe Brown's sister, the curvy one?"

"Yeah, Lisa. Looks like she could keep a guy awake all night long, that's for sure."

"Well, maybe that's it. Anyhow, Peter Foster's a good man. If he's voting with Harry Brown, I just might do the same."

"I thought Carding Academy would be a good fit for White River Junction," Edie Wolfe said as she accompanied a realtor down the village's

main street, "since you already have one school here."

"The Center for Cartoon Studies," the woman said with a smile. "Yes, as well as a theater, and lots of artists in studios all over the village." She waved her hand in a circle. "And a meditation center, good places for coffee, and…"

"…buildings that could use some care and attention," Edie observed as they stopped in front of a large stone structure, a former department store that stood vacant and yearning on the village's main street. She tilted her head up to cast an appreciative eye over the decorative fan-shaped window above the large front doors. "Hardly anyone takes the time to make buildings beautiful any more."

"That's for sure. Have you ever seen anything uglier than a big box store?" the realtor asked as she unlocked the doors.

"Two big box stores," Edie said as they stepped over the threshold. "The only thing they're good for is demolition when they fail. And they all fail, sooner or later. Remember Bradlees?"

"Yep, and before that there was Woolworth's and Zayre and King's. They all fail eventually, leaving their ugly buildings behind. And what can you do with them? They all look the same, all built on the same inhuman scale. Blight in the making, in my opinion."

With those words, the realtor snapped on the lights, and Edie gasped. A subtle mosaic of tile stretched across the floor. Large, open archways delineated what Edie presumed had been different departments. Though the place needed TLC and elbow grease, its lovely bones pleased her.

"Is the tile work like this on every floor?" she asked.

"It's less intricate upstairs, and the floors in the offices are wood not tile," the realtor said. "But Mr. Giamatti—he's the man who built this store—liked his tile. I understand his father was a stone cutter. Come, I'll show you."

As the two women slowly ascended the wide staircase to the second floor, Edie began to wonder if she should reconsider her desire to stay in Carding at all. Harry might be doing the academy a favor with his ancient road scheme.

One of Peter Foster's favorite little-boy memories was of his parents reading stories before bed. While he and his brother liked adventures such as *Johnny Tremain* and *Treasure Island*, their sister wanted nothing but *Dr.*

Dolittle books. Peter swore she became a veterinarian because of Hugh Lofting's tales. After all, horses, dogs and cats are a lot easier to talk to than people, and that suited his shy sister just fine.

The only thing Peter remembered about the *Dr. Dolittle* books was a creature called Pushmi-Pullyu. Depending on your point of view, the Pushmi-Pullyu was blessed or cursed with the head of a gazelle at one end, and the head of a unicorn at the other so that it could go in two directions—or no direction—at the same time. As town meeting day ticked closer, Peter thought about that mythical animal often because he'd felt like one ever since Harry concocted his ancient road scheme.

Every minute of every hour of every day crawled by as the good folks of Carding argued, discussed, and debated the fate of the Carding Academy of Traditional Arts, and the advantages or disadvantages of a large condominium project in the center of town. Peter heard it all as so much background noise, barely discernible over the roar of his heart. As he expected, tempers flared, and eruptions occurred among the town's normally placid social groups. For the first time in anyone's memory, a town meeting lunch would not be organized by the elementary school's PTA because one half of the group wasn't speaking to the other half.

Harry jumped all over the PTA squabble, seeing an opportunity to curry favor with voters by getting the wives of his crew to cook town meeting lunch. But that idea quickly died, speared at the end of Cate Elliot's sharp tongue. Alone of all the people associated with Brown & Sons, Bruce's wife openly defied Harry's edict, declaring she would rather "do without" than go against the academy, "the soul of Carding," as she called it.

"And if you think I'm going to slave over a hot stove for you and your cockamamie idea," she snapped at Harry, "you've got another think coming. You want catering from me and the other wives, you'll pay for catering from me and the other wives, you pitiful old miser."

His wife's outburst made Bruce's life miserable at home and at work. Harry harangued him constantly about making his wife vote for keeping the ancient road public until Peter intervened. He pointed out that needling Bruce made all the men uncomfortable, and if the ancient road vote went to a paper ballot instead of a hands-in-the-air count, people like Bruce might take advantage of the secrecy to vote "nay."

After that, Harry became honey itself, smiling and greeting the men who worked for him every morning. He bought them all donuts and coffee which they reluctantly ate and drank, looking over their shoulders all the time. "This is giving me the creeps," Sam the Younger remarked, and everyone in earshot nodded.

For Peter, the worst hours were the ones he spent in the office after the crews were dispatched to their morning tasks. Harry paced back and forth, assessing and reassessing who'd vote which way. Peter joined in as little as possible except to reassure Harry that the crew members would vote his way.

To keep his sanity, Peter hid his true feelings from everyone. He believed Harry's plan would devastate Carding forever. He shuddered awake from dreams about excavators tearing up the land behind the school, felling the old oak trees to make way for a bunch of look-alike buildings constructed of the cheapest materials but sold for the highest prices. In his view, Carding Academy brought life and passion to the entire Corvus Valley. In comparison, Harry's Cinnamon Hill Estates would bring nothing but short-term jobs, and long term resentment between the condo crowd and the townies. It was an old and unhappy story all over Vermont.

His situation at home wasn't getting any better, either, because he and Lisa weren't talking much. One morning, he stopped off at his house to pick up a pair of heavy work gloves, arriving the same time as Ruth Goodwin and the mail. As they greeted one another, she pulled a sizable box marked Cherries Jubilee from the back of her vehicle. Ever a modest woman, she blushed as she handed it to Peter who blushed when he saw the return address, and its provocative logo.

As he walked through his garage among the forest of Lisa's exercise equipment, Peter struggled against the urge to pitch the box into the rubbish. The last time Lisa ordered from that place was just before their first anniversary, and he didn't sleep well for a whole week. Peter enjoyed physical intimacy but to him, that meant cuddling on the couch, holding hands on a walk, kisses in the kitchen, and lovemaking between the flannel sheets on his bed.

To Lisa, however, intimacy was all about performance. Once that Cherries Jubilee box showed up, their intimate acts took on aspects of Olympic events. Peter felt like they were auditioning for one of the HBO-TV series that left nothing about the human body to the imagination. In retrospect, he now believed that that moment was when his marriage began to fall apart. Lisa's physical needs disgusted him, pure and simple.

He stood in the kitchen, box in hand, wishing it would disappear.

Maybe he could address it to someone else, and put it back in the mail. The idea had its appeal. Or maybe the box could just get "lost" in their attic. But then Lisa would check on it, and Ruth would have to tell her she'd handed it to Peter personally.

Just then, a niggling notion popped into his head. Lisa had been quiet in their bedroom for a while. That could mean two things—either she had plans to reheat their marriage, and that's what the contents of the Cherries Jubilee box was for...or...she was heating up someone else.

Peter put the box down as he retrieved his work gloves, rolling the alternatives around in his head, assessing the possibilities. It would be easy enough to find out which one of his alternatives was true.

On his way back out the door, Peter left the box in the place where Ruth would have put it if he hadn't showed up. Lisa would be home for lunch soon. If Peter never saw the box or its contents again, he'd know the answer to his question for sure.

Pushmi-pullyu.

After her encounter with Peter in Edie's driveway, Chloe changed her routines so their paths no longer crossed. The force of her anger scared her. Peter had seemed like such a decent man, so different from the two-faced Browns. Peter was all the things she desired in a man—kind, perceptive, intelligent, funny. They both adored the *New York Times* crossword puzzle. They both guzzled the mocha specials that Diana served at the bakery. He always asked about her latest design projects, and she liked to hear about his songwriting. Not enough to build a whole relationship on, maybe, but it was far more than Gideon ever offered on his best days.

"I can't believe Peter would turn his back on...you," she ranted to Edie as they made tea in the academy's kitchen. The older woman gave Chloe a quizzical look.

"He's loyal," she finally said. "A rare quality these days."

"Loyal? To Harry Brown? Why would anyone be loyal to Harry Brown? That man's never done anything to earn anyone's loyalty."

"Not to Harry, my dear," Edie said. "Peter's loyal to the men on the Brown & Sons crew. Harry will fire them if they don't vote his way, and Peter knows they can't afford to lose their jobs. He's sacrificing what he believes in to protect them."

Nearly moved his head from side to side, following the trail of the human sound. Then he sighed as loud as he could. Didn't anyone remember he needed a walk?

"That's ridiculous. Bruce and Sam and the rest are grown men. They can take care of themselves," Chloe protested. "Why should they follow Peter?"

Edie shook her head. "In any given situation, only ten percent of the folks involved know what's true and what's not. The rest of us, the ninety percent, look for someone we trust to provide the information we need. For example, if we needed information on fishing, we'd ask Bruce Elliot, right?" Chloe nodded. "If it was tearing apart an engine or welding, we'd go to Sam the Younger. If it was art quilting, it would be you. The same principle applies here. I guarantee you that the first thing old Harry did after Gideon told him about the ancient road question was corner Peter. Harry may be dumb about a lot of things but he is smart enough to understand that people don't like him or listen to him. He needs Peter's cooperation to pull this ancient road thing off, and Harry's not above a little emotional blackmail, believe me."

Edie sipped her tea. Chloe did not pick up her mug. "How can you be so calm about this?" she finally asked.

"Age—and practice," Edie said. "You're sitting here all glum, fixated on a future that may or may not come to pass. When you do that, you give Harry Brown control over you because you're reacting to his need for the future to turn out in a certain way. Years ago, I refused to be owned in any way by Harry Brown. I still refuse to be owned by Harry Brown. I would suggest you do the same. Now, I've got to take Nearly for a walk, and see my grandson, Carding's infamous Little Crow, so he can spread the word that Carding Academy will be fine, no matter the vote." She patted Chloe's hand. "And we will be. You'll see."

Gideon wouldn't have believed it possible that his wife could grow any colder toward him. But after the ancient road news hit the streets of Carding, Chloe became a glacier. Instead of the civil exchanges that passed for a relationship between them, she glared. If he even so much as nodded at her, she hissed in response.

"What did you expect?" his mother asked when he took his complaints to her. "You destroyed your marriage because you can't keep your zipper zipped any better than your father. And now you're destroying Carding Academy, the place where she works, the place that made her a renowned quilt designer. Did you think she was going to thank you?"

"But Chloe's famous among quilters everywhere," Gideon protested. "She teaches all over the country. She can get another job just like that." He snapped his fingers.

His mother shook her head, amazed that she'd raised a son as obtuse as her husband. But then Gideon had always coveted his father's good opinion. That was his problem.

At least I have Lisa, Gideon reminded himself. True, her sexual athleticism was daunting but he was determined to enjoy the challenge. The charge on his credit card from Cherries Jubilee had made him gasp but he had no doubt it would be worth it. A man needed a little affection in his life, Gideon reassured himself. He just hoped that Lisa's new cowgirl outfit didn't come with spurs. That didn't appeal to him at all.

TWELVE

THE HILL AWAITS

New post on Carding Chronicle blog: February 20

Carding Ski Team Fundraiser This Saturday at Mount Merino
by Little Crow

The Carding Regional High School Ski Team qualified to compete in four events at the New England Regionals at Jay Peak Resort.

This is a really big deal for our Alpine athletes, folks.

The team trains and races on Mount Merino during the school year. So it's no surprise that the resort's support continues in the form of a grant to send our team north to vie for medals in slalom, giant slalom, and freestyle skiing in half-pipe and moguls.

The Merino grant is a matching grant. In other words, for every dollar donated at the Ski Team Fundraiser this Saturday, Mount Merino Resort will match it with two dollars.

To encourage participation, local merchants have donated gifts for a daylong silent auction including a weekend for two at the Carding Inn, coffee-and-muffin cards from the Crow Town Bakery, a pizza party from Fiorello's Pizza with music by Thieves of Fire, a hand-knit cable sweater and scarf from the Green Apple Crafts store at the Carding Academy, an original wall quilt designed by Nancy Graham, a boxed set of quilt books by international designer Chloe Cooper Brown, an original fireplace screen sculpted by Jeffrey Sass, a mosaic mirror by Carrie Fradkin, and an exquisite wooden jewelry box crafted from cherry and chestnut by J.C. Davis, among many other prizes.

The money raised will underwrite the costs of transportation, food, and lodging for the weeklong competition. Let's give our athletes the support they need to make us all proud.

I'll be looking for you.

Little Crow | February 20 | Categories: Local Sports

After their day on the Campgrounds' slope, Ted enrolled his niece in the sixth grade at Carding Elementary School. Fortunately, the first person he spotted in the hallway was Edie's granddaughter, Faye Bennett. Faye immediately took to the role of "guide for the new girl," and Ted left feeling that Suzanna was in good hands.

Each afternoon, Ruth pulled up to the school in her Jeep to pick Suzanna up for delivery to the post office. Even though the sun still retired early, the uncle and niece managed to fit in some skiing time on the little slope at the Campground. When Edie found out, she encouraged Faye to join them. The result, in a short period of time, was two new best friends.

At first, Ted resented the addition of Faye to his family party, but that didn't last long. The two girls, each quiet on her own, chattered together like birds newly arrived for the first day of spring. Faye, it turned out, had an encyclopedic knowledge of everyone in the elementary school. She even knew the true story behind the principal's toupee. Ted was spellbound. He'd known Otto Caitlin for years and never knew the man wore a toupee.

"It's because of cancer," Faye pronounced in a low, solemn voice. "And he beat it."

"Really? Otto had cancer?" Ted said just as the two girls slid over the crest of the hill so he never heard Faye's reply.

"Hey Mr. Owens," she said when they reappeared, "why don't we take Suzanna to the mountain on Saturday? The weather's supposed to be good, and I think she's ready."

Suzanna looked up, her eyes as big as pie plates. Ted nodded. "I was just thinking the same thing." He grinned at his niece. "How do you feel about skiing on the mountain?"

"Will you stay with me?" she asked.

"He can come with us on the big hill but he's too big for the bunny slope," Faye said. "I'll go with you on that a few times, and then the three of us can do the Easy-Peazy Trail together. Right, Mr. Owens?"

Ted couldn't help himself. He laughed. "Absolutely, Faye."

"Why are you laughing?" the girl said.

"Because you sound so much like your grandmother."

Faye lifted her skis into the back of Ted's truck as she said, "Yeah, I know. My mother tells me that all the time. But I think Gram is terrific so I take it as a compliment. Even though I'm not so sure Mom means it that way."

"Well, I mean it as a compliment," Ted said. "So, can you two get up early on a Saturday morning? I love to hit the slopes when they're freshly groomed."

"You bet."

Almost fifteen years had passed since Ted set a ski boot on Mount Merino or any other slope. That Saturday morning, as he pulled into the resort's parking lot with the two excited girls, the pain that lay coiled up in him like a sleeping dragon reared its ugly head. He'd expected something like this to happen but the force of it took him back. He hadn't expected his feelings to still be so raw.

His hands shook, and he fumbled as he tried to open the tailgate of his truck. But before Suzanna noticed, Faye stood at his elbow, helping. She knew, as she seemed to know everything about Carding's denizens, what had happened to Ted's mother on Mount Merino, and her grandmother had schooled her in how to help Ted so that Suzanna's first day of skiing would not be marred. As she later reported to her brother: "Mr. Owens looked at me with the most miserable eyes you can imagine. But then Peter Foster showed up, just like Gram said he would, and everything was OK after that."

In fact, Edie had done more than call Peter Foster. Once Faye alerted her to the ski excursion, she told Andy Cooper the news, and he, in his turn, spread the word among the members of Ted's high school ski team. They'd all been waiting for this day for a long time.

Enveloped in grief, Ted was only dimly aware of the people who accompanied him from the truck to the base lodge. Oblivious to their real reason for being there, Suzanna accepted the knots of familiar people as just more evidence of the richness of life in Carding. For her part, Faye supported that belief in every way possible.

Andy Cooper paid for the girls' lift tickets when they got to the base lodge and walked with them to the bottom of the bunny slope. Ted rallied himself as the girls moved toward the rope tow and slid effortlessly into the role of coach.

"OK, this is just like the Campgrounds tow rope, only longer," he told Suzanna. "There's nothing here that you haven't done before. I bet you could even do this one-handed." He winked at the tow operator who nodded. "One-handed" was Mount-Merino code for "watch out for this one."

"Let Faye go up first, give her a heartbeat or two, and then you grab hold." Ted gave his niece's shoulders a squeeze. "You can do this."

Faye stepped up to the circling rope, bent her knees, grabbed it with her mittened hands, and zipped up the hill. Suzanna was right behind her, and she skied off the rope at the top of the small hill without a hitch. Down below, she heard her uncle's whoops and a burst of mittened applause.

"Who are all those people?" she asked Faye, pointing at the motley crew of knitted hats and colorful windbreakers standing in a loose circle around her uncle.

"Friends of his," Faye said. The answer seemed to satisfy. "Are you ready?"

Suzanna glanced down the freshly groomed slope where they would make the first marks of the day. Just then, the sun splintered the morning clouds, fingering the spruce trees on the hills that rose behind Carding, and the girl grinned. I belong here, Suzanna thought. "Meet you at the bottom," she yelled. And with that, Suzanna pushed off.

Faye stayed behind her friend, relishing the role of guardian angel.

Ted's eyes never strayed from Suzanna's pink jacket as she arced her way down the hill. She moved with some of the hesitancy of a newbie, he realized, but that would wear off over time.

"She moves like you," Peter said quietly.

Ted grinned. "You think so? I think she skis like my mother. See the way she folds her poles under her arms? Mom did that."

When she reached the bottom of the hill, Suzanna slowed only long enough to circle around to the tow and zip back up to the top. When she waggled a pole in Ted's direction, the whole company cheered. The sound startled him, and for the first time, Ted noticed the group standing around him. His high school ski team—a bit older, a bit more filled out—grinned back at him.

"What are you doing here?" he asked.

"A beautiful day like this is wasted indoors," Peter said.

The rest of them nodded then turned to glide toward the chairlift, keeping Ted in their midst. His heart thudded, and he suddenly realized he'd never intended to ski himself.

"I don't think I can do this," he muttered.

The group pressed closer. Hands reached out to touch his arm or squeeze his shoulder. Andy patted him on the back. No one spoke.

Ted stopped at the chairlift, breathing hard. "I don't think I can do this. I can't."

"We're not going without you, Ted," Paula Bouton said. "We've been missing you for far too long. You've come this far by yourself. We're going to help you go the rest of the way." She reached out to grip his hand. "You need to ski again because that niece of yours needs a good teacher. Come on, Andy, ride up with me." And with that, she jumped into the next open chair, and they started toward the top.

"Come on," Peter said. "It's time."

Ted tried to swallow and looked at his friend. Panic made him feel rigid, but then its hold was broken by a soft push from Sam the Younger. Stiffly, Ted followed Peter to the lift, a chair scooped them up, and his skis left the ground. He gripped the bar in front of him, forcing himself to breathe. Mom, he called in his heart, please come help.

Sunlight rolled down the trail system, glinting off the snow and the trees. Ted looked up. Not a cloud remained in the sky, blue as far as the eye could see. Down below, he could just make out the speck of pink that was his niece as she circled about the bottom of the bunny slope.

"She'll be ready for bigger and better as soon as we get down to the base lodge," Ted said.

"Yeah, I think you're right," Peter said. "One run, and we'll go collect them. OK?"

Ted leaned back, and closed his eyes. "Thanks," he said softly.

"Any time."

As he slid off the lift at the top, Ted wondered if this is what an out-of-body experience felt like. He sensed the mountain shouldering up against his skis, and the loose snow squeaked as he glided across it. His friends seemed far away, vague specters whirling in the light. He heard the thud-thud of Paula's ski poles as she stabbed them into the snow, freeing her hands to pull her goggles into place. Always the organized one of the group, she ran her eyes over them, spending an extra few seconds on Ted. Then she said softly: "The hill awaits."

Ted nodded as the words hit him, his mother's favorite expression at the start of a ski session. The serpents of grief that he'd tended for so long hissed to life. "Remember us," they called. "We are your oldest and dearest friends."

He turned to look down the slope, the base lodge now hidden beyond a curve in the trail. His cheeks felt cold, very cold, as if his flesh would freeze. A touch on his arm made him turn and Sam the Younger handed him a folded red bandana. When a question mark formed on Ted's face, Sam touched his own cheeks. Ted nodded then raised the scarlet gift to his face.

I'm crying, he thought, and the sensation brought a strange release and exquisite pain.

Still our angel of peace, Sam is, Paula thought. Somehow he makes talking seem overrated.

"Take all the time you need going down," Peter said. "You're not alone. You've never been alone."

Ted sensed, though he could not see, the group move close to him—Paula, Andy, Peter, and Sam.

Paula glanced around. They were ready. "On my count," she said to Ted. "OK?"

He took another swipe of the bandana across his face, stuck it in his pocket then nodded.

"One…two…three."

Ted's hands could barely grip the poles as he pushed off, and Peter saw his friend struggle to keep his balance. Inside, Ted's ghosts screamed with anger at this threat to their supremacy. He stopped at the crest of the first rise, and the group slid to a standstill. Ted's whole body trembled and shook. He gasped for breath.

"I can't believe how hard this is," he muttered.

They stood together, breathing deeply, making small clouds in the air. Ted shook his head.

"This is nonsense," he said.

Sam mouth curved up. "Not nonsense," he said. "Just difficult."

And the faces of his friends crystallized in those words. Ted stared at them, suddenly aware that they'd been living his pain too. He drew in a long, shaky breath then dug the tips of his poles into the snow.

"The hill awaits," he said, and he felt his mother's voice stir inside him, as if she'd waited for this moment for far too long. "On my count—one…two…three…"

And they pushed off across the beckoning expanse of freshly groomed snow.

Andy checked his watch when they reached the bottom of the mountain. "I've gotta go," he said. "We're shorthanded at the store today." Before he left, he took a good long look at Ted's face. The bright eyes of the young man he remembered from years ago had returned. "I think you'll do," he said.

"Do? For what?" Ted felt edgy.

"You'll do just fine." Andy nodded at Suzanna, now part of a larger circle of girls drawn by Faye. "Your niece needs a father, and I think she's chosen you for the job. And you will do just fine."

Ted shook his head. Standing on Merino reminded him of how much he hated his sister, and it choked him. "I don't know about that."

Andy watched Suzanna for a moment. The little girl was radiant. There was no other word for it. He'd known the Owens family all his life, grew up with Ted's parents, Anna and Robert, watched Ted and Allison since they were born. He knew for a certainty that Suzanna swam in the same gene pool as her grandparents and her uncle. No trace of Allison, thank goodness.

"I never told you this because your father tries to be a fair man, tries to see both of his children with equal love," Andy began.

"Dad never says a word against Allison," Ted interrupted. "Won't let anyone else, either. It's the only thing we ever argue about."

Andy nodded. "I know, that is his way. But make no mistake, Ted, he's known what Allison is since she was a little kid." He paused. "We all do."

Ted took a long sip of this information. Did he want to know the rest? Secrets, once revealed, could not become secret again. Then he heard Suzanna laugh, and decided he needed to know.

"And what is she, my sister?"

"Crippled," Andy said. "Emotionally crippled. Some people aren't born with the same feelings the rest of us have. And your parents knew that about Allison by the time she was in kindergarten. I know they took her to a couple of specialists in Boston who more or less confirmed what they already knew. Your sister can no more feel hate than she can love."

"Personally, I think she's a vampire," Ted said.

"Vampire?"

"Yeah. She has no feelings of her own so she has to suck them out of other people," Ted said. "Did you ever notice, when we were kids, how all the fun in a room died when she walked in?"

Andy considered that for a moment, paging back through his memories. "Now that you mention it." He tilted his head in Suzanna's direction. The girls were teaching her a clapping game, and she squealed with delight every time she mastered a new sequence. "Allison never did stuff like that," he said.

"Not unless she got to be in the center of the circle," Ted said. He watched his niece for a moment. "She's really nothing like her mother, is she?"

Andy looked up at the mountain. "Look, I know this is hard for you but Sam's right. This is worthwhile. You're putting the pieces of yourself back together, and maybe finding a place for some new ones. That girl needs you to fight for her."

Ted stood still, his arms crossed over his abdomen while he chewed over Andy's words, turning over the rocks of his childhood to see what lay underneath. "She's toxic, Allison is."

"It's OK to keep Allison out of your life, you know." Paula slid herself into the conversation. "Just because you share a genetic ancestry doesn't mean you have to let her poison your life."

Peter and Sam glided up just then. "I think Faye's itching to take your niece up the hill," Peter said. "It's time, don't you think?"

Paula patted Ted's arm. "The hill awaits."

As soon as she heard Peter's truck leave their driveway, Lisa reached for her cell phone, and punched in Gideon's number. He'll be surprised to hear from me so early in the day, she thought. But I can't wait to tell him.

"Hello?" To Lisa's ear, her lover's voice sounded restrained. Was there someone else there? Had her sister forgiven him, and was she even now lying beside Gideon? Lisa was shocked to feel a spurt of jealousy.

"Are you alone?" she asked.

Gideon snorted. "Of course I am. I'm just being cautious in case Peter uses your cell to talk about this ancient road thing. This business can't be over soon enough for me. It's making the whole town crazy."

"Oh, that." Lisa yawned. "It's all anybody's talking about at town hall. I don't know what the big deal is. Your father will win, take down that nasty old pile of a house, and Edie Wolfe will move the academy to

White River Junction. Big deal."

"So it's certain then, about Edie moving the school?"

"Well, I heard her telling Paula that she hadn't signed any papers yet but that all in all, it would be a good move," Lisa said. She stretched, and made a groaning sound that put Gideon's body on high alert.

"Are you in bed?" he asked.

She giggled. "Oh yes. Are you?"

"Yeah." Then, before he could stop himself, he asked: "Where's Peter?"

"Oh, he left early to ski over at Merino. Claimed it was some kind of emergency or something, for a friend." She groaned again. "Hey, guess what came in the mail?"

"A package?" The image of the exhorbitant charge on his credit card bill floated across Gideon's mind.

"Yes, and you're gonna love what I got. I promise. And you know what else?"

"What?"

"Dad let it slip that he and Uncle Andy finally finished the sauna at the cabin so we can christen it. Won't that be fun? Just you and me and all that steam." Lisa giggled. "Make sure you bring more of that champagne. We're gonna work up a thirst."

"Champagne it is," Gideon said, and a smile stretched across his face. The timing for their overnight couldn't be better. It would be three days before town meeting, and an evening with Lisa promised to be the perfect stress reliever. Suddenly he had a thought. "Hey, there's no chance that Peter saw our package, is there?"

Lisa grinned. She liked how Gideon called the box from Cherries Jubilee "our package." That was a hopeful sign.

"No way. I found it right where Ruth leaves our stuff when we're not home," she said. "The mail gets here at 11:30, and I left early for lunch that day. Besides, Peter doesn't notice much these days. He was so tired last night, he fell asleep on the couch in the den again. But it was just as well, because he left before the sun was up."

"So what was this skiing emergency?" Gideon made a mental note to himself about the fact that Peter wasn't sleeping with his wife every night. That could be an early warning sign of trouble. He just wanted to borrow Lisa, not have her on his hands permanently.

"I don't know too much about it." She pulled the covers over her shoulders, wishing Peter had turned up the heat before he left. He knew how she hated a cold house. "Something about his old ski team getting together again."

Gideon sat straight up in bed. "The ski team? Are you sure? Did he say anything about Ted Owens, by any chance?"

"The post office guy? Yeah, I think he was going too. Must be some kind of reunion. Why?" Lisa yawned. She didn't like it when Gideon's attention drifted away from her.

"Ted Owens was the best slalom skier in New England when we were in high school," Gideon said. "He would have made it all the way to the Olympics, he was that good."

"So what's that got to do with skiing on Mount Wooly today?"

"The night before the national trials, his mother died on Merino," Gideon said. "She skidded on ice into a tree."

"Oh, I thought that's what happened to Alli-O's mother. I read all about it in on her Facebook page," Lisa said. Gideon swore he could hear her synapses firing as she struggled to make sense of the relationship between Ted and Allison. "So does that mean Ted-the-post-office-guy is Alli-O's brother? Do you know him? Do you know Alli-O?"

Gideon's mouth went dry. He'd barely known Anna Owens but her death ripped such a big hole in Carding, everyone felt it. How could Lisa not know what happened? That's it, he promised himself, after next Saturday night, I'm done with this one.

"I'm surprised you never heard the whole story," he said in an attempt to educate his paramour. "Ted and his father were in Colorado at the national trials but his mother stayed home with Allison because she had a part in some sort of a pageant at the ski resort. That night, when they closed the mountain, no one could find Allison, and they were afraid she was lost on the slopes. Anna went up with the ski patrol to find her."

"Oh." Lisa threw back her covers, raced for the thermostat, jacked it up then raced back to bed. "So where did they find Alli-O?"

"In a downstairs supply closet with some guy from out of town," Gideon said.

"Oh." Lisa considered this bit of information then shrugged. How was Alli-O supposed to know her mother was going to die? "So is that why what's-his-name, her brother, is that why he stopped skiing?"

"Yeah, said he couldn't face it so he gave it all up," Gideon said.

"Is that why Alli-O left town? I read that she moved out to the west coast because somebody saw her picture and asked her to be in a television show." Lisa smiled as she heard the furnace come on. "She must have been really pretty back then."

"Hmph, Allison's been telling that lie for a long time," Gideon said. "The truth is, she didn't seem to care that her mother died looking for her, and everyone shunned her. She caught a bus for the west coast on the night she graduated from high school, and I doubt anyone cared. I know Ted hadn't spoken to her since she left, so it was a big surprise when she dumped her kid on his doorstep."

"Oh, speaking of her kid, I saw on Facebook that Alli-O's going to be on the cover of *Celebrity Parent* because of some new line of children's clothes she's designed so I expect she'll be in Carding soon to get the kid back," Lisa said. "Since you know her, would you introduce me? I'd really like the chance to meet her. I think we have a lot in common."

Gideon shook his head. How did he get himself into this mess? "Yeah, I think you do have a lot in common. Two peas in a pod."

Lisa giggled.

Ted couldn't recall a finer day in his life—ever. Paula, Peter, and Sam skied with him and the girls until the sun's sudden drop over the horizon gave them all a chill.

"Cocoa," Paula announced, and they all clumped into the swirl of the base lodge. While the four adults sat with their hands wrapped around their mugs, Faye and Suzanna flitted around the building like fairies who'd had too much coffee, checking out all the stuff in the auction, and figuring out if Carding's ski team would make enough money to travel to the New England regional competition.

Peter chuckled as he watched. "My father claims that that kind of energy is wasted on the young."

"Oh, I don't know about that," Paula said. "Somehow, I can't imagine what any of us would look like running around like that. A bit ridiculous, I'd wager."

Sam laughed, a hearty sound all the more appreciated because it was so seldom heard. "They might make good models for wind-up toys."

Paula counted on her fingers. "Oh my gosh, Sam just spoke eight words in a row," she said. She stared at the speaker. "I hope you didn't hurt yourself."

Ted laughed. "Sam's right. Just look at them go."

"Uh-oh, there's the first yawn," Paula said as Suzanna's mouth gaped open. "Guaranteed she's asleep before you're done with supper.

She did really well today, didn't she? Tackled everything as if she'd been on skis all her life."

The whole table chimed in, recounting their pleasure in watching Suzanna's fever pitch as she negotiated the small moguls, and then raced Faye to the bottom of the mountain. And though they didn't recount them out loud, Ted's friends silently noted the changes in him as well.

As the conversation dropped off, Paula let her hands fall on top of Ted's. "I hate to ask but I have to know," she began.

He shook his head. "Not a word from Allison," he said. "But I did have a long talk with Charlie Cooper about getting custody of Suzanna. He says it won't be easy but we're going to try."

Paula curved her head in Suzanna's direction. "How about her? Have you talked it over with her, let her know what might happen?"

Ted shook his head. "Not in detail. The first day we skied at the Campground, she told me she doesn't want to go back to living with Allison."

"But you have to make absolutely sure she wants to stay in Carding," Paula said. "Forgive me, Ted, because after today, seeing you two together, I have no doubt that's what she wants. But in a custody fight…"

"If Allison fights me," Ted interrupted. "She may not."

"True," Paula agreed. "But a whole lot will ride on what Suzanna says so if you get her used to talking about staying in Carding with you, she'll be ready to answer a judge's questions, if it comes to that. It's a lot for a twelve-year-old girl to take on."

Just then, a small arm snaked around Ted's neck, and Suzanna laid her cheek on his shoulder. "Tired?" he asked. She nodded, and her face split open in another, bigger yawn. "How's the auction going?"

"Good," she said. "Faye and I have decided to be on the ski team when we get old enough. And she took some pictures of me up on the top of the mountain that she's going to print out so we can bring them to Grampa." She grinned, savoring the taste of the word on her tongue. She had a real, live grandfather. Then she yawned again, and felt her jaw snap. "Can we go home now?"

Suzanna sat silent, except for her jaw-cracking yawns, all the way back to the house. Then, as Ted turned off the truck, she wriggled around in her seat to face him "I think today was the very best day of my life, ever."

Ted squeezed her hand. "You did so well, Suzanna. I was so proud of you. You're quite the skier."

She latched onto his fingers. "Uncle Ted? Faye said your mother—my grandmother—died on Mount Merino. Is that true?" Her voice reached her uncle's ears as if from a long way off. He drew in a breath.

"Yes, she did. It was an accident."

Suzanna digested this for a moment, and then said: "Can I tell you something, and will you promise not to laugh?"

"Of course."

"Sometimes, I felt a little scared up there," she began.

Ted nodded. "I understand that. I think it's healthy to have a bit of fear up there. Mountains need to be respected."

Suzanna nodded. "But that's not the strange part. You see, every time I got really scared and wanted to quit, it felt like someone came up behind me to hold me. Faye said she thinks it was my grandmother. Could that be true?"

Ted felt grateful for the dark in the truck. After a couple of silent mouth openings, he finally said: "Yes, I do believe it's true. I felt her up there today, too. I think her spirit has waited for us for a long time."

Suzanna examined her fingers with great concentration. "Which is why I can't leave Carding, don't you see? I have to live here forever. I have you, and Faye, and a grandfather now." She turned to look at him, and Ted felt her eyes pressing him for the promise he wanted to make. "Can I?"

"Suzanna," he began.

"My mother doesn't want me," she said. "Not really. That Bruno who called me Zee had it right. It's true, I am the last thing she thinks of. If I can't stay with you, Faye says she'll ask her mother if I can stay there, with her family.

"Suzanna Owens, if you think for one minute that I would let you stay in Carding and live anywhere but in the house that belongs to our family, you are quite mistaken," Ted said. "I wasn't sure this uncle and niece business was going to work out. But I think we're getting the hang of it, don't you?"

Suzanna did a little fist pump, accompanied by an exuberant "Yes."

"Now, let's get the skis out of the back, get some supper into you, and then I think it's off to bed for the both of us," Ted said. "It has been a long but wonderful day."

Ted sent his niece off to get into her pajamas while he whipped up grilled cheese sandwiches and tomato soup. When she trudged back to the kitchen, he slid a steaming bowl and a sandwich onto the table then turned back to the stove to tend to his own sandwich.

"You know, this is what my Mom and Dad made for us after we'd been skiing all day," he said. "Not gourmet fare, to be sure, but filling."

"Uh huh." Behind him, Ted heard Suzanna's spoon rattle as he flipped his sandwich to toast its second side.

"Back then, Mom had to buy that awful American cheese because it was all you could get in the store," Ted said, watching his favorite Vermont cheddar ooze out from between two slices of bread. "I never liked that stuff, especially after I took high school chemistry and found out what made it so yellow." He slid his sandwich onto a cutting board, and sliced it in two. When he turned back around, he had to chuckle. Suzanna had her head propped on one hand, the remains of her grilled cheese in the other, her eyes shut.

At that moment her head started forward, and Ted reached her just before her chin hit the soup. "Come on, young lady, I think we'd better get you into bed."

"Uh huh."

Ted cajoled Suzanna up on her feet, and steered her down the hall to the guest bedroom. No, he told himself firmly, Suzanna's room. He peeled back the bed quilt just before she flopped down then covered her up. "Your grandmother made this quilt," he told the sleepy girl.

"Uh huh."

As he reached for the light, he took a good look at the faded wallpaper. This whole room needs a good sprucing up, he thought. I wonder what Suzanna's favorite color is.

It wasn't until he got back to the kitchen that Ted noticed the blinking light on his answering machine. He punched the button, took a huge bite of his sandwich, and then nearly choked on it when he heard the recording.

"Hi Ted, it's Allison. I'm calling to check on my little girl. I miss her so much, and I hope she's not being a bother. Please tell her how much her Mommy loves her, and that I'll see her soon. Bye."

Ted looked at the telephone as if it had just spat at him. The silence in the house thickened. He tiptoed down the hall to check that Suzanna still slept, pulled her door closed then listened to his sister's message again. Yes, the sound in the background was unmistakable. Allison had called from a casino.

Jamming the last of the grilled cheese into his mouth, Ted hustled to the living room, and opened his laptop. A moment later, he was reading the latest news about his sister. "Alli-O selected to be cover story in April issue of *Celebrity Parent*!"

Well, the custody battle is on now, Ted thought as he punched in Charlie Cooper's phone number. She's going to need Suzanna for the photo shoot.

Lady Mary Grantham of *Downton Abbey* had just discovered a dead body in her bed when Charlie's phone rang. He thought about ignoring it until Agnes read the caller I.D. "Ted Owens," she said.

"Oh gawd, I hope Allison hasn't shown up to take that little girl away," Charlie muttered. "Hello?"

"Allison will be here soon," Ted said, "and Suzanna definitely wants to stay in Carding."

"We'll be ready, never you fear," Charlie reassured him. "Suzanna may not have been born in Carding but she'll grow up in Carding. Try not to worry too much."

Agnes had her computer open before Charlie finished his conversation. "Any more developments on what you found before?" he asked.

Her fingers flew over the keyboard. She read, clicked, scrolled, and then read some more. Finally, she managed a grim little smile. "Yeah, take a look at this."

THIRTEEN

THE GIFTS OF FRILLY UNDERWEAR

New post on Carding Chronicle blog: February 26

No Lunch for Town Meeting
by Little Crow

Town Moderator Andy Cooper just emailed the *Chronicle* with news that no lunch will be served at this year's town meeting.

In the past, lunch at Carding's town meeting was put together by a combination of members of the Carding Quilt Guild, the local PTA, and the Rotary Club. But sources tell the *Chronicle* that feelings on the ancient road question are running so high, none of these worthy non-profits can muster enough members to make lunch for the 300+ people who normally attend because folks aren't speaking to one another.

Harry Brown, owner of Brown & Sons, tells the *Chronicle* he has hired a lunch wagon to serve hot dogs, burgers, and fries at the noon recess. Diana Burke at the Crow Town Bakery has offered to put up brown bag lunches for people who call a day ahead to make a reservation.

"It's a sad day for civility," Andy Cooper said. "This is the first time in my memory that lunch will not be served at Carding's town meeting."

The countdown has begun. Only five days to go.

I'll be looking for you.
Little Crow | February 26 | Categories: Local Politics

The package from Cherries Jubilee unleashed Lisa Foster's inner seductress, and for the first time since he'd dated Candy Croft, Gideon felt pursued. At first he was amused by Lisa's steamy text messages. But as they became more graphic and frequent, Gideon began to worry. That's when he doubled down on his vow to make Saturday night the last he would spend with Lisa.

She, of course, had no idea that her aggressive flirting bothered her prospective playmate. This is fun, Lisa thought as she fired off another sext from the ladies room in the town hall. At lunchtime, she rushed home to don her Jubilee outfits each day, admiring the effect in her many mirrors.

She'd become quite fond of the cowgirl outfit, an all-white teddy with deep cuts on both sides, and fringe dangling from all the right places so that it accentuated her hip and chest movements. Gold studding highlighted the deep plunge of the bra while wiring and pads pushed up from below.

"Eat your heart out, Dolly Parton," Lisa murmured when she looked at herself from the side.

The cowgirl special even came with a pink clip-on bandana and a white hat.

"But it needs something to make it more fun," Lisa told her reflection. She considered handcuffs and ropes but quickly rejected both ideas as too confining. She liked freedom of movement, lots of movement. Then another idea struck her as she hid the outfit in her closet, and she giggled as she thought it over. Oh yes, that would be fun. She grabbed her phone, her thumbs flying over the tiny keyboard. "Gone toy shopping. More fun on Saturday. XXX"

When Gideon saw her message, he groaned.

Louisa Brown had given up dislike of her husband in favor of disinterest long ago. Dislike, in her opinion, took more energy than she was willing to spend on Harry. "He's not worth the effort," she confided in Rita, her hairdresser. "Know what I mean?"

But Harry's cockiness increased so much as town meeting approached, Louisa reconsidered her emotional position. He bragged at the dinner table, counting up the number of condos he could cram into Cinnamon Hill Estates. (Such a stupid name, Louisa thought.) He savored the consternation he would see on the faces "of all those fools and artists" when he took possession of their precious school.

"Fools and artists, aren't they the same thing?" Gideon chirped. He now ate dinner at his parents' house every night to scheme with his father. Louisa shot him a look of such loathing at these words, Gideon sank in his chair.

How could I have raised such a toady for a son, she wondered. But a second look at Gideon's face softened her heart. Her boy—she always thought of her eldest son as "her boy"—was all too visibly miserable.

"I'm sorry Mom," he mumbled when he brought his dirty dishes out to the kitchen. "I'm sorry about everything."

She reached out to squeeze his hand. "It'll be over soon," she said.

But Gideon shook his head and slanted his eyes toward the living room where they could hear Harry pontificating to his younger sons. "I'm afraid it's just begun. If he wins, it will only get worse."

Unfortunately, Louisa knew that what Gideon said was true. So after she turned on the dishwasher, she tiptoed to her sewing room—Harry never crossed its threshold—and opened the laptop he still didn't know she owned. Ten minutes later, she'd booked four plane tickets for Florida, one for herself and one for each of her sons. Departure date: March 5, the day after town meeting. Return date: unknown.

Long after her computer's screen darkened, Louisa sat in the dimly lit room, her manicured nails drumming on the arm of her chair. No one would ever describe Louisa Day Brown as a daring woman. She craved comfort and consistency. Anything outside her carefully constructed routines disturbed her. But maybe it was time, she thought, and a small flutter of fear knocked around inside her chest. The old goat's latest scheme had shredded her peaceful life. Half the people in town now turned their faces away when she entered a room. She saw it at her sewing circle, and in her church's after-hours coffee klatch. They think I can stop him but that I choose not to, she thought. But no one ever stopped Harry from doing anything.

Except Edie, and it appeared as though Edie would fail this time.

Louisa sniffed, and reached for a tissue to blot her face. The best I can do is get us all out of here for a while, she thought.

Later, as Harry took his evening shower, Louisa sent a text message to each of her sons: "Tix bought 4 Florida. Leave March 5. Meet Manchester Airport at 7:30 in morning. xxxMom."

As the calendar shed its last days of February, a steely silence gripped Carding's throat. After a flood of hot bile, folks on both sides of the ancient road argument simply stopped talking to one another. Bruce Elliot, in a fit of domestic wisdom, made no further attempts to persuade his wife to vote with Harry Brown. Though he didn't dare say it out loud, he agreed with her, and wished he felt free to vote as he chose. Not that he thought Harry would keep his word about the good jobs to come if the ancient road vote went his way. No, Bruce had worked for Brown & Sons for too long to believe that.

But he believed Harry would keep his word about firing anyone who went against him.

"Just because he wins the vote, there's no reason to think he'll hire Carding men for any of those jobs," he told Peter. "Can't we get him to sign a contract or something?"

Peter considered that for a moment. "But then couldn't someone accuse Harry of bribing us?"

Bruce snorted. "What do you call his firing threats?"

"Coercion."

"Which is only bribery by another name," Bruce said.

"True." The two of them sighed together. They'd had the same conversation several dozen times, always coming to the same conclusion.

"How are you voting? Decided yet?" Bruce asked.

"I vote that it snows so bad, the only people who show up are those within walking distance, which is Edie Wolfe and her friends," Peter said, "and the rest of us are stuck at home."

"Kinda cowardly, that, don't you think?" Bruce observed.

"Yeah, it is."

Bruce nodded, and re-checked the weather report that the *Carding Chronicle* sent out every morning. "They're predicting a storm for Sunday," he muttered. "But it'll be all cleaned up by Tuesday."

"What's the weather for Tuesday?"

"Sunny."

The two men sighed again.

"Light," Chloe sighed as she stepped into her studio. "I need light." She grunted as she pulled on the narrow ropes that parted her studio curtains. The afternoon sun, now flirting with the Green Mountains off in the distance, winked and glared at her. The sudden brilliance made her smile. But it also revealed the layer of dust on the creative detritus she hadn't touched in so long. The trouble with having a lot of space, she thought, is that you collect a lot of stuff to fill it.

She pivoted slowly, arms folded over her chest, taking in her stash of fabrics, her tools, the archaeology of projects-that-seemed-good-ideas-at-the-time but now lay in boxes awaiting a return of interest on her part. She counted back the months since her marriage collapsed. Close to a year, she realized with a start. I've been a zombie for nearly a year.

Without waiting another moment, Chloe stepped over to a jumble of totes, and pulled at the one on top. She put it on her worktable, popped its lid, and then exclaimed out loud. Ribbons! In every hue from teal to lemon, emerald, scarlet, and eggplant. She reached in with both hands, scooped up the colors, and held them to her face. "Where did you come from?" she asked out loud.

Then she remembered finding a craft store going out of business on her way to a conference in Boston. Chloe would have bought everything in the store but thought better of the idea, opting instead for a large bag of ribbons that cost only twenty dollars.

Excited by her find, Chloe returned to the tote jumble, chose a second one, popped its lid, and abracadabra—a nest of bright fabric scraps in all sorts of patterns.

"Cleaning house?" a voice broke into her reverie. Edie and Nearly stood in her studio doorway. "I don't think we need to make plans for moving the school yet. Even if that old fart Harry wins at town meeting, he's going to have a heckuva time knocking down this historic building. Historic preservationists are pretty tough when it comes to fighting for a place they love."

"Old fart." Chloe laughed. "I don't think I've ever heard you refer to anyone that way before." Edie grinned, and then she started to laugh, too. Nearly glanced from one woman to the other as they made that odd human noise. Then he sat down and slipped into waiting mode. In his experience, this odd noise usually heralded a lengthy human-to-human interaction in which he played no part. He would be stuck here for a while so he might as well make the best of it.

He scanned the area for a likely place to sleep, and spotted a sunny rectangle on a piece of carpet at the far end of the room. He ambled over. After casting a long, reproachful look at Edie, the dog sprawled on his side.

"Oh my, where did you get these?" Edie asked as she fingered a scrap of brilliant green covered with oversized yellow flowers.

"They're left over from that workshop I took at the Houston Quilt Show," Chloe said. "Aren't they amazing?"

Edie nodded as she took a look around the dusty studio "I'm glad to see you're getting ready to make a change in your life with Gideon. It's time."

Chloe stared at the older woman. "Sometimes, Edie, you are downright spooky. How did you know that? I've barely started thinking about it myself."

Edie smiled, and patted Chloe's hand. "You forget, I've watched you at work for a while now. You're usually the most organized of hoarders. You sort your fabrics by color, and print style. Each kind of embellishment has its own place on your shelves. Your thread collection is always neat. So this," Edie pointed to the jumble, "is out of character. It started when you caught Gideon cheating on you. But now you're organizing it, and for you, organizing is a meditative act. That tells me you're mulling over a decision or you've made one."

Chloe shook her head. "Edie Wolfe, Carding's answer to Sherlock Holmes."

Edie made a small bow. "At your service. Now, would you like some help or is this a solo project?"

"If you've got the time, I'd love to have the company," the younger woman said.

"Oh good, I love digging through other people's stuff." Edie took off her coat.

"Really? Why?"

"Because I'm not responsible for making the 'should this stay or should this go' decisions. I just get to enjoy the looking."

One by one, the women dragged totes and boxes out of the pile. Chloe's whole face began radiating a sparkling charm as she rediscovered a box of scrap fabric from South America, all hot colors, that took nearly an hour for the two of them to fondle, fold, and appreciate. They were trading stories about "the fabric that got away" when Edie peeled a wide strip of packing tape from a beat-up cardboard box, flipped open the top, looked inside, and muttered a distinct "Oh my."

Chloe reached in, and fished up a fistful of scanty panties and pushup bras. She snorted. "This is all the sexy stuff that Gideon bought for me." She held up a scarlet thong decorated with black lace. "Can you imagine actually wearing this? One of my college roommates called thongs 'butt floss.'"

Edie smiled. "How accurate."

"I can't imagine anything more uncomfortable unless it's this." Chloe pulled a out a bra festooned with fake ostrich plumage. "Now where would I wear this stuff? Shopping at the Coop?"

"Maybe Gideon hoped you'd wear it just for him."

Chloe shook her head. "I'd be embarrassed to wear it even in the privacy of my own home. I'm not a Cherries Jubilee girl. I thought about giving all this to Lisa after Gideon…" She threw the feathered bra back in the box. "I obviously didn't."

Edie fished out a bit of bright pink netting edged in more feathery fluff. "Lisa wears this stuff? Really?"

"Yep, she's always thought of herself as starlet material, an Alli-O wannabe," Chloe said.

"I can't imagine any part of Allison Owens that anyone in their right mind would want to emulate," Edie dropped the pink thing back in the box. "Why is your sister still in Carding if she wants to be a starlet?" she asked as she closed up the box. "I would think she would have followed your mother out to California instead of marrying Peter Foster, if that's the case."

Chloe turned her face away but not before Edie spotted two red circles burn her cheeks. Might as well get this out right now, the older woman thought, while you're cleaning and organizing your husband out of your life.

"Move out to live with our mother?" Chloe's voice squeaked. "But don't you know that Mother is too busy. She's either just moved so she's 'still settling in' or she's about to move again, and 'it's not a good time for company.' Personally, I don't think she wants anyone out there to know that Angela Cooper—astrologer to the stars—has children as old as Lisa and me."

"Astrologer to the stars? Is that what she's doing now?" Edie asked. "Last I knew, she was pushing some sort of voodoo vitamin tonic on a shopping channel."

Chloe nodded as she re-taped the box full of sexy underthings, and marked it "For Gideon." Then she kicked it toward the door. "Let him give these to his next wife or girlfriend or wear them himself," she said.

"Does he have one? A girlfriend, I mean?" Edie asked, remembering the rose scent she'd caught downwind of Gideon.

"I think so," Chloe said. "He was gone until real late last Friday, and I can't imagine my dear husband sitting up with a sick friend." She kicked the box again. "Oh, how can Peter Foster say he's going to vote for that ancient road thing?" She went at the box again, kicking it out the door. "What a coward."

"A coward? Really?" Edie said.

Chloe whirled around, her fists clenched. "Harry's not going to fire everyone. He'd have to close down if he did that, and my darling father-in-law kept Brown & Sons open the day I got married, and gave Gideon a hard time because he took the morning off."

Edie's face clouded over as she picked up another tote from the jumble. When she removed its lid, she found a neatly folded cache of linen guest towels from the 1950s. "Let me tell you something about Harry Brown. The man enjoys wielding power over other people. He enjoys it more than he enjoys money. And based on little bits of gossip that have floated in the air to me, I believe Harry has a Plan B if he loses this vote, and that Plan B does not include keeping Brown & Sons in business. What's more, I think Peter knows it as well as I do. The men who work there are his friends, and he believes he can protect them."

"But he knows how much the academy means to me." Chloe nearly choked on her words.

Edie stepped closer to the young woman and hugged her. In return, Chloe sobbed on her shoulder, and Edie rocked her from side to side until the first anguish subsided. "Tackle one man at a time, my dear. If you want to end your marriage to Gideon, then do that. It will be enough to handle. Then take some time to decide what you want to do next. It may include Peter Foster or it may not. It may include the academy or it may not. Breaking the connection to Gideon opens up lots of possibilities, and that's as it should be, don't you think?"

Chloe nodded, and Edie handed her one of the linen cloths to dry her face. Chloe hiccupped, and then laughed. "I feel so muddled."

"I'm sure you do," Edie said. "But I have something that may help clear the clutter in your heart."

"What's that?"

"A question."

"A question?"

"Yes, it's the one I asked myself when I was trying to decide whether to leave Harry so many years ago." Chloe looked up, expectant. Edie smiled. "It's really simple: Is this the way you want to live for the rest of your life?"

"You mean the part with Gideon?"

"Yes."

Chloe shook her head. "No. I can't trust him from the waist down."

"Then there's no more reason to wait. Call your father, and have him draw up the divorce papers. You'll need a place to stay while this all sugars out, and Nearly and I would like to extend an invitation to stay with us as long as you wish. We'd both enjoy having you. Our house is too big by half so we won't trip over one another. Your work with the academy goes on no matter what that…"

"…old fart…"

"…old fart does or does not win at town meeting," Edie said.

Chloe dabbed at her face then heaved a giant sigh. "Do you suppose that box would survive if I kicked it all the way down the stairs?"

"Only one way to find out, my dear."

Chloe ran to the door, drew her foot back, and then with a yell that came up all the way from her toes, she sent the box of lingerie down two flights of stairs. Edie and Nearly joined her at the top to watch the cardboard container's crash landing.

"Son of a gun," Chloe said when it came to rest. "It did."

Edie laughed. "The sense of change can be so invigorating, can't it? How about joining Nearly and me for a bit of supper? I have a chicken stew in the crockpot, and Ruth is bringing wine and dessert. I'll ask her to get a second bottle."

"Love to," Chloe grinned. She felt lighter than she had in a long time. Even the throb in her toes felt good. "I'll close up my studio, and be right along."

That first supper, as Chloe called it, gave her a new regard for Edie Wolfe. Even though she'd known Edie all twenty-seven years of her life, Chloe had never sat at a table with her as an equal. Edie had either been "Mrs. Wolfe" or her boss at the academy and not much in between. But underneath Edith Wolfe's neat white hair there lay a caustic wit. Chloe not only laughed until she begged for mercy, she learned a whole lot about life with Harry Brown.

"So he thought all he had to do was issue a command, and you would obey it?" she asked as Ruth opened a second bottle of cabernet. "Did he not know you at all before he married you? It's not as if people in the 1960s never heard of divorce."

"Ah, but Harry is a tyrant who believes in the rightness of tyranny."

Edie sipped. "And Peter understands that. That's why I can't be angry with him for what he's doing."

When Chloe turned her face away, Ruth and Edie exchanged a look. "If the economy was better, and Peter knew the guys could get other jobs, I have no doubt he'd vote against Harry," Ruth said. "The man may harbor a musician's soul but he earns his daily bread as an engineer. He's pretty good at calculating the odds."

"And everyone knows how Bruce and Sam the Younger feel about Peter," Edie chimed in. "They'd walk on hot coals for him. Peter won't betray that kind of loyalty."

Chloe tried to swallow but gave up the effort when she realized her heart was in the way. "I shouldn't have yelled at him the way I did that day on your porch," she finally said.

The older woman smiled. "I bet he'll give you the chance to apologize in person when you're up to it." She patted Chloe's hand. "And you will be, once you've taken care of your Gideon problem."

"Gideon problem?" Ruth asked. "Has that pup done something new that I should know about?"

"Nothing new, no." Chloe wrapped her hands around her wine glass and smiled. "But I have decided to divorce him, finally. It doesn't make any sense to keep living my life this way."

"Well, it's about time," Ruth said. "I think this calls for some chocolate, don't you?"

Chloe left Edie's soon after she finished a small piece of Ruth's notorious double-trouble chocolate cake. Her house was dark when she pulled in the driveway, so she was grateful Gideon had installed a garage door opener and lights she could activate from the car.

As she climbed the steps to the back door, she promised herself to call her father before crawling into bed. He'd waited a long time to hear this news. Charlie Cooper no longer handled divorce cases because, as he once explained to his daughter, he'd grown tired of witnessing the pain that people could inflict on one another. But Charlie would make an exception for her. That was understood between them.

He answered on the second ring. "Chloe, your timing is perfect. Agnes and I were just sitting down to watch *Downton Abbey*. We'll make more popcorn if you want to join us."

"Oh do come," Agnes called in the background.

Chloe grinned. Though both of them claimed an aversion to marriage, Chloe felt certain that her father and Agnes had each found a partner for life.

"No, thanks Dad. I just got home from having supper with Edie and Ruth."

Charlie's eyebrows went up a fraction when he heard his daughter refer to Edith Wolfe as Edie but he let it go without remark. *My eldest daughter is twenty-seven,* he reminded himself. "Was this a pow-wow over the ancient road vote?"

"No, not exactly," Chloe said. "Though I sure got an earful about my soon-to-be-ex-father-in-law."

Silence filled the phone line for a heartbeat or two, and then Charlie said: "Soon-to-be ex-father-in-law?" Agnes whipped around to stare at him, putting her hands together as if in prayer. "Is it time, Chloe?"

"It is, Dad." She drew in a breath. "I want a divorce from Gideon. Will you help me?"

"Help you? My darling daughter, I've had the paperwork drawn up for almost a year." Agnes began to clap. "Have you said anything to Gideon yet?"

"No, I just made the decision today and wanted to talk to you first."

Agnes handed Charlie a brimming wine glass, and they clinked.

"Do I hear the sounds of celebration over there?" Chloe asked.

"You do, indeed. Now, as I see it, we'd be wise to move quickly on this in order to drop it on Gideon just before the town meeting vote. He'll be distracted, and I think he'd be more likely to sign the paperwork we need for an uncontested divorce. How does that sound?"

Chloe thought about the battered box of frilly underwear in the back of her van. *I'll put a big bow on it,* she thought, *and attach the divorce papers to it.* "I think that's perfect, Dad."

Even though Edie adhered to her daily routine of walks with Nearly, work at the academy, and coffee at the bakery, she sensed a whirlpool swirling around her. Carding writhed with uncertainty. That made Chloe's move into her house all the more welcome.

"Nonsense," Edie said when Chloe protested she needed only a single bedroom. "You must have a place to lounge, a place to read, and room to mess about in."

"But I don't know how long I'll stay," Chloe said, "and I feel like I'm taking over your whole house and that's not right."

"Nonsense," Edie said again. "It doesn't matter how long or short you stay. You still have to spread out a little."

For his part, Nearly felt compelled to keep up appearances as the supervisor of the house. He met Chloe at the door every time she arrived, trotted up the stairs before her, and then snuffled over every box she deposited on the floor. Chloe had always laughed at the way Edie talked to Nearly as if he was human. But then she'd never had a pet. Her mother didn't like dogs (or cats or anything outside herself, for that matter), and her father never rocked that boat because there were so many others perils in their marriage.

So Nearly Wolfe represented Chloe's first sustained person-to-dog contact. She ignored him as she emptied boxes, hung up clothes, and arranged her personal stuff in the room. For his part, Nearly sat quietly attentive, studying her every move. After a while, Chloe realized she responded to subtle cues from the dog about where to stow her things. For example, when she moved her grandmother's bentwood rocker closer to the windows overlooking the green, Nearly stood up, his stumpy tail aflutter.

"Oh, you approve of that, do you?" she said.

When she put her clock radio on a bedside table, she heard the dog snort in unmistakable terms of derision. On closer inspection, she discovered that the clock's cord would never reach the outlet so she moved the timekeeper to a bureau on the opposite side of the room.

"Is this better?" she asked, and swore Nearly grinned at her.

"So, is my little friend helping you settle in?" Edie asked when she appeared at the bedroom door. "Nearly has to approve of everything, you know. Or at least he thinks he does." Edie reached down to scratch behind the dog's ears.

"He's got quite the persuasive personality," Chloe said as she accepted a proffered cup of tea.

Edie laughed. "Have you started talking to him yet?"

Chloe's blush was enough of an answer, and Edie laughed again. "You'd better watch out or some people will figure you've become a batty old lady like me."

Later that day, the dog endeared himself to Chloe for life when he started bringing her presents from his private cache of treasures—a fuzzless tennis ball, a rubber duck with a missing beak, and then a rope toy with which they played a raucous game of tug-o-war. Then he showed up with a magazine, its binding held carefully between his teeth. He waited until he had her full attention then dropped it at her feet. A glance told Chloe it was the latest issue of *Patchwork Life*, and the cover photo made her gasp.

It was an Amish-style quilt pieced in vibrant solids. "Quilting in the home of the Amish," the headline read. "Alsace, France." She picked it up, entranced by the quilter's use of color, and studied the photograph closely in order to understand how it was pieced together.

"Alsace," she murmured. "I've always wanted to visit France."

Nearly's tail fluttered, and he shifted from side to side. Chloe fixed him with a stare.

"Are you some sort of messenger from another world?" she asked. "Am I supposed to go to France?"

Nearly sat down, and stared back at her, swinging the pendulums of his ears forward.

"Edie set you up to do this, right?" Nearly stood up, his tail a blur. Chloe laughed. "Lead on."

The spaniel turned, and raced down the stairs to the kitchen where Edie sliced onions for soup—French onion was one of her specialties. "I love eating this soup," she said, wiping tears from her face with her sleeve. "I just wish making it wasn't such an emotional experience." Then she caught sight of the magazine in Chloe's hand, and she smiled. "Isn't that an amazing quilt?"

Chloe agreed. "But I never knew Alsace was where the Amish began. I thought the Mennonites were of German origin."

"I traveled all over that area when I lived in France. Over here, we forget how tightly intermingled the German and French cultures are in Alsace." She slid rings of onion into a heavy pan where they joined others simmering in butter. "Personally, I think all cultures benefit when they rub elbows with one another. You can get the worst of both worlds at times but more often, I think you get the best."

Chloe turned the magazine over to stare at the cover again. Edie glanced down at Nearly, gave him a wink, and then offered him a piece of cheese from a block sitting on the counter. He accepted his due, swallowed it, and then headed toward the bed next to the stove where he'd have a clear view of the action. Chloe dragged in about an acre of air.

"Is April in Paris as lovely as the songs would like you to think?" she asked.

Edie slid the last of the onions into the pan, and covered it. "The only month I would not recommend being in Paris is August. Way too hot, just like every other city in the northern hemisphere, and many things are closed because the locals are all on vacation. Otherwise, it is lovely." She opened her spice cupboard and scanned the racks of glass jars. "I still have friends who live there...and they welcome guests."

Chloe traced the quilt picture's pattern with her finger. "I don't have any classes scheduled from mid-March to mid-April but if we have to move the school..." Her voice trailed off.

"Why don't you wait until after town meeting to make a decision about Paris," Edie said.

"Dad wants me to tell Gideon that I want a divorce just before town meeting. He figures Gideon will be so stirred up, he'll sign the paperwork I need without a fight." She smiled. "I've never given any serious time to studying European quilting."

"Well, that's an oversight that's easily corrected," Edie said. "Hand me that spoon, will you?"

FOURTEEN

MAXIMUM COMFORT QUILT

New post on Carding Chronicle blog: March 1

National Weather Service Predicts Sunday Blizzard
by Little Crow

It's that time of year again, folks. We're coming out of winter into spring, and that means heavy, wet snow. That's what we've got on tap for Sunday, starting early in the morning.

Temperatures are expected to hover around freezing which means that it will snow sometimes, sleet sometimes, and rain the other times while coating every available surface with a thin glaze of ice.

Fun, eh?

Green Mountain Power is warning about widespread power outages because the heavy precipitation will pull tree branches down. Andy Cooper reports that the battery supply at the store is running low, and Stan over at the gas station says there's a steady flow of customers filling cans for their home generators.

Stay warm, stay dry, and if you can, stay off the roads starting Sunday morning. Sorry to Reverend Lloyd over at the Episcopal Church!

I'll be looking for you after the snow stops.
Little Crow | March 1 | Categories: Local Weather

It's a widespread belief among Vermonters that just about the time folks are weary of their heavy jackets and clunky boots, March will roll out storm after storm across the Green Mountains, each with its own unique mix of frozen water. A hint of the windy month's coming attractions popped up on the weather radar the morning of the second—a low pressure system oozing down from the Canadian maritimes to mate with a storm sliding east from the Great Lakes. At first, the national weather people pooh-poohed the coupled system as much ado about not too much. But Vermont's local weather gurus quickly pegged the mass as just the type of storm to embrace the mountains and hang around for a while.

As the storms got closer to their rendezvous in the Green Mountains, they picked up speed and moisture. Snowfall predictions rose from 4–6 inches to 12–15 with, as the weather guys put it, "local icing," a term that has nothing to do with cake.

"We're gonna catch it," Coop shoppers told the cashiers as they rushed in to buy milk, eggs, bread, and batteries. "Remember that ice storm back in '87? We lost power for three days."

Andy sighed and shook his head over the mini-stampede in his store. "You'd think we'd never had a big storm hit town before," he told Edie when she stopped by.

"Well, the weather guys on Dirt Road Radio have bumped the accumulation up to 18 inches, last I heard. With ice," she said. "You have to admit that's a sizable storm, Andy. It'll be Monday before we're all dug out, and things get back to normal." She looked down at the wine, tea, and dog treats in her own basket. "One must have the necessities at hand, don't you agree?"

Andy laughed. "Don't know why I'm complaining, do I? It's all good for business." He picked up the wine bottle and approved Edie's choice. "We still on for dinner and cribbage tomorrow night?"

"Of course. Maple chicken's on the menu. How's that sound?"

Early risers on Saturday morning luxuriated in a brilliant blue sky, and temperatures that teased with the promise of more warmth to come. All over town, radios and computers tuned in to the various weather outlets tracking the storms. In Vermont, following the weather is as close as you can get to a state religion.

"Looks like the storm coming down from Canada got hung up on the White Mountains," Bruce said as the crew at Brown & Sons scurried to check on their plowing equipment. He nodded at Peter. "Should give you plenty of time to get to Montpelier to play with the Thieves. But I'd stay put until Monday morning, if I were you."

Peter glanced up at the sky where the thinnest wisps of white had started taking the edge off the sun's promise. "Yeah, I'll make it, and you're probably right about hanging out until Monday. I'll throw in some extra clothes when I go home to pack."

Lisa was just about to put her cowgirl outfit on to make last-minute adjustments when she heard Peter come in the back door of their house. She flung the fringed satiny thing to the bottom of her closet, closed the door, and sat down at her jewelry box.

"I'm leaving earlier than expected," Peter said as he threw socks, jeans, and shirts into his bag, "to get ahead of the storm. And I may stay over until Monday morning, depending on how bad it is." Then he stopped moving. "I'm surprised you're still here. You usually go shopping on Saturdays."

She heard the annoyed notes in his tone but decided to ignore them. She wanted him gone as much as he wanted to go.

"Oh, I felt one of my headaches coming on," she sighed. Peter winced, waiting for the expected gusher of complaints.

Well, I guess the honeymoon's definitely over, Lisa thought as she turned back to her jewelry. Then she caught him looking at her in the mirror, and was startled to see worry and fatigue dragging at his face. What did he have to mope about?

"The latest forecast has it that the snow won't start here until early tomorrow morning," she said. "I'm surprised Harry's going to let you go to Montpelier."

"Oh, Gideon usually rides herd on the snow crews. I'm pretty much in the way." Peter zipped up his bag.

"Gideon? Really?"

"Yeah, why?"

Lisa shook her head. "Nothing. Just surprised is all. It seems that Harry has you do everything."

"There's not much to the snow plowing, really. We wait until the town crews make their first pass on the roads then our drivers take off. Nothing different from what we were doing back in December, and I didn't have to be around for that. " He picked up his bag, and started for the bedroom door.

"Wait a minute," Lisa called. "Don't you want a kiss?"

Peter stopped. She moved close to him, put her arms around his neck, and he bent to kiss her. As he did, she snuggled her prominent breasts into his body, and he pulled away. They parted, and looked at one another without a clue what to do next. Not now, they both thought. There will be plenty of time later.

"Well, good-bye," Peter said. "See you Monday."

When she heard the door close behind him, Lisa lunged for her cell phone. "Come at 6. Peter already gone. xx" she texted. Gideon's body tingled all over as he read her words. When he replied with his "OK," he changed his mind again about letting this relationship go on after town meeting.

The clouds' color resembled tarnished silver by the time Ted and Suzanna got back to Carding from their visit with Robert. With the storm coming, Ted knew he'd never get to Woodstock on Sunday, so niece and uncle decided to forego skiing on Saturday morning. The old man had studied the pictures that they'd brought of his granddaughter on the slopes of Mount Merino, and Ted swore he saw tears in his eyes as Suzanna pinned one of the photos to the wall near his bed. Robert asked a lot of questions, and smiled the whole time the girl chattered.

"And how about you?" he finally asked his son. "Did you ski?"

Heavy questions floated in the air between them until Ted finally nodded. "Yes. A lot of the old team was there, Peter and Sam and Paula. Andy Cooper came, too."

Robert leaned back in his wheelchair and nodded. "Good," he whispered. "Good."

The flag in front of the assisted living center hung limp against its pole as they left. When they turned south on Route 37 toward Carding, they spotted Peter's truck heading in the other direction, and Suzanna gave him a big wave. Next they saw Ruth in her Jeep, and Suzanna waved again.

"I have never had anyone to wave at before," she said, settling back in her seat. "That's fun. Do you think we can still get to the mountain today?"

Ted hunched forward to scan the sky, shaking his head. "I think this storm is starting sooner than the weather guys predicted, and we don't want to be that far from home when it does," he said. He took her sigh of disappointment philosophically.

"But I thought snowstorms were good for skiing," she muttered.

"They are." A single crow darted in front of their truck when Ted turned down their road. He tensed, straining to see if any strange cars loitered in front of his house. But the street lay empty.

His movement did not escape Suzanna's notice, and she looked at her uncle. Faye checked Alli-O's website every day so Suzanna knew about the "celebrities and their children" photo shoot. The girls also knew that Ted meant to fight Allison so that Suzanna could stay with him but just in case that failed, Faye and Wil had concocted a plan to hide their friend.

"It's just until your mother goes away again," Faye promised. When Suzanna wondered about telling her uncle so he wouldn't worry, Wil said it was just as well not to trust adults in this matter because they had "too many rules they had to obey about kids."

In the truck, Ted turned toward his niece. "We can get some cross-country ski time in. That will keep us closer to home so when the storm starts, we can get back easily. How's that sound?"

Suzanna grinned as she opened the truck's door. "Race ya to the snow!" she yelled.

The single crow, now perched on the fence dividing Ted's yard from his driveway, exchanged a look with the man, cawed twice, and then flew off. Ted looked around again but the whole street had nothing more on its mind than getting ready for the storm. Still, he knew he'd been warned.

The bright-eyed little girl had already pulled apples from the fridge and cookies from the cupboard by the time Ted arrived in the kitchen. "I beat you," she said. But she stopped bustling when she noticed his face. "What's wrong? Aren't we going skiing?"

"Yes, yes we are." He turned a chair around and sat. "I just need to talk to you first…about your mother."

Suzanna's eyes flew about. "She's not here, is she?"

"No, but we both know she will be, sooner or later, right?"

"Yeah." The girl wrapped her arms over her chest. "But I'm not going anywhere with her. Ever."

Ted grinned. "On that, my dear niece, we are in complete agreement. Now, I've had several talks with Charlie Cooper about this."

"He's the lawyer guy, right? The one who knows about the rules that adults have to follow?"

Ted was confused by her choice of words but he plunged on. "Right. Charlie and I have figured out a way for me to get custody of you. At least, we're pretty sure what we plan to do will work." Suzanna clapped her hands.

"Charlie thinks we better our chances if we act fast when your mother arrives, and I want to keep the argument between her and me, not you. Is that OK?"

"My mother is very good at screaming," Suzanna said.

"Oh, I know. Only too well." Ted paused for a moment then pushed his memories to one side. "Here's what I need you to do if she shows up." Ted stood, and walked down the hall to Suzanna's room, carrying a kitchen chair with him. He placed it just inside the door when they arrived.

"This room really needs a good sprucing up," he said when he stepped in. "Since it's going to be really bad out tomorrow, maybe we can get the wallpaper stripped off if we don't lose power. I've got a steamer down in the basement."

"Can we paint the walls instead of putting paper back on them?"

"Sure. Anything you want."

"Can I pick out the colors? I love blue and yellow cuz they remind me of summer," Suzanna said.

Ted grinned. "Blue and yellow it is."

"Yellow on the walls and blue on the ceiling?" Suzanna had seen a room painted like that in a book, and she'd loved it.

"You bet. Now," Ted turned toward the door, "there's no lock on this so you'll have to use the chair to keep it shut." He closed the door, slid the chair under the knob then demonstrated how it worked to keep people out.

"So, if we pull up in the truck, and your mother is here…" Ted said.

"I'm to take my house key, open the front door…" Suzanna continued.

"And come in here, shut the door, and push the chair under the knob," he said. "And not come out until I ask you to. That part's really important. If she gets ahold of you…"

"She won't," Suzanna said. "I run a lot faster than she does in those stupid high heels of hers." Suzanna looked up at Ted with her best, encouraging smile. She knew he meant well, and she gloried in the fact that someone really wanted her. But she didn't think much of his plan. Just hiding behind a door held shut by a chair wouldn't stop Alli-O. No, the plans Suzanna had made with Faye and Wil were much better. She wished she could confide in her uncle but she remembered Wil's caution about adults with their rules so she kept her own counsel.

"Come on." Ted patted her shoulder. "Let's get a little skiing in before we lose the light altogether."

The sky had darkened even more with the promise of snow by the time they trudged to the end of their dead-end road, their pockets stuffed with apples and cookies, skis on their shoulders. A soft wind slid over the sloped terrain, and its icy fingers made them both shiver.

"I think this is going to be a short run," Ted said, zipping the collar of his jacket closed.

"Why? We'll be close to home, right?"

"When it snows in this kind of low light, it's easy to get lost because you can't make out the trail." He bent down to help Suzanna adjust one of her skis. Though still very new to cross-country skiing, Ted thought her steady enough on her feet for the local trail. And if something went wrong, they wouldn't be far from home.

"I got lost out here once when I was a kid. Mom told me not to go off the little loop we're going to do. But I figured I could get down to the Campground and back before it snowed." He slid his hands into the straps of his poles.

"What happened?"

"Oh, I got down to the Campground all right, and had started back up the trail when it started," Ted said as they pushed off with slow, easy strokes. "The snow got heavy right off, and in just a few minutes, I couldn't make out the trail, couldn't find my way out."

"Were you scared?"

"Oh yeah, I was a lot younger than you, about seven, I think. No food, no water, no shelter, and I knew if I got turned around bad enough, I could end up over the falls." The two of them pulled their skis together to slide down a short slope.

"What did you do?"

"More or less froze in place until someone came to find me."

"Who found you?"

"Dad."

"Was he angry with you?"

"Oh yeah, but only after making sure I was OK."

As they panted up the next rise, Ted in the lead, Suzanna reached up to touch the breast pocket of her jacket where she'd zipped in Ted's cell phone. She'd promised Faye to call when she disappeared. She hoped Uncle Ted would forgive her when he found it missing.

Snow—and the hush that accompanies it—started making its way to the ground before Peter had traveled more than two exits on the interstate. But he didn't notice. Images of Lisa and Chloe swirled through his heart, sometimes superimposed on one another but mostly distinct, as they were in real life. The more he got to know Chloe, the more he realized how much she resembled her father, and he'd always liked Charlie. As for Lisa, well, Peter realized she longed to be just like her mother—famous in her own mind—and that she'd likely succeed.

He shuddered at his recall of their last kiss, and wondered, yet again, why he had married the woman. Had it really been nothing more than the sexual pleasure of their early days? He suspected it was so and kicked himself for being so shallow. Now that he knew Chloe, everything about love and commitment seemed so…well, he'd better not think about that now. Too confusing.

The snow changed to sleet, and its ping on the hood of his truck finally grabbed Peter's attention. He sat up straighter in his seat, redirecting all the truck's heat to the windshield to keep it clear. Suddenly, the van he'd trailed for the last few miles swerved across the road in front of him, skirting the median strip before the driver regained control. Peter eased off on his gas pedal. It promised to be a long, slow ride.

As soon as Peter drove away, Lisa dove into her closet to scoop up her evening's outfits. She folded them carefully into their pink boxes, grabbed a paper bag from under her bed, and swooped into the kitchen to collect the treats she'd gathered for the occasion—chocolate, smoked salmon, special crackers, and a container of Boursin she'd hidden behind a pickle jar in the fridge. Snowstorm or no snowstorm, she would have her date with Gideon.

The sight of a pair of Peter's gloves on the kitchen table made her flinch as she remembered their parting. Then she straightened her shoulders. She'd outgrown Peter, OK? And he still had his music, didn't he? Probably the only part of him she'd ever been attracted to. Everyone knew that Lisa had a weakness for boys in a band. Deal with it.

She glanced around again, skipping over the gloves with their silent accusation, just to make sure she'd not left anything incriminating around. Gideon's cautions rang in her ears, and since he had more experience in this stuff than she did, Lisa heeded his warnings.

As she opened the back door to the garage, she hesitated, her bags and box in one hand, car keys in the other. An odd, somewhat queasy sensation clutched her center, and for just a moment, she saw the home where she'd been Mrs. Peter Foster as if from the wrong end of a telescope—small and far away. Then she blinked, and the hallway, her house, and her life came back into focus. She stepped over the threshold. She had to get to the Campgrounds before Gideon.

"Why don't you stay here tonight, dear?" Edie asked. "We'll be snowed in, there's plenty of food, and a woodstove for heat if the power goes out."

But Chloe shook her head. "No, but thanks, Edie." She glanced around her cozy two-room suite, now filled with her books, quilts, knitting bag, lamp, and chair. Odd how the place felt warmer and more welcoming, than the house she'd shared with Gideon. Is this all it takes to leave an old life behind, she wondered, moving your favorite things from one place to another?

"This will be my last night at my...my old place." Chloe's voice cracked, and she sagged in the doorway. "Oh Edie, I feel like such a failure. How could I have been so blind about Gideon? This whole mess makes me doubt myself. Am I that bad a judge of character?"

Edie's gaze grew very soft as she looked at the young woman, now temporarily crumpled by life. She knew with a certainty that Chloe would, eventually, be fine. That she would right herself and sail with confidence into her future. But right now, Edie reminded herself, she doesn't know that and can't feel it. She reached out a hand, and gently placed it on Chloe's arm.

"I know you feel like something stuck to the bottom of a shoe," she began, "and you're worried that this is how you're going to feel for the rest of your life."

Chloe blinked and turned her face away.

"Do you remember when you first came to work at the academy?" Edie asked.

Chloe nodded, and sniffed. "I felt like I had no ideas, and I couldn't understand why anyone would pay me to teach them anything."

"And now?" Edie prompted.

Chloe sniffed again, then smiled. "Now I can't get my ideas down on paper fast enough, and there's a waiting list for my classes."

"Exactly. Time moved on. Circumstances changed. You changed. Happens all the time, if we let it," Edie said.

Chloe shifted. "But this is different."

"Not in the fundamentals," Edie argued. "I'm talking about how change happens in our lives. While we can and do act quickly in reaction to an event—like when you pushed Gideon into living in the basement of your house—the emotional adjustment to those events always lags behind. We make emotional accommodations over time."

She could tell that Chloe hung on every word, so Edie chose them with great care. "Look at the time it's taken you to accept the idea of divorcing Gideon," she began. "You've thought about it, considered it, imagined it, and lived with it for quite a while. Without realizing it, you've been gathering your strength for this moment in the privacy of your own heart. Divorce, like marriage, is a public undertaking. You're dissolving an unsuccessful partnership, one that involves a lot of pain, and you needed to be ready for the public part of that. And now you are or you would never have accepted my invitation for a place to live. So it's reasonable, at least to me, to figure you won't feel the way you're feeling now for very long. What do you think?"

Chloe knew the answer right away. "I thought I would die when my mother and father divorced. I was just twenty, and I thought my life was over then. But by the time I was twenty-one, I realized my life had improved a lot because I didn't have to listen to Mom screaming at Dad." She smiled. "And I got to have Dad more to myself."

"Ah yes, the unexpected silver lining," Edie said.

"But I still have to ask—how could I have fooled myself about Gideon? I really talked myself into believing that he loved me enough to change."

"But he does love you," Edie said. Chloe shook her head hard from side to side. "No, it's true, Chloe. It took me years to understand how much love varies from person to person. On the day you were married, Gideon was besotted with you. That much was apparent to anyone with eyes to see. But Gideon's personal interpretation of love doesn't include his body. He's kind of like Nearly here." The dog lifted his head, ears cocked forward, and Edie smiled at him. "He loves me, is intensely loyal after his fashion but I know he'd follow anyone who promised a handout of Vermont's finest cheddar."

Chloe laughed, and brushed a hand over her eyes. "Is that what Gideon's other women are, so much cheese?"

Edie lifted one eyebrow. "It may be a bit more complex than that," she admitted. "Gideon's self-image relies, in part, on his physical prowess with women. But that activity doesn't touch his heart."

"Only because his heart is located above his waist," Chloe said.

"Exactly. Which explains why he couldn't understand why you didn't just 'get over it' when you found him in bed with another woman." Edie sighed. "Gideon's lifelong problem is that he admires his father, and wants Harry's approval so he thinks he has to do everything that Harry's ever done. That's the part I don't understand because he knows how much Harry hurt Louisa, and from what I can tell, he cares about his mother."

Chloe shook her head. "Some mysteries are never going to be solved, I guess." She leaned over to hug the older woman. "Thank you for everything."

"Don't mention it. I'm glad to help." Edie clapped her hands. "Now, what about France? Have you given any more thought to travel?"

The young woman beamed. "I decided not to wait for town meeting. I booked a ticket for Paris this morning."

Edie crowed. "Excellent!"

Gideon slowed his truck as soon as he turned onto Beach Road, swinging his head from side to side to make sure there were no other cars. Even though no one lived on the short access road, the town kept it clear of snow for parking for those who loved to ice fish. But the anglers left with the setting sun, making the deserted parking lot the perfect place to leave his truck for the night.

As soon as he set the emergency brake, Gideon checked the National Weather Service report on his phone. The storm was coming in quicker than expected but it would be the wee hours of the morning before he'd be needed for plowing. Plenty of time to spend with Lisa though he'd have to go slow on the champagne so he could drive later. He looked at the four bottles that he'd brought but tucked only two into his backpack along with a change of clothes. Lisa loved champagne so he didn't worry about having to lug full bottles back to the truck. The empties would be heavy enough when he returned later, and he counted on having a lot less energy than he did now.

He clicked on his big flashlight then laid it on the ground so he could see to tighten the straps of his snowshoes. Then he shouldered the pack and headed for the path that led to the Campgrounds.

I wish this storm had waited for another day, he thought as his light bobbed across the snow. Though maybe a whole night of Lisa would be too much. Then he grinned. Nah, a whole night of Lisa would be just about right.

Gideon quickened his pace when the lights of the cabin came into view. Lisa was obviously watching at the window for him because as soon as he got to the bottom step of the porch, the door opened. There she stood, backlit by soft lights, her every curve clearly outlined.

"Hmm, nice," he said. "Very nice." Then she stepped out into the cold night air, and Gideon was stunned by the view. Lisa smiled, her dark hair brushed to its fullest, her lips very red. She wore a black lace body stocking that covered everything and nothing at the same time. She stepped forward on black stiletto heels, and the air whooshed out of Gideon as though he'd been hit in the abdomen.

"Hello," she said, moving toward the immobilized man. Lisa reached for the zipper of Gideon's jacket, and lowered it slowly. Then she unbuttoned his shirt. He hissed at her touch. She tugged on the backpack's straps. "Now, what have you got in there?"

"Champagne," he said. She looked magnificent.

"Well, why don't you bring it inside where we can enjoy it," she said, and then she turned to saunter into the cabin. Gideon groaned, and rushed up to grab her, pinning her against the wall of the cabin.

"Oh Gideon, so eager," Lisa cooed.

"Oh yes," he said. "You have no idea."

As Lisa peeled off his shirt and pants and dropped them on the porch, Gideon never noticed the cold air slithering over his skin or that it had started to snow.

Peter leaned closer to his windshield, struggling to make out the yellow line in the middle of the road. Icy crystals coagulated on his wipers and bounced off his truck. Driving through snow was one thing but only an idiot stayed on the road during an ice storm, he thought. And that's what we're having, a full blown ice storm.

Finally, the towering gas station sign that heralded the approach of Exit 4 pierced the gray, a mere smudge of red and white in the swirl. He released the breath he'd been holding for the past mile. Now, if he could just pick up a cell phone tower.

He lumbered off the interstate, careful to tap the brakes with just the lightest of touches, and slid into the station. The cell phone signal was weak and crackling but it was strong enough to get through. Bruce picked up at the other end.

"Peter, they just called here from Montpelier looking for you because your phone wasn't working," he boomed. "The dance is cancelled. Turn around and come back if you can. Harry's in a total twist because Gideon's nowhere to be found."

"Has it started snowing there yet?"

"It just did. Latest report says it's moving slower than expected so it's got time to dump even more snow than they predicted. It's gonna be a beauty."

Peter heard someone yell in the background. "I expect that's Harry."

"Yeah." Bruce sent a huge sigh over the phone. "What's it doing where you are?"

"It's been sleeting since I got out of Bethel, and the interstate's not in good shape." As Peter spoke, the ice crystals morphed into fat snowflakes that splatted on the asphalt illuminated by his headlights. "And I think it just changed back to snow."

Bruce sighed again, even bigger this time. "Great, my favorite. March slop. Do you think you can make it back?"

A flash of yellow light swept over the gas station's front windows, and the ground underneath Peter's pickup shook. "The state plow truck is just going by." Peter cleared the fog off his side window to watch the giant waddle up the ramp to the interstate, leaving a spray of sand and salt in its wake. "It's heading south. If I can get in behind it, I'll do all right."

Bruce glanced over his shoulder at the fuming Harry Brown as he paced back and forth, shaking his cell phone in his fist.

"That would be great," he told Peter. "The sooner, the better."

As soon as Chloe snapped the lights on in her old house, as she now called it, she considered going right back to Edie's. This was not her home any more, not this barren place. Sure, all the furniture remained the same—she didn't want it because she'd picked it out with Gideon—but all the doodads that made the place hers now lived somewhere else. It was as if all the color had been vacuumed out of the room.

The silence made her uneasy. For once, she wished Gideon was home. The overspray from his incessant television would have been comforting. Then she realized, with a start, that she had a television too, and wondered if Gideon's cable subscription covered it as well.

She slid an old recliner into viewing distance then opened the cabinet doors that hid the "big eye." Chloe hated TV with the same intensity she reserved for all shoddy art. But sound was sound, and boring company was, under these circumstances, better than no company at all.

As she walked past the open guest room door, Chloe paused to look at the gaily wrapped and battered box she'd put there. Somehow, returning Gideon's sexy gifts this way seemed petty to her now that her anger had passed. She knew her father would not approve of the gesture. Too much like something Mom would do.

And that thought settled the matter for Chloe. It belongs in the dumpster with the other trash from my studio, she thought. As she bent down to pick it up, she noticed a bit of color sticking out from under the bed. Curious, she dropped to all fours, and pulled a clear plastic bag toward her.

"Oh my." It was her first quilt, made in the summer she turned twenty. She'd felt so uncertain about life then, with the aftermath of her parents' divorce and all the recriminations that went with it. To comfort herself, she'd cut pieces from all her old clothes—school skirts, summer blouses, a flowered pair of pajamas two sizes too small—and sewed them together. Agnes, who'd just become part of her father's life, called it "Chloe's maximum comfort quilt," and it became a fixture in her dorm room when she went back to school. Delighted to find her old friend, Chloe hugged it to her chest, grabbed the frilly underwear box, and hauled them both into the living room. She draped the quilt over the recliner then wrestled the box out to her van. She'd bring it to the dump later and be done with it.

As she closed the van's back door, snowflakes melted on her face. She stood for a few moments to watch their descent, clinging to one another as they rounded off the sharp edges of every angle. Amazing how the most important events of every day happen in utter silence, she thought. Sunrise, snow falling, hearts breaking. Finally she turned back to the house, hoping she'd find a channel showing an old movie to go with her wine, melancholy, and popcorn. Tomorrow, she'd present Gideon with the papers drawn up by her father, and tell him that their marriage was finally over. He could do whatever he wanted with whomever he wanted. She had made other plans for her life.

The hush of the anticipated snow settled in the spaces among the bare trees guarding the network of trails that led to the Campgrounds. Ted and Suzanna moved their skis in an easy glide. The trail forked at a tree adorned with signs that pointed downhill to "Great Falls" and uphill to "Royal Buchanan," the street where they lived. Ted paused at the base of the tree, and pointed at them.

"My mother made these after I got lost down here so I'd always know the way home." His voice cracked a little on the last word but then he smiled at Suzanna. "If you're ever down here by yourself, be sure to stay away from the Great Falls path, OK?"

"Why?"

"It's very steep, sheer rock in some places, and the spray from the falls means the stones are always wet and slippery," Ted said. "Even in summer, it's not a smart place to hike."

"Has anyone ever fallen down the falls?" Suzanna asked.

"My Dad can tell you a story about someone who died down there back in the 1940s. He says that folks around here have avoided that trail ever since." Ted slipped his hand back into the straps of his ski poles. "The snow's gonna catch us if we don't move along. Ready for a little uphill work?"

Suzanna smiled back, hoping with every cell in her body that Faye and Wil's plan would work. She just had to stay in Carding. Her Uncle Ted would be lonely without her. And to tell the truth, she'd be lonely without him.

They slid down a short slope then leaned forward to dig in their poles, spreading their skis out in shallow Vs to herringbone up a rise to the next plateau. By the time they reached the top, they were both panting hard.

"Whew, just two more," Ted gasped. "Then it's supper and settling in for the night."

"Can we have pancakes with maple syrup?" Suzanna asked.

"For supper?"

"Yeah, I love maple syrup."

Ted laughed. "OK, I guess so."

As they set off again, snowflakes settled on Suzanna's nose. She looked to the right and then left, wondering if she could find her way through the woods to the Campground by herself. Between the twilight and the thickening snow, one leafless tree looked so much like another.

As she followed her uncle up the final rise, Suzanna heard a single, sharp caw. The sound was so loud she started and whipped her head around, half expecting to find a black bird on her shoulder. Then she heard a second sound, the one she'd been dreading for weeks.

"Well, hello Ted," a female voice called, its normal screechy edge dulled by the snow.

Her uncle jerked to a stop, and Suzanna heard him gasp. She turned, silently kicked off, and followed their tracks back downhill, her heart thumping in her chest. She wanted to scream "No, no, no" all the way down but she never opened her mouth. She counted the slopes—one, two, three—then veered to her right, looking for the sign her grandmother painted so long ago.

It was then that the clouds opened like feather beds split with a sharp knife, and flakes clotted in the gloomy air around her. Suzanna could barely make out the tips of her skis. She strained and strained to see through the murk. Finally, she spotted the tree with the signs. Spinning to the left, she listened for the sounds of someone following her but all she heard was her own thundering heart.

She moved faster, praying that the trail into the Campgrounds would somehow, miraculously, be visible enough to guide her skis home to the Owens family cabin. Suddenly, the trees fell away on both sides. With the last light of day, Suzanna realized she was standing on the edge of the field that lay behind the Campgrounds. Then the dark closed in, and she could barely see her own mittens, never mind the huddled cabins that were her journey's end. She stood still, afraid to move forward, sure she would never go back.

Snow covered the shoulders of her jacket, and she shivered. She shifted her feet from side to side to clear the white stuff from her skis. Then she remembered her uncle's cell phone. She wrenched it free of her pocket, and turned it on. But all she got for her trouble was a message about the "lack of service from your location." Tears flooded her eyes as she jammed the useless thing back in its hiding place.

What to do? What to do?

Then she saw…something.

At first, Suzanna thought the pinprick of light was just a trick of her eyes. She blinked, squeezed her lids down tight, and then slowly opened them again. It was no trick. The light was real. Was someone already looking for her? Had Faye and Wil told? Suzanna hung her head, waiting to hear her mother's demanding scream shred the darkness.

But there was no sound. Instead, Suzanna spotted a second light, this one advancing over the snow, away from her and toward the cabins. As it drew closer to the first light, a rectangle of illumination appeared, and Suzanna thought she saw something or someone move. She flicked her eyes from side to side, and picked out enough fuzzy detail to understand that the lights came from the cabin owned by her uncle's lawyer friend, Charlie.

"Well," she said aloud, "I can't stay here all night." With a bone-deep shiver, she dug her poles into the fluff at her feet, and headed toward shelter.

FIFTEEN

TERRA COTTA AND
RUBBER BOOTS

"So, where is my darling girl" Allison said as she walked up to Ted, swishing her fur coat, and flaunting a big smile. "Suzanna?" she called. "Where are you girl?"

Ted swallowed hard but did not turn his head to look behind him. He hoped the child had heard, hoped she was prepared to flee into the house, and lock herself in her room. Ted had no doubt that if Allison had the chance, she'd whisk Suzanna off before he could call Charlie Cooper. He realized that this situation was an argument for always carrying a cell phone.

In the street behind his sister, Ted saw a large car idling in front of his house, a tall man leaning against its trunk.

"Do you have any idea how much gas you waste when you're idling?" he asked.

Allison laughed. "Oh, you Vermonters are so green," she said. "But I, for one, appreciate your saving ways. More for the rest of us to waste." She stopped just under the only street light on Royal Buchanan, and Ted thought the makeup around her eyes had been applied with a too-heavy hand. The faint smell of marijuana drifted through the air.

"Where's my darling girl?" Allison repeated, rocking unsteadily on her high heels. In snow, Ted thought. Now that is stupid. "And what are you doing on skis, Teddy boy? I thought you were never going to ski again."

The surge of hate that flared through Ted would have frightened him if he'd seen it in someone else. He marveled at how pure it felt, and how much he would enjoy hitting his sister. Allison sensed the coil of his loathing rise up between them, and she stepped back, wobbling on her silly, useless shoes. The man lounging against her car stood up, squared his shoulders, and it suddenly struck Ted as so much bad theater.

He started to laugh, not a timid "woo-hoo-hoo" but a genuine, full guffaw that rolled out into the night. Allison cringed at the sound and stepped back from her brother. Ted glided past her while he was still giggling. The man near the car obviously had other ideas for Ted and ran to head him off at the end of the driveway. The motion sensor lights on the garage blinked on, and Ted saw the features of a boy loom out of the dark.

"Where's Allison's daughter?" the boy asked in much too loud a voice. Ted heard Allison wobble up behind him, and squelched the desire to laugh again. There was no time to waste. Suzanna was stranded in the cold, and Ted had to get this odd couple out of the way so he could get his niece safely inside.

"My gawd, Allison, this Bruno is awfully young, even for you," Ted said, raising his voice.

Confusion knitted up the young man's brow, and he glanced at Allison. "Bruno? Who's Bruno? My name is Justin," he said in a voice that sounded like Marlon Brando's *Godfather* filtered through Kermit the Frog.

Ted couldn't resist. "And how old are you, Justin?"

The words "seventeen" and "don't answer that" hit Ted's ears at the same time as he shot up the driveway. As he kicked off his skis and swung the back door open, he hoped Suzanna wouldn't hear his next words. "I didn't want your daughter any more than you did. She's living with Diana Bennett and her family behind the bakery in the center of town. Go and get her there."

He slammed the door but its dramatic impact was muffled by the snow. Ted raced to the living room window to watch Allison and her Bruno leave. As they got in the car—the boy in the driver's seat, his sister in the back—their loud voices crackled through the air, punctuated by spiky gestures. The limo's back tires spun, spraying dirty snow.

"Come on," Ted urged. "You can get out if you just tap on the gas."

Finally, the dark car lunged away from the curb, fishtailed, and then pivoted to go back from whence it came. Ted grabbed his flashlight, and ran for the trail head, skidding across the road.

"Suzanna? Suzanna! It's safe now. She's gone," Ted called. He covered and then revealed his light, hoping she'd see it through the gloom. "Suzanna!"

He crept down the hill in his ski boots, clinging to the trees on the side of the trail, calling louder and louder. A muffled caw made him whip his head around, and he stumbled into the tree holding the signs that read "Great Falls" and "Home."

"Suzanna! Suzanna!" Had she heard what he said? Please don't let her believe it if she did. Please. "Suzanna!"

Ted flicked his flashlight over the trail, studying the marks now nearly invisible under the falling flakes. She'd stopped here, that much he could make out. But which way did she go? He raised his flashlight, willing its beam through the gloom. "Suzanna!"

The watching crow lifted off from a spruce branch, making it drop its snow load to the ground. The bird was satisfied. She'd delivered her message, and it was time to get to her own roost to wait out the storm.

Over in their home behind the Crow Town Bakery, Faye Bennett's cell phone made a tiny squawk as she made her way down the stairs to answer her mother's supper call. She touched the screen to make Suzanna's text message appear: "In cabin—mother here—no food or light yes heat—S."

Wil clattered up behind her, and read over her shoulder. The two siblings exchanged a look. Concocting an adventure was one thing. Living it was quite another. How on earth were they going to get food to Suzanna in all this snow?

"How long does it take someone to starve to death?" Faye whispered to her brother.

Before he could answer, the phone in the family kitchen trilled, and they heard their mother say: "Oh, hi Ted" followed by an explosive "What?" and then "You go search. I'll call Charlie."

Faye and Wil looked at one another again, and she was worried that her brother looked worried.

"What's going on?" they heard their father ask. "Is Ted's no-good sister in town?"

"Yes, Allison's in Carding," Diana said as she frantically punched the buttons on her phone. "In fact, she's on her way here, to this house, right now. And Suzanna's disappeared, out there in this storm. Ted's terrified she'll go over into the falls."

Wil and Faye crept a bit further down the stairs, each hoping no one would hear their thrumming hearts. "Charlie? It's Diana Bennett. Ted just called. Allison's in town. Ted told her Suzanna was here so this is where she's headed. But Suzanna's disappeared. They were skiing on the Campground trails when Allison arrived, and the girl took off."

Charlie grabbed his coat while he talked to Diana. Agnes ran to get his car keys then helped him snake his arms into his sleeves. "I'll be right there, Diana. Try to keep Allison at the door if she gets there before me. Stall her, argue with her. That shouldn't be hard."

As he snapped his phone shut, Agnes pressed a file of papers marked Owens into his hands. "Suzanna's run away because her mother is here," he said. "Ted's out looking for her, and…"

"No time. I'll stay by the phones," Agnes said, pointing to her cell and their land line. "I'll call for help. Go!"

As Charlie fled out the door, Stephen Bennett looked up the stairs to where his two children stood. He couldn't remember when he'd seen facial expressions that displayed guilt better than theirs.

"I do hope," he began, "that neither of you plans a career as a professional poker player. You're both as easy to read as a book." Just then, a fist banged on the door leading to the Bennett's family's living quarters. He eyeballed Faye and Wil. "Stay right where you are, and don't say a word. We're going to have a little chat as soon as your mother and I take care of the problem standing at our door."

"So now what do we do?" Faye whispered to Wil as their father turned away.

"Get closer," Wil said. They crept down the stairs as far as they dared, to a spot where they could hear better.

As soon as he and Diana met at the door, Stephen raised a finger to his lips, took off one of his slippers, and placed it where it would jam under the door. Then he nodded to his wife who carefully turned the knob, and pulled the door toward her. The slipper caught, leaving the door opening too narrow for anyone to get through.

"The bakery's closed," Diana said. Stephen, Wil, and Faye looked over her shoulder to the pinched face beyond. So that's the famous Alli-O, Faye thought. She's a mess. The kids heard their father sniff, and understood immediately that Suzanna's mother was a smoker. Their dad hated the smell of cigarettes.

"Doesn't look anything like she does on TV, does she?" Wil whispered. Stephen turned around to glare at them.

"Diana," Allison squealed with all the fake delight she could muster. "It's been years. Teddy tells me you have my darling girl here. I'm sorry about that. I can't believe he pawned her off on you. Anyway," she clapped her hands, "I'm here and ready to take her home."

She pushed on the door but when it wouldn't move, Allison noticed Stephen, his arms crossed over his chest, standing foursquare behind his wife. She turned on her five-star smile but when it got nothing in response, she dropped the effort.

"Look, maybe you don't understand. I have come all this way to get my daughter—*my* daughter," Allison hissed. "Go get her and bring her to me. Now." She signaled Justin to come closer but before the boy could obey, a car skidded to a stop in the street right next to the black limo, and Charlie Cooper jumped out. As soon as she heard Charlie's voice, Faye's fingers darted over the keyboard of her phone: "Mother at our house. Charlie here. We come soon."

Allison made a sour face at Charlie. "Why, if it isn't the family solicitor. Come to do what? Keep me from taking what is rightfully mine?" She pushed on the Bennett's door again but Stephen's slipper, now joined by his shoulder, held.

"Suzanna!" Allison screamed through the narrow opening. "You come here this instant."

Charlie easily moved Justin to one side so he could stand next to Allison. The boy looked positively relieved.

"Get away from me," she growled. Charlie held up a piece of paper. She scanned it, and said: "That's nothing. Nothing at all." Then Charlie held up a second piece of paper, and suddenly Allison eyes were riveted to its surface. "What does this mean?"

Charlie smiled. "It means we need to have a private conversation, Allison." He nodded toward her idling black car. "In there will do." Then his smile broadened to include Justin. "You should be a part of this too, young man. It seems your mother is very worried about you."

The young man reacted as if Charlie had slapped his face, and turned without a sound.

As Allison and Justin moved toward the car, Charlie turned to Diana and Stephen. "Call Agnes," he said in a low voice. "She's coordinating the search for Suzanna with Ted."

Diana worked her husband's slipper loose as he looked up the stairs toward their children. "Were you helping your friend hide from her mother?" he asked. "Because if you did, that's a worthy goal and I'm proud of you."

"But..." Wil said.

Stephen smiled. "But she's lost on the Campground trails, and that can be very dangerous in the dark and snow. We've got to find her. If you know anything at all..."

"Can Mr. Cooper keep Suzanna here?" Faye interrupted.

"Judging by what I just saw, I think there's a very good chance he can do just that," Stephen said.

Faye sighed. It would have been far more exciting if she and Wil had had to sneak out of the house to bring food to Suzanna, and even more exciting if they had had to walk to Canada to free her. Faye had always wanted to sneak out of the house. All her favorite heroines did that at least once in every book.

"Faye? Where is Suzanna?" her father asked.

The girl sighed. "She's OK, just hungry."

"How do you know?" Diana asked.

"She texted me. She's hiding in Ted's cabin in the Campground." When she raised her head, Faye's tears tumbled over her cheeks. "Please don't make Suzanna go with her mother. You have no idea how horrible her life has been, and how much she wants to stay here." She sniffed, and Stephen opened his arms to hold his daughter. Then he looked up at his son.

"Go get our snowshoes and find all the flashlights you can. We'll have to hike into the Campgrounds to get her."

Suzanna rolled up one of the towels she'd found in the cabin's bathroom, placed it under her head, and then dragged a second one over her body. She rechecked the lighted dial on the gas heater to make sure she had it turned all the way up. Then she curled into the tightest ball possible. A shiver swept over her body.

The relief she felt when she managed to open the cabin door had been shortlived. Now the cold permeated her flesh, and her stomach protested its lack of food. The earliest Faye and Wil could reach her was probably tomorrow afternoon—if they got her message. She pulled Ted's cell phone out of her pocket again. Maybe the battery had a little juice left in it. But it was just as dead as it had been the last time she checked it. With a big sigh and another shiver, Suzanna drifted off to sleep, dreaming of Uncle Ted's pancakes.

Peter followed the state plow truck all the way back to the Carding exit, careful to stay out of range of its sand and salt spray. Behind him, a line of drivers, grateful for the chance to crawl behind the truck's flashing lights, stretched into the night. "The second safest place to be in a snowstorm is at the head of the line behind a plow truck," Andy Cooper always said. "The first safest place is home in bed."

As they neared his exit, Peter turned on his blinker to alert the drivers behind him about the coming change. Just as he did, some idiot in a gas guzzling, too-high-off-the-road four-wheel-drive SUV sped past everyone, including the plow. Snow and sand smeared across Peter's windshield, blinding him for a heart-stopping minute.

"Damn Joey," he muttered.

He held his breath as he eased his truck toward the slush-filled exit ramp. Just as he made his move, the speeding SUV's headlights cut crazily through the dark as it spun in the middle of the road. Then it slid in front of Peter, and his headlights illuminated a frightened man, one hand gripping his steering wheel, the other gripping a cell phone.

"Jerk," Peter muttered as he hit his flashers, and delicately tapped his brakes. He willed the Joey into the breakdown lane. Please don't hit anybody else, he begged. Please don't hit anybody else.

The SUV slammed into the guardrails just as Peter left the highway for the snowy ramp, and Route 37. He risked an upward glance as he passed under the highway, enough to ensure him that the SUV's driver was still conscious, and at least aware enough to turn his own emergency flashers on, a warning to others of the wages of stupidity.

Peter sighed, and looked in all his mirrors. No one else on the road as far as he could see. He stopped to fish his cell phone out of his jacket pocket to call 9-1-1 but it rang before he punched a button. He checked the caller ID. Agnes Findley. Why would she be calling him?

"Yeah."

"Peter? Allison Owens showed up, and Suzanna's run away." Agnes sounded out of breath. "Ted's frantic. We found out she's hiding in the Owens' cabin in the Campgrounds, and we need someone to plow a way in. It's sleeting here."

"Did you call…"

"Yes, I already called Harry but he cut me off. Says the town's called his plows in for backup because they can't keep up with the ice on the roads and he's one man short so he can't spare anyone. Stephen and Wil tried to snowshoe in but they turned back because the snow is so deep. Bruce said you might be headed back to town. Are you?"

"A man short? Are you sure that's what Harry said?"

"Yes, very sure. Wait a minute, I've got a call on the other phone." Peter heard her frantic voice in the background then she came back to him. "Are you on your way Peter? We can't leave her there all night."

"Yes, I am and we won't leave her there all night." He checked his rearview mirror again. "Call Ted. Tell him to wait for me at the end of his street. I should be there in about ten minutes. I'll get someone to plow a way into the Campgrounds, Harry Brown be damned."

Peter turned his heater up to high, checked his mirrors again, and rubbed the inside of his windshield with one hand while he punched Bruce's number into his phone with the other.

"Yeah?"

"Bruce, it's Peter. We've got a situation. I'm about ten minutes from town. Can you meet me at the beginning of Campground Road?"

"Campground Road? Really?"

"Yes, really. I'll explain when I get there," Peter said. "And please don't tell Harry."

"Don't worry."

"Ease off the gas. Ease off the gas," Peter chanted to himself as he followed the curves of Route 37 into Carding. He sensed Ted's anxiety inflaming the night. He couldn't lose Suzanna, he just couldn't. First his mother dying on the mountain, then his father's Parkinson's disease, and his sister dead to everyone but herself. Not fair, Peter thought. That really would not be fair.

As he skidded around the last corner into town, Peter sighed in relief when he saw lights in Edie Wolfe's house. That meant the power was still on. Suddenly, a figure jumped from the front porch carrying flashlights, and waved him down.

"Agnes called. We've been watching for you," Andy Cooper yelled. "Here are the keys to our cabin. Use whatever you need from it when you get there. Diana and Faye are here, Stephen and Wil are waiting with Paula and Sam the Younger up at the Campground Road. We're making food for everyone so come back here after you get Suzanna."

"I'm picking up Ted, and Bruce is going to plow us in." Peter took the keys, and zipped them in a pocket. "Any word on Allison?"

"No, nothing yet." Andy waved. "Good luck."

Peter nodded and eased out the clutch. His tires spun then grabbed. Raindrops spattered his windshield as he pulled away. "March slop," he muttered. "Bruce's favorite."

Ted hurled himself out of his truck as soon as he spotted Peter's oncoming headlights, his arms full of snowshoes. Without a word, he dropped the equipment in the back of Peter's pickup then joined his friend in the cab.

"Bruce is meeting us there," Peter said.

Ted nodded. "We'll have to walk ahead of him to spot the way. You won't be able to tell road from stone wall in his mess."

"Yeah, Stephen, Wil, Paula and Sam are there, too." Peter patted his pocket. "And I have the keys to the Coopers' cabin if we need anything."

Ted nodded again, his fists clenched in his lap. "Diana's kids...they had a plan to hide Suzanna." He swallowed, or tried to. "I should have done more, should have acted sooner. The poor kid. She must be so frightened. But Charlie said to wait until Allison showed up...said it would be easier to work on her in person...to get custody. But what kind of guardian am I? Look at this mess."

Peter cut down Stumpfield Road, passed the elementary school, and then turned toward the Campgrounds. "You are and will be the best family of any kind, anywhere, for your niece. You are what she needs," he said. "You know that as well as I do."

Then his headlights picked out the hulking shadow of an idling snow plow with a small crowd of people clustered around it, each carrying a flashlight. Without another word, Peter and Ted jumped down, grabbed snowshoes, and joined the group.

Bruce leaned from the window. "What's the plan, Peter? Harry's squawking like a rooster who just lost his favorite hen." They all heard the nasty snarl rising from the truck's radio. "Gideon's nowhere to be found, and Harry's threatening to nail his you-know-whats to the wall when he shows up. And this time, he just might do it."

"Look, no matter what happens, no matter what Harry says, you tell him that you were following my orders," Peter said. "Understood?"

Bruce considered for a moment, nodded, shut off his radio, and then pointed at Wil. "And you don't write about any of this in that bloggy thing of yours. Got it?"

The shock of Bruce's words made Wil turned whiter than the falling snow. He turned toward his father, a mute protest pasted on his face but Stephen only grinned. "Worst kept secret in Carding, son. 'Little Crow?' Not hard to figure out."

The boy's face flipped from white to red. Paula was sure Wil would have welcomed a big hole under his feet, and opened her mouth to say so when Sam the Younger slapped the boy on the shoulder. "Don't worry about it. We all read it. Good stuff."

"But there's a time and a place for everything," Stephen said. "Until we know for sure that Suzanna's safe and staying with Ted, nothing about this in the *Chronicle*, understood?"

Wil nodded, and the flames in his cheeks died back a little. They read it, he told himself. They actually read it.

"Right. Now there's stone walls on both sides of the entrance and for quite a ways down the road. There's no way Bruce can see them under all the snow so we have to guide him," Peter said. The rain changed back to snow as he spoke. "I think if we pair up—Ted and Paula, Stephen and I, Sam in the middle with flashlights—we can mark a trail for him to follow."

"What about me?" Wil had never felt so young.

Peter dangled his truck keys in the boy's face. "I want you to drive my truck behind Bruce's. I know you don't have your license but I do know you can drive. I don't want to have to walk out with that little girl. I want to be able to put her inside a warm truck and drive her out of here. Just take it real easy, OK?"

Wil's face lit up. "Yeah, totally."

Every time he retold the story of that night, Bruce Elliot called it "the slowest plowing job ever." The walkers had to plod through a Vermont winter's worth of accumulated snow and ice, stopping now and again to push their ski poles into the frozen precipitation to make sure they stayed just inside the stone walls that marked the Campground Road. Sometimes the surface of the densely packed snow held them up. But in the next second, they'd break through, sinking in white stuff past their knees. Just ten minutes into their ordeal, and they had to strip off their scarves and unzip their jackets in an effort to cool off. Every twenty feet or so, they switched places to spell the trail breaker.

Bruce downshifted into his lowest gear, steering carefully between the paths made by the snowshoers. Wil waited until the plow was several lengths in front of him before he moved Peter's pickup, carefully pressing on the gas pedal just enough to keep inching forward.

As they got closer to the cabins, Ted strained ahead of Paula, refusing to switch places with her. Finally, she grabbed his shoulders to make him stop. "It's you Suzanna will want when we get there," she argued over Ted's protests. "You've got to save some of your energy for her."

"OK, OK," he agreed. Which is why Paula was in the lead when they reached the crest of the last hill before the land dropped away to the cabins and Half Moon Lake. She stopped, momentarily fascinated by the blaze of lights streaming from the Cooper family cabin.

"I thought the kids said Suzanna was holed up in Ted's cabin," she said. "What's this?"

Under other circumstances, Gideon would have admired the quality of the new tile floor in the Coopers' kitchen. He had an eye for that sort of thing. But waking up cold and stiff on squares of terra cotta did not leave room for any sort of polite consideration. He heard someone groan, and then realized the sound came from him. My gawd, he thought as memories of recent events flooded back, that woman is an amazing athlete.

"Oh Giddy," a female voice cooed. "I have the sauna all hot and bothered. Care to join me? The steam will do you good." Lisa stood in the doorway, sheathed in a pale blue robe. "Come on. It'll be fun."

Gideon had his doubts. Saunas made him lazy and sleepy.

"Come on, Giddy." Lisa's voice took on a note of urgency because she knew if she didn't get him into the sauna, it would ruin her plans for the cowgirl outfit. She reached out a hand, letting the front of her robe part to reveal one of her legs all the way to the top.

He grinned as he rose to his feet in order to hide his grimace, hoping that his back wouldn't go out on him for real this time. His head foggy with champagne, he let Lisa lead him on.

The atmosphere of the sauna was indeed hot, bothered, and very steamy. Gideon sank gratefully onto the nearest bench, maneuvering himself until he felt some support for his back muscles. Then he sighed quietly, hoping the moist heat would ease any oncoming pain before he had to move again.

Lisa reclined on a a bench opposite his so that Gideon could appreciate her peaks and valleys without effort. Now he understood why Peter had married her. In Gideon's opinion, most men married in a sexual fog, and Lisa was obviously good at generating that.

So what did that say about his marriage to Chloe, whose approach to sensual matters was so different from her sister's? As Gideon closed his eyes, his wife's delicate features swam into focus. Not now, he told himself. This is hardly the time to think about her.

And yet he felt dimly aware of the hurt he'd inflicted on Chloe. He'd loved her, truly loved her, on their wedding day. Loved her still, he suddenly realized. Then, just as his eyes began to sting, Lisa spoke:

"Whew, I am thoroughly baked. Let's go play in the snow."

"Yeah." Gideon cleared his throat. "I'm ready too."

A pile of rubber boots lay in a jumble on the dressing room floor. As he fished about for a pair that fit his feet, Gideon didn't notice Lisa slip behind a dressing screen until he heard a loud "Yahoo!"

Gideon spun around just in time to get hit in the chest by a jet of cold water from one of the squirt guns in his playmate's hands.

"Yow!"

"Ha ha, gotcha." Lisa holstered her weapons, put her hands on her hips, and lifted her chest, watching closely for Gideon's reaction to her white-fringed bustier with its matching hat, and pink clip-on neckerchief. Why look at that, she thought, he's stunned. I'm as good as any of those models in the Cherries Jubilee catalog. I knew it.

But Gideon's only thought was: How can something with so little fabric cost so much money?

Lisa laughed, and opened the door to the night beyond. "Come on, Giddy-up, let's go play in the snow."

Ah, what the hell, Gideon thought. Might as well be in for a dollar as a dime. "No fair," he said. "I don't have a gun."

Lisa giggled, and pointed to a box on the floor. "Honey, I got you a pair just like mine. Clap them on, and let's go."

At first, Gideon felt foolish running around in the snow, his steaming body clad in nothing but a pair of rubber boots while carrying a pair of water pistols. But Lisa's excited squealing, and the way her body peeked in and out of her costume ignited his playful lustiness. The two of them romped behind the Cooper cabin, laughing and sliding, ambushing one another from behind trees.

He was so focused on Lisa's new game, Gideon's mind failed to register the falling flakes. "I'm gonna get you," he yelled, twirling his guns in the air. She whooped and raced to the cabin's front yard, her Giddy-up in hot pursuit.

Suddenly, Lisa's left foot skidded out from under her. With a loud "Oof," she leaned forward to catch herself while lifting her shapely backside to the night sky. And at that very moment, Bruce Elliot's headlights lit up the Campgrounds.

For a single frozen moment, the walkers, the truck drivers, and the gunslingers stopped. Then Bruce raised his cell phone, hit speed dial for home, and said to his wife: "Honey, you won't believe what I'm seeing through the windshield of this truck."

"What?" Cate asked. She was used to getting progress reports when Bruce plowed but this time, an urgent note in her husband's voice made her wifely antennae rise up.

"Well, let's just say that it gives the song 'Moonlight Over Vermont' a whole new meaning," he said. And then Bruce started to laugh.

So that's what was in that Cherries Jubilee box, Peter thought as he looked at his wife. At that same moment, he spotted a movement to his right, and turned his head just in time to see a retreating male backside hightailing it through the trees. That's when Stephen heard him say, "Well, well, well. Thank you Gideon Brown."

SIXTEEN

CONSTRUCTION-GRADE
TRASH BAGS

"Suzanna! What have you done with Suzanna?" Ted's voice boomed across the frozen landscape.

"What are you talking about, and what are you doing here?" Lisa gave up trying to protect her cowgirl outfit, plopped down in the snow, and then immediately snapped back up when she realized that the residual heat stored by her body from the sauna was long gone. She raised a hand to block the glare of the headlights. "Who's Suzanna?"

"Lisa, have you seen a little girl?" Peter asked. Later, when she retold the story of that night, Paula often remarked on how calm his voice was then. In fact, she found it remarkable that Peter never asked his wife how she came to be romping in a skimpy cowgirl outfit in the snow.

"Little girl?" Lisa's body shuddered. "There's no little girl out here. Just me and…and…" She looked over her shoulder, and shut her mouth when she saw no one there. She sensed that keeping Gideon's identity to herself might have its advantages.

"Suzanna!" Ted bellowed. He turned toward the Owens' family cabin, and his friends followed. Bruce kept his headlights on Lisa, talking to his wife as fast as he could.

"Did you say water pistols?" Cate asked. "And she's wearing a cowgirl outfit cut up to here and down to there?"

"With fringe in all the important places," Bruce said.

Cate whooped. "Oh my gawd! Can you take a picture of it with your phone? I gotta see this."

At first, Lisa didn't move, stunned when Peter turned his back on her. How dare he? But then she figured she could tell Peter off just as well when she got warm again so she walked off toward the cabin as Bruce snapped a photo with his phone, and described her every jiggle to his giggling wife.

"Suzanna!" Ted called again when he reached the cabin door. He fumbled with his keys, tore his gloves off, and then dropped them in the snow. Paula scooped them up.

"Get your snowshoes off," she told him.

Just then, the cabin door swung open a crack, and little voice drifted out of the opening. "Uncle Ted?"

"Yes, yes, it's me."

The door swung open all the way, and the little girl threw herself at him, gripping him about the neck so tightly Ted couldn't breathe for a moment.

"I want to stay with you," Suzanna said. "I hate my mother. I hate her. Please don't make me go with her." Then all of the tears and sobs she'd been storing up for weeks tumbled out. Ted hugged her close, patting her hair. "There there," he murmured. "There there."

Paula stooped down. "Charlie Cooper has talked to your mother, Suzanna," she said. "I think everything's going to turn out just the way you hope."

"But you don't know my mother," Suzanna wailed. "She always gets her way. Always!"

"Oh, I beg to differ." Paula laid a hand on the girl's shoulder. "Everyone standing here does know your mother, and we are all quite determined that you stay in Carding where you belong."

Suzanna looked up, and Paula felt the girl's eyes pin her to the night sky. "Where I belong?" she asked. "Really?"

"Yes, really." Paula used the special firm tone she normally reserved for members of the selectboard when she needed them to make a decision. "It's perfectly obvious to all of us that you belong here with your Uncle Ted, and he belongs with you."

Tears spilled down the girl's cheeks again but they were the waters of relief, not fear. After a deep breath, the little girl turned to her uncle. "I'm hungry. Can we have pancakes now?"

At that, the five walkers laughed softly. Then Wil appeared on the edge of the crowd, holding a blanket he'd found behind the seat of Peter's truck. He looked a bit sheepish, Stephen was glad to note. Suzanna noticed too.

"Promise me you won't be mad at Wil and Faye," she said. "They were just trying to help."

"Promise me you won't run and hide like this again," Ted said. "You cannot imagine how scared I've been."

Suzanna buried her face in his shoulder so only he heard her muffled "I won't. I promise."

As the group moved toward the waiting trucks, Peter broke away to have a private word with Bruce. "That was who I thought it was, am I right?" he asked.

Bruce drew a breath. "I didn't see the face, just the back...side," he said. Under other circumstances, he would have been rolling on his truck's seat, laughing until he lost breath. But his respect for Peter squelched the impulse. Then there was the matter of Gideon's treachery.

"It was Gideon, wasn't it?" Peter asked.

Bruce sighed then nodded. "We played football together when we were in high school," he said, "and I saw plenty of that backside in the locker room. I'm sure that's who it was."

All the muscles in Peter's face compressed as he struggled to sort out his feelings—anger, relief, a touch of sadness. But most of all, he was embarrassed to have the sham of his marriage exposed, literally, in such a public way. What would Chloe think when she heard? He looked at Bruce. "This puts a whole different spin on the ancient road vote, am I right?"

The two of them looked at one another until understanding gelled on both sides. "It does indeed," Bruce said. Then he nodded at the approaching group. "Who do you want to ride back with you?"

Peter considered. "Wil, Sam, and Stephen," he said. "We're all meeting at Edie's. I'll call to let her know we're on our way."

When Wil handed the pickup keys back to Peter, he said: "Dad and I will ride in the back. It's not far now that the road's plowed." He couldn't bring himself to look at the older man. Seeing Lisa Foster all but naked in the snow was interesting but confusing at the same time, and he needed a private word with his father.

"You're sure?" Peter asked, looking at the boy-man twisted up in his awkwardness. Wil nodded.

Though he'd never say it out loud, Peter felt relieved to have Sam's company all to himself on the short ride back. About halfway down Campground Road, Sam cleared his throat. "So, are you going to sell the house?" he asked.

The question made Peter laugh because he'd been thinking about that very thing. "I don't think so, not right now," he said, shaking his head. "With this economy, it's not a great time to be selling a house."

Sam nodded. "Yeah, that's what I thought. You can stay at my house until you figure it out."

Back in the Cooper family cabin, Lisa watched in amazement as everyone piled into the two trucks, and drove away. Wasn't anybody going to check on her or give her a lift back to her car? As the truck headlights faded, she stomped her foot in frustration. Here she shows Gideon a good time, and she's the one stuck cleaning up the cabin. It was so not fair.

She stooped to pick a wet towel off the floor. This is the last time I'm showing that man a good time, she promised herself. He's so ungrateful.

"What? What? Who's there?" Chloe sprang from the recliner where she'd been dozing, scattering popcorn, and clutching her quilt. On the TV, a black-and-white Lauren Bacall put the moves on Humphrey Bogart.

"Who's there?" Chloe called again.

"It's me, Gideon. Please let me in. I lost my house keys."

Chloe shook the sleep out of her head, trying to clear it. This was the moment. This was the time to get Gideon to sign the divorce papers.

She shuffled into the kitchen, peered through the back door's window to make sure he was alone, and then let him in. Snowflakes decorated the curls of his hair, and Chloe realized she would have found that very appealing once. Now she stood taut as a bowstring, wondering how to ask this man to sign divorce papers.

Gideon assumed, since Chloe didn't yell at him right away, that news of his latest transgression had not reached her ears yet. She was tousled with that sleepy-little-girl look that had always moved his heart. He thought about the tsunami of consequences headed his way, and sighed. Better make this quick, he told himself.

"Thanks, Chloe." He rubbed his cold hands together. "Sorry to wake you." Then, with a shock, he realized how bare and colorless the room was. He looked closely at his wife, standing barefoot but fully clothed, wrapped in an old quilt, and he knew.

"You're moving out," he said.

She nodded. "I'm pretty much gone, actually. I was just waiting to talk to you."

Drops of melted snow slid down Gideon's face. "It's OK. I understand."

Chloe straightened her shoulders. Time to be a big girl, she told herself. "I want a divorce, Gideon. I have some paperwork for you to sign, if you're agreeable." She indicated a sheaf of papers lying on the kitchen counter. "If you agree, we don't have to go to court. I'm not asking you for anything. This house was yours before we got married, and there's no reason for that to change, as far as I'm concerned. And…"

Gideon raised a hand to stop her. "Did your father draw those up?"

"Yes, yes he did."

Gideon nodded. "Have you got a pen?"

"Yes." Chloe opened the small drawer where the two of them used to stow paper and writing implements. "You should read them," she urged. "I'll wait in the living room while you do."

"No need." Gideon flipped through the pages, looking for the places that required his signature. He needed to get out of Carding as quick as he could. "You've always been more fair than I've deserved. And I've trusted you even when you couldn't feel the other way around."

Is this it, Chloe asked herself while she watched him scrawl his name. Years of courtship, love, marriage—gone in a few pen strokes? "There's a second copy of everything there…for your records."

Gideon twisted the pen between his fingers. "You know, I loved you the day we got married," he said.

Chloe hesitated. She wasn't sure she wanted to have this conversation. But the opening proved irresistible. "What about after that?"

Gideon's body jerked. "Every day after that," he said, "including today. It's just that…it's just that I don't…I can't…" He stopped. What, exactly, was he trying to say? "My mother claims that I've looked up to my father all my life, and that's why I…"

He stopped again, took in a lot of air, and then looked his wife square in the face. "I was blind and stupid and I thought I could do what my father did, and get away with it. So I never bothered to think for myself." He pulled a trembling hand across his forehead. Chloe did not move.

"What I'm trying to say is that I loved you then, and I love you now. But I'm not very good at love, I guess." He shifted from one foot to the other. His urgent need to get away became more urgent with every passing second. But he wanted so much for this woman to understand. He leaned forward to kiss her softly on the cheek.

"Believe it or not, I am sorry," he said. Then he walked to the basement door, opened it, turned on the stairway light, and walked out of Chloe's life.

She stood still for a long time, her hand resting on the place his lips had touched, wondering how much of what he said was true. It was only afterwards, when she heard the whole story about the search for Suzanna, and the finding of her sister Lisa, that Chloe realized the only thing Gideon had on the last time they talked were the coveralls he kept in his truck in case it rained and a pair of rubber boots.

Peter didn't stay at Edie's. As soon as he dropped off his passengers, he turned toward home. With a box of construction-grade trash bags in hand, he emptied Lisa's closet, bureau, and bathroom, dumping clothes, cosmetics, and assorted doo-dads all together. The full bags piled up in the garage next to the pieces of her unused exercise equipment until the mess filled up the space where his wife—his soon-to-be-ex-wife—customarily parked her car.

Satisfied with his handiwork, Peter ran to the basement for his cordless drill, a handful of long screws, a padlock, and a hasp. Within minutes, his windows were all locked, his front door screwed shut, and the padlock in place on the door leading from the garage into the house.

As he backed out of his driveway to head toward Sam's house, he anticipated the peace of his friend's silent companionship.

Gideon dressed and was back out of his house in record time. The snow faded as he crossed the border from Vermont to New Hampshire, heading south to Manchester airport. His cell phone rang incessantly until he finally located it in the dark and turned it off. He and his father didn't have anything to say to one another any more.

By the time he reached the airport, a weak morning sun struggled to make its presence known. Weary beyond weary, Gideon parked his truck in the long term lot then boarded a shuttle bus headed for the terminal. But then a Holiday Inn sign made him change his mind.

"I'll stop here," he told the driver. Sleep and a shower, that's what I need.

The young woman behind the hotel's counter looked perkier than anyone should so early in the morning. She welcomed Gideon with a practiced smile, an expression that stayed on her face until she ran his credit card.

"I'm sorry, sir," she chirped. "But this card appears to be maxed out. You've reached your credit limit."

"What?" Gideon was wide awake now. "That can't be."

"I'm sorry, sir," the young woman said. Then she turned to assist a tan family with two tired kids on their way home from Disney World, turning a deaf ear to Gideon's protests. She'd heard it all before.

Stunned, Gideon walked to the far end of the lobby, and turned on his cell phone to call his mother. A dancing envelope announced the presence of a text message. "Hey Giddy-up," it read. "Still had your credit card number. Need to visit mother so got cash advance. Know u will understand. Luv L."

Harry finally gave up trying to raise Gideon when the sun rose. Exhausted—a man his age shouldn't work all night—he tumbled into his favorite recliner as soon as he got home, so he was probably the last person in Carding to hear the story about his son and Lisa Foster.

Everyone in town assumed Louisa would break the news to her husband as soon as he got home from plowing. But as she said to her two youngest sons: "Do I look that stupid?" Noah and Jacob agreed she wasn't, and even recommended she leave for Florida before their Dad woke up. In fact, they were packing their stuff in Jacob's van to leave for Manchester airport right now. Wouldn't she like to join them?

Louisa thought about it long and hard. But somehow, she didn't feel right about abandoning Harry to face Carding all alone. Yeah, he was wrong about the ancient roads thing. She knew as well as everyone else that that foolish fixation had more to do with his ancient hatred of all things Edie Wolfe than it did any road. And yes, she knew all about his affairs, and his regrettable influence on his sons. But as she laid a blanket over him, she didn't feel right about letting Harry clean up Gideon's mess all alone. He was her son too, after all.

Of all the people feasting on the particulars of Lisa Foster's escapades in the snow, only Louisa listened to Gideon's side of the story. He managed to reach her as she drove to church on Sunday morning, spilling words of loss, bewilderment, anger and pain into her ears. No one came up to her as she sat in her favorite pew at Our Lady of the Assumption Church. She briefly considered talking to her priest but what did a celibate man know about the heartbreak of children and the stupidity of obstinate husbands?

So it was with great relief that Louisa saw Edie Wolfe standing by her Cadillac when the service ended. The two women sat in silence in

Louisa's car for a long time before her tears started to flow. Edie handed her tissues as needed.

Harry didn't wake up until mid-afternoon that Sunday. He found Louisa in the kitchen, cooking in a strange silence.

"What's wrong?" he asked. "Someone die?"

Louisa looked up, read the mood on his face, and said: "No, nobody's dead. Just a quiet day after all that snow. Twenty-four inches in some places, I hear."

Harry nodded. All his muscles ached. "I'm taking a shower."

"Feel like watching a movie while we eat?" she asked.

"I thought you didn't like the TV on during dinner cuz we're supposed to talk," he grumped.

"But I know you're tired," she said, sprinkling lemon juice on two swordfish steaks with more than her normal degree of care.

"Hmph, I'm always tired nowadays." Harry started to stump off, and the tension eased in Louisa's shoulders. But then he turned back. "Have you heard from Gideon?"

Louisa heard the latent growl in his voice, and decided to get it over with sooner rather than later. "I talked to him this morning, on my way to church," she said.

"He didn't happen to explain why he abandoned me, did he?" Harry sighed and rubbed his face. "Probably some new girl he's sniffing around. You can't trust that boy around women. But he has no right to leave me hanging like that in an ice storm. So where was he?"

As Louisa turned around to face her husband, she envied Edie Wolfe, envied Chloe. Why had she stayed all these years? New cars? Luxury vacations to places she didn't care about but could brag about? Life in the biggest house in Carding? She made fists of her hands, placed them on the island counter between them, and leaned forward.

"Gideon was doing a lot more than sniffing last night—with Lisa Foster," she began. "The two of them were caught up at the Campgrounds together, playing in the snow in front of Andy and Charlie Cooper's place."

Harry stared at her. "Lisa Foster? Peter's wife?"

Louisa nodded. "And Chloe's sister."

Harry stared some more. "In the Campgrounds? But how did they get caught up there? Those roads are closed."

"Ted Owens' niece ran away because her mother showed up. She ran to Ted's cabin. Peter got Bruce to plow the Campground Road so they could rescue the little girl, and they saw…" Louisa swallowed. "Lisa was parading around with hardly anything on in front of the Coopers' cabin with our son, and he was wearing nothing but a pair of boots. She stayed. He ran."

Harry shook his head, and braced himself in the doorway, muttering. Gideon? And Peter's wife? He shook his head again, like a dog stuck by a porcupine. Try as he might, he couldn't dredge up any memory of Lisa Foster's face. But then, he seldom remembered any woman from the neck up. He tried to think if he'd ever known anyone as stupid as his eldest son. But he failed in that too. So he grabbed at the only thing that made sense to him.

"Bruce shouldn't have used that plow for that job. Could have broken it." And with that astonishingly obtuse statement, Harry Brown turned away to take a very long shower, after which he went straight to bed. Louisa ate her swordfish alone.

And enjoyed every mouthful.

As Sam the Younger told the other guys gathered in the Brown & Sons parking lot on Monday morning, "Peter may come in or he may not. Barely said a word all Sunday."

"Fit right in with you, did he?" Bruce said.

The little group edged about nervously as they talked and slurped coffee, watching for Harry's truck but hoping for Peter's. What they got was Louisa Brown's Cadillac.

The woman who rose out of the driver's seat was smaller than the guys remembered. She gave them a shaky smile then carefully picked her way across the icy asphalt.

"Poor woman," Sam murmured, and at that signal, the men moved to meet her halfway. A keening wind, busy clearing out the last remnants of the storm made them all shiver.

Louisa wore no makeup, leaving the papery folds of her skin pale against her fur hat. She knew she had to speak first because the men had no idea why she was there. But she hadn't settled on an opening line.

She glanced quickly from face to face. "Peter's not here," she said flatly. They shook their heads. "Any idea if he's coming in?"

Before anyone could answer, Peter's dark green pickup rolled into the lot. He stopped next to Bruce's truck then marched toward the group. "What are you doing here," he said, looking straight at Louisa. She raised an eyebrow at his take-no-prisoners tone. Surely he couldn't blame her for this situation? Then Peter turned his face toward the crew. "Sorry I'm late. I went to check on my house, to make sure no one broke in. Lisa took her bags of clothes and face paint and left me a note." He pinched his mouth into a thin line. "Pretty good trade, I'd say."

Then he fixed his eyes on Louisa again. "Where's your husband? Hiding your no-good son?"

Louisa stepped back. "It's not my fault."

"Maybe not." The rage boiling inside Peter shocked him. "But you're hiding them, doing their dirty work. They're cowards, both of them, and Harry is nothing more than a bully, threatening folks' jobs so he can turn that land behind the academy into a playground for Joeys. Tell him for me that I quit."

When he turned, the wind grabbed Lisa's note from his hand but Peter made no move to retrieve it. He just wished he could erase his wife's last words from his memory: "Darling, why are the doors locked? Guess you must be angry. I'm off to mother's. Please send me money there. Not sure how long I'll stay. Don't sell the exercise stuff. I'll need it. L."

SEVENTEEN

PREVAILING WINDS

Early in the morning on the first Tuesday in March, the prevailing wind shifted to the south. It wouldn't last, everyone in town understood that. But it was taken as a good omen that spring planned on returning to Vermont's hills once again.

Harry Brown heard the change in the wind as he lay in his bed, wide awake, next to Louisa. The temperature would rise with the sun, he knew, and the ritual melting of winter would begin. He imagined all the pairs of muddy boots stomping into town hall to perform that other ritual heralding spring in Vermont—town meeting.

The night before, Harry told Louisa he wasn't sure he'd attend town meeting this year. He didn't need to say it, but she knew he'd heard more of the details about Gideon and Lisa's great adventure, and he felt embarrassed about facing anyone he knew.

He and Louisa had not talked much since Sunday morning. When Charlie Cooper called to ask for Gideon's mailing address so he could send him copies of the signed divorce papers, Harry said nothing until he remembered that Charlie was father to both Chloe and Lisa. "Sorry about all this mess," he muttered. "I used to think the hard part about raising kids was when they were little, and you were afraid they'd drown or fall or something. Now I think it's harder when they grow up."

"Yeah, sometimes that's true," Charlie agreed.

After some more silence, Harry asked: "What happened to Allison Owens and her kid?"

"Hmph, wouldn't do her image much good if she got arrested for endangering a minor now, would it?" Charlie said. "The boy who drove her up here was only seventeen, a runaway she picked up in Reno. He flew back home yesterday to finish high school, and Allison drove herself out of Carding this morning after she signed over permanent custody of her daughter to Ted."

"Good riddance, I guess," Harry said.

"Yeah, I agree with you there, Harry," Charlie said. "Good riddance to bad rubbish."

Louisa rolled over in her sleep, murmuring what sounded like an incantation, and Harry took advantage of the moment to ease himself out of bed. He looked down at his wife before he left the room. Good old Louisa. He'd have to buy her something really special this time.

By nine o'clock, the season's first zephyrs had melted the top surface on every icy spot in town, making the walking slicker than slick. Everyone, even the youngest kids, had to shuffle to stay upright. Chloe decided against attending town meeting at the last minute. She told Edie she still had a lot of packing to do before boarding her plane to France. But the older woman knew better.

Chloe had finally talked to Lisa on Monday night—at their mother's insistence. Afterward, she could only shake her head over Lisa's excited chatter about California and the warm weather and "all the awesome people Mom knows."

"Not one word of sorry, not one word of regret," she told Edie over breakfast. "It was like nothing ever happened. How can anyone be that dense? Do you know she had the nerve to ask me to contact Peter and tell him not to sell her exercise equipment?"

At that, Edie's mouth popped open. "She asked you to get in touch with Peter?"

"Yes. Since he wouldn't answer her phone calls or text messages, could I contact him for her." Chloe shook her head. "What planet do you suppose she lives on?"

"Planet Lisa, I imagine."

As soon as Edie left for town meeting, Chloe grabbed her keys. The box of frilly underwear was still in the back of her van, and now was the time to get it to the dump. "Hey Nearly, want to go for a ride?" she asked. The dog immediately made himself comfortable in the passenger seat, and the two companions took off under a cloudless sky that grew brighter by the minute.

Chloe felt vaguely separated from her body as she drove along, as if she'd imbibed way too much caffeine. As they rounded the flank of Mount Merino, she counted all the major events that had happened since Friday. One, finding out her husband was cheating on her with her sister. Two, Gideon signing their divorce papers. Three, moving into Edie's place. And four, buying a ticket to Paris on a plane that was leaving tomorrow.

"How can I feel so numb and excited at the same time?" she asked the dog. Nearly fluttered his short tail.

Once at the landfill, Chloe backed her van up to a dumpster, and let the box of skimpy bras and ruffled panties tumble to its bottom. She was just about to pull out when a familiar truck pulled in beside her. She waited until Peter's head emerged then she called over, "I owe you an apology. I shouldn't have popped off on you that day you showed up at Edie's to tell her about Harry's ancient road scheme."

Peter started. He'd been so fixated on dumping Lisa's junk, he'd never noticed Chloe's van. He stared at her. He had no idea what to say.

Chloe cleared her throat. Should she say anything more? And if so, what was appropriate under these bizarre circumstances?

Then Nearly, catching a familiar scent, whined a hello.

"Hey there, Nearly." Peter stepped over to the van to pat the dog's head and looked at Chloe. "I'm not sure what to say to you."

"Yeah, kinda weird, isn't it?" She got out of the van. "So what do you think—will Harry's scheme pass?"

Peter frowned. "Hard to say. I think a lot of air's gone out of it. But folks still need jobs, and Harry maintains he's a job creator."

The two of them laughed. "What a stupid term that is, 'job creator,'" Chloe said. Then she noticed Peter's cargo—exercise equipment. "I talked to my sister last night. Mom made me do it. Lisa wanted me to call you and say not to sell this stuff. Says she'll need it."

Peter grinned as he let down his truck's tailgate. "But I'm not selling it." He pointed to the landfill's scrap metal pile. "I'm recycling it."

They stared at one another for a long moment, and then shared a slow smile. "Need any help unloading?" Chloe asked.

"I could use a hand, sure."

No matter how he felt on a personal level about issues in town, when Andy Cooper stood up to moderate a town meeting in Carding, he buried his own opinions so deep not even Edie could tell what they were. He kept a careful eye on the growing crowd as he stood at the front of the high school's auditorium chatting about the meeting's agenda with

Paula Bouton. The anti-Harry Brown crowd arrived first—Edie, Diana, and Stephen leading the way. Charlie Cooper and Agnes arrived next, Ted Owens right behind them. Wil sat on the edge of the stage, balancing his laptop on his knees, ready to blast bulletins into digital space. He never did write about that night in the Campgrounds when they rescued Suzanna. He didn't need to because it's all anyone talked about, and in Carding, gossip was faster than blogging.

As the clock ticked off the minutes to the ten o'clock start, Andy whispered to Paula, "Have you seen Harry?"

"No," she whispered back. "I can't believe he'd miss this no matter what happened."

At that very moment, Harry Brown was sitting in the passenger seat of his wife's Caddy in the municipal parking lot, watching for Peter Foster. A rugged silence had settled between Harry and Louisa ever since she'd let him know over breakfast exactly what she thought about his scheme to get rid of the Carding Academy of Traditional Arts.

"It's all about Edie," she said. "It's always all about Edie. You live more in the past than anyone I've ever known. I won't raise my hand in public to vote against you. But if someone asks for a paper ballot on the ancient roads thing, don't count on my vote. And I'll bet I can say the same for a lot of the folks in town that you've been bullying."

So Harry sulked in the Caddy's soft seat, his eyes riveted on the men gathered around a pickup across the parking lot, men whose livelihoods depended on Brown & Sons, hoping they'd remain true. In such a small town, it didn't take many votes to sway yea to nay. Bruce Elliot and his wife Cate arrived last. Once they got out of their pickup, the group started walking toward the school.

"Come on," Harry growled to Louisa. "Let's go."

Some of Harry's usual cockiness returned as he cut through the crowd. He shook hands, greeted people he usually ignored, and glared at Edie for good measure. She smiled back and wagged her fingers at him. Then the clock struck ten, and Andy stepped to the podium.

Most articles on the warrant passed with little discussion. People asked questions, raised a point here and there. But it seemed to Andy that the whole crowd perched on the edges of their seats, straining to get to Article Nine.

They finally arrived, and a murmur rose in the hall. Andy read the article aloud, as he was required to do. "'To see if the town will abandon the portion of Academy Road under the former Joseph Stillman Croft house as drawn on the town map of 1810. Is there any discussion?"

People stirred, and a couple of folks started to rise from their seats when a single, loud voice boomed from the back of the hall. "I move that we vote yes on Article Nine, and legally abandon that section of Academy Road," Peter Foster said. "That road should be officially discontinued by the town."

Everyone started talking at once. Edie managed to look across the room, and catch a glimpse of Harry's stony, red face. She was only vaguely aware that Chloe sat down in the last seat in the row. Andy banged his gavel repeatedly on the podium, trying to restore order. Wil's fingers flew over his keyboard. Diana and Stephen looked at one another and grinned.

Then another loud voice cut through the hall. "I call the question," Bruce said.

"I call for a paper ballot," his wife Cate said.

"I second that," Louisa shouted, and looked triumphantly at Harry.

"All those in favor of casting a paper ballot on Article Nine, please signify by saying 'aye,'" Andy said. The vote for the paper ballot was deafening.

"All those opposed?" A few voices twittered in protest. Harry sat silent and unmoved.

"Will the board of civil authority please get ballots ready for voting," Andy called.

Thirty-seven minutes later, when all 343 ballots had been cast and counted, the final tally was 237 for abandoning the ancient part of Academy Road, 106 against.

"That's it," Andy banged on his gavel. "Article Nine passes, and the section of Academy Road under the former Joseph Stillman Croft house is legally abandoned by the town of Carding."

Edie smiled as several hands reached over the seats to pat her shoulders. Chloe put her face in her hands, uncertain whether to laugh or cry. Harry and Louisa Brown quietly slid out of their seats, and left for the seclusion of their Cadillac. Once home, Louisa dropped Harry at their front door, turned on her CD player, and headed south to the airport to join their sons.

"What am I going to do while you're gone?" Harry asked before she drove away.

"I have no idea, Harry. I have no idea at all."

New post on Carding Chronicle blog: March 5

Road Under the Academy Discontinued—The School Stays Here
by Little Crow

Well, it's now official. That little chunk of Academy Road that's under the old Croft house has been discontinued by the town which means the Carding Academy of Traditional Arts can stay right where it is.

"I am so pleased," Edie Wolfe said after moderator Andy Cooper announced the voting tally of 237 to 106. "I know some people will be disappointed but I hope that all the hard feelings can be forgotten."

Harry Brown, who wanted the town to keep that part of Academy Road public, left as soon as the vote was announced without talking to anyone so we don't know how he feels.

Here's a little poem that Sam the Younger wrote after town meeting. He says I can share it with you.

The Road Unsalted
by Samuel Willis (who hopes that Robert Frost will understand)

We shall long tell the tale of this do-or-die vote,

And the people who showed such good sense.

We had a road that was questioned in Carding town,

And we chose to keep it unsalted.

For us, that has made all the difference.
Little Crow | March 5 | Categories: Local Government

"*Fifteen two, fifteen four, fifteen six,* and a double-double run for twenty-four points." Andy moved his cribbage peg forward on the board with an exaggerated air of triumph.

Edie laid down her cards. "You're killing me," she said, looking at the paltry number of points in her hand. "I think it's time for a glass of wine." Someone knocked on the back door. "I'll bet that's Ruth. She's probably got that bus tour settled at the inn."

"I hope she brought some of that chocolate cake of hers." Andy rubbed his hands together.

Edie raised an eyebrow in his direction. "I thought you were supposed to be on a diet," she said. "Something about doctor's orders?"

Andy grinned. "Just an ugly rumor, that is."

Ruth did indeed have cake, a dark unfrosted variety made from a recipe she'd found in a World War II era cookbook of her mother's.

"No frosting," Andy said, poking his piece with an exploratory fork.

"Oh go on, try it," Edie said. Andy did, letting the sweet taste dissolve over his tongue. Then he grinned.

"Not bad. And since there's no frosting, I can have two pieces."

Ruth settled down with her own plate and glass. "Well, you'll never guess what I heard."

Andy and Edie looked expectant.

"Allison Owens' new line of clothes was yanked from the stores. Something about shoddy construction." Ruth sipped her wine. "She texted Ted that she won't be able to get to Vermont for her Easter visit."

"Well, Suzanna and Ted will be celebrating extra over that news," Andy said. "Judging by the faces they've been carrying around the last few days, they weren't looking forward to an Alli-O visit."

Ruth looked at Edie. "The ladies on the bus were disappointed that Chloe wasn't on the teachers' roster. But I assured them that they'd have just as much fun with Nancy Graham."

"Did you show them samples of what they're going to learn?" Edie asked.

"Oh yes, that's what persuaded them that it was a good swap—dyeing, painting and stamping. They'll be happy," Ruth said. "Speaking of Chloe—any idea when or if she's coming back?"

Edie smiled, and handed Ruth a printed copy of the email she'd received that morning. "I think another couple of weeks ought to do it. April in Paris should not be missed."

Ruth looked over the top edge of the paper at her smiling friend. She knew, without asking, that Edie was deep in memories of her own time in the City of Lights. As chatty as Edie could be, she'd never revealed much about the man who fathered her twins, Diana and Daniel. Ruth suspected that those memories were so few, Edie hoarded them for special occasions.

"Well, I know I'll be glad when everyone's back in Carding." Andy squashed the last crumbs of cake with his fork then lifted them to his mouth. He didn't even miss the frosting. "I saw Gideon yesterday. I gather he's back working for Harry. Louisa and the other two boys are on a cruise somewhere. They'll be back around Mother's Day. I guess Noah officially came out of the closet while they were in Florida."

Edie laughed. "And I'll bet the only one who was surprised was Harry. The whole town's known Noah Brown's gay for years. Even my granddaughter knew."

"Is Gideon back living in his house?" Ruth asked.

"Just long enough to spruce it up to rent," Andy said. "Says he plans to live in White River. My guess is that it's better for him not to be too close to Harry too often."

"Have either of you heard from Peter?" Ruth asked.

"Not since he left to visit his sister," Andy said. "Though I don't see why he won't come back to Carding now that Lisa is staying in California. Is it true she got a part in some movie?"

"Yeah, according to Charlie," Ruth said. "Though I notice he's not saying what kind of movie it is."

Edie couldn't resist. "Maybe it's a western."

Even though she was deep under a quilt, the scents of fresh coffee and brioche penetrated to Chloe's nose. She inhaled deeply, glad as ever that she'd chosen a miniscule flat over a bakery for her stay in Paris. She stirred and stretched luxuriously. She had to get up. The foggy light near the river didn't last long, and she wanted at least one day more with her latest painting.

Then she heard the flat's door open and close. The sound made her smile. He'd brought her fresh coffee and rolls every morning since he moved in.

"Here," he said. "I thought we'd get an early start. Get to the river before the tourists."

Chloe giggled. "But we are tourists. We're not from here, and some day, we'll have to go back."

He sighed, and stroked her hair. "Do we? I've been thinking about staying here...with you...forever."

ABOUT THE AUTHOR

Sonja Hakala is the author of *Your Book, Your Way: How to Choose the Best Publishing Option for Your Book, Your Wallet and Yourself* (Full Circle Press LLC) as well as its upcoming companion book, *The Independent Publisher's Handbook: A Fingers-on-the-Keyboard, Step-by-Step Guide to Independent Publishing* (Full Circle Press LLC).

She is a quilter and the editor of *American Patchwork: True Stories from Quilters* (St. Martin's Press) and the author of *Teach Yourself Visually Quilting* and *Visual Quick Tips Quilting* (Wiley Publishing). She is past president of the Northern Lights Quilt Guild and the current secretary for the Green Mountain Quilt Guild. She is also a founding board member of the Children's Literacy Foundation (www.CLiFOnline.org), and the founder of the Parkinson's Comfort Project (www.ParkinsonsComfort.org).

Sonja has written for numerous magazines and newspapers, and worked on many book projects as an editor and designer. In recent years, she has become an advocate of independent publishing, and has successfully guided many authors through the process. She teaches classes and workshops, and is currently developing an online school for independent publishers.

Sonja lives with her family on a river in her beloved Vermont.

You can visit Carding any time at www.CardingVermont.com.

ABOUT THE CARDING ACADISTS

While the characters who take the age in *The Road Unsalted* are fiction, many of the artists who ma o appearances in the Carding Academy or whose work is featur silent auction at the Mount Merino Resort are very real. They the area known as the Upper Valley, the place where Vermont a Hampshire meet around the towns of Hartford and Norwich, at and Lebanon and Hanover, New Hampshire. This area is exce y blessed with a population of creative folks in all the traditions.

You can see these artists at eative best any time on www. CardingVermont.com, and I wa ank them for the privilege of putting them on the page.

Nancy Graham, quilter and artist. She made the quilt that's on the cover of this book.

J.C. Davis, woodworker ex naire who can make any storage area into a work of art.

Jeffrey Sass, metal sculptor n eye to all the possibilities of his medium.

Carrie Fradkin, mosaic arti a magical eye for color.

Joanne Lendaro, who sure s how to have fun with a longarm quilting machine.

THIEVES RE:
THE SECOND OF CARDING, VERMONT

If possible, the interior Windsor County courthouse was gloom-
ier than the November outside. Edie Wolfe touched the waiting
room's radiator then sigh

"No hope?" Agnes F asked.

"I guess that custodiaght—no hope of heat," Edie said. "But
there's always hope of anod. Come on, let's see if that coffee area
is warmer than this. Even n't want to drink the stuff they serve,
at least we can wrap our hound the cups to warm them."

The two women rose, d their scarves, and opened the doors
to the paneled hallway.

"Ah, Mrs. Wolfe, I'm e Kidder from the *Valley News*." A
youngish man loomed in f her, his pen gripped by fingers pro-
truding from his gloves.

"Ms. Wolfe," Edie corre

"What?"

"It's Ms. Wolfe. There is r. Wolfe unless you count my father,
who's deceased, or my son, w Boston," Edie said. "I thought you
might like to start this intervi on the correct foot."

"Oh, right, Ms. Wolfe," porter said, making a note. "You're
the chairman of the board at t ademy, right?"

"No. I am the executive d of the Carding Academy of Traditional Arts," Edie said.

"Oh, right." Another not le. "Got it. And you are…?" He
looked at Agnes.

"This is Agnes Findley, Ms lley, and she is the chairwoman of
the academy's board of directors e said.

"Right, right." More scribl "Got it. Now, what's this case
about, exactly?"

"Property rights," a voice p Barbara Croft extended a hand

covered by a pink leather glove that matched her pink high heels. Edie made a note that her daughter, Candy, hovered in the dim distance.

"Oh, and you are?" George asked as he flipped a page in his reporter's notebook.

"Mrs. Barbara Croft," she said. "Plaintiff. I brought this suit. This is my attorney, Martha Rosen." Edie stared at the short, darkhaired woman standing next to Barbara, trying to make out if she'd had plastic surgery to make her sneer permanent. "I'm here as the rightful heir to the Joseph Stillman Croft estate. I mean to restore his home and the rights to his artwork to his family…where they belong."

The reporter hesitated. "I thought this was about some school and a strange will," he said. "At least that's what my editor told me."

Edie and Agnes stared at Barbara, anticipating the reaction they were sure would come. Edie spotted a flicker in the woman's carefully made-up eyes as Barbara contemplated strangling the impertinent reporter. How could he not know who she was? But then her mask dropped into place, and Barbara stretched a tight, teeth-clenched mouth across her tan face. Still the same old Barbara, Edie reflected. The only thing genuine about that mask is the venom behind it.

Just then, the courtroom door swung open and Charlie Cooper stuck his head out. "The judge is ready," he called.

Edie felt Agnes's fingers grip her arm as they followed their lawyer.

"We can talk later," Barbara purred to the reporter as she handed him a business card. "I'm sure to say something quotable. I always do. Did you bring a photographer by any chance?" She looked around but there was no one with a camera. "Well, come Candy. We mustn't keep justice waiting."

George stayed behind in the vacant hallway, thumbing the thick paper of Barbara's card. He'd learned long ago to avoid people who asked about photographers because unrestrained ego was an ugly thing to behold. Besides, his editor didn't expect much more than seven paragraphs for page three from this gig. He didn't have to stay if he didn't want to because the court's clerk would make him copies of the judgement, and all George had to do was rewrite it in English and he'd be done. So his real decision was between coffee at the Tuckerbox where he could chat up his new favorite waiter or listening to some dry legalese.

He'd just pocketed his notebook when a cry of rage made the whole building hold its breath. George raced to the courtroom door.

"What do you mean, I have no standing?" Barbara roared at the judge. She shook off her lawyer's restraining hand. "I am Joseph Stillman Croft's niece—his last living heir."

The judge looked over her glasses. Good lord, she thought, a screamer. And so early in the morning, too. What a way to start the day.

"It is quite evident that you are not Croft's last remaining heir," she told Barbara. "You are his great-nephew's widow which is a position of no standing at all as far as Croft's will is concerned. The will clearly states that his true heir never shared his last name."

"An old man's imagination," Barbara said. "He was hardly in his right mind when he left Carding."

The judge made a show of shuffling her papers. "I don't see any medical records here," she said. "No statements to that effect."

George reopened his notebook. This story might be more fun that he'd expected. He hadn't been out to Carding in a while. Maybe that waiter had the afternoon off, and they could make a day of it.

"My uncle Joe died in 1930," Barbara snapped. "Of course there are no medical records. But everyone knows he was a broken man when he left Carding."

"Everyone?" The judge let her gaze sweep the room while all the people in it, except Barbara, froze in place. Edie and Agnes both risked a look in Candy's direction. The young woman sat curled over, most of her face hidden from view behind a screen of hair. Neither of the older women cared much for Candy. Her abrasive style did not invite soft feelings. But this wasn't the first time they'd pitied Barbara Croft's daughter.

The judge swept all her paperwork into a single pile then tamped the edges of the pages until they were even. "Let the record show that the suit filed by Barbara Croft vs. the Carding Academy of Traditional Arts is dismissed."

"Let the record show that this judge failed to take all of the evidence into account..." Barbara screeched. But the court stenographer had already followed the judge, and Barbara's attorney was long gone. You could say one thing about Martha Rosen—her exit strategies were impeccable. If all went well, she'd eat dinner in Phoenix, a nice warm place where no one knew her, a great place for a woman of her questionable legal talents.

"Lunch?" Agnes asked Edie.

Edie smiled. "Absolutely. Where would you like to go?"

"The Tuckerbox has great soups and sandwiches," George broke in. "I'm headed that way, and I'd love to talk with you if you'll join me."

Edie glanced over at Barbara's rigid face. "Let's do that," she said. "And quickly."

CPSIA information can be obtained at www.ICGtesting.com
Printed in the USA
BVOW05s0327250215

389217BV00001B/1/P